I0645211

Such a sweet little boy, such a tragedy…

Suddenly, my son, Dannie, ran into the room. His wide eyes held fear. His panting slowed as he caught his breath and shouted loudly, "Mommy, Mommy, Joey fell in the pond!" Joey lived at the far end of the street nearest the pond.

Suddenly, memories of a chubby little boy with reddish-brown hair and a dazzling twinkle in his big brown eyes flashed through my mind. Younger than the other boys, he had one slightly shorter leg that caused him to limp when he walked. He loved sports. Although a little awkward, they allowed him to play anyway. Nate affectionately took on the role of Joey's big brother. I remembered Nate tossing him the football in our backyard. Joey reminded me of an angel with a broken wing. My own angel experience flooded my thoughts as I recalled that one icy day when God dispatched an angel to protect me. Joey always found some excuse to show up at our house around dinner time. He loved my cooking. I knew Rita, Joey's mom, but didn't know his father, Charlie. He attended a function every once in a while. But, for the most part, he kept to himself.

Five years into their marriage, Rita gave birth to Joey. "The doctor told us that we would never have children, but then Joey came. Charlie's heart exploded with pride at the birth of his son." Rita said.

Then I thought of something Joey said once as we sat together at the kitchen table snapping peas for dinner. He looked up at me with those adorable brown eyes, "My daddy hit my mommy," then he leaned his head against my shoulder. My heart ached for Joey. Our tiny community had no secrets. Everyone knew Charlie had lost his job and started spending more time in bars. His drinking got worse. We also suspected that he let his temper get out of hand on occasion. Yet each of us stood by and waited for someone else to act first on our suspicions. As Joey and I grew closer, my guilt eased. Joey had chosen my house as his safe haven. Dannie's tug at my arm snapped me back to the present. Startled and gripped with fear, I dialed nine-one-one and provided the emergency personnel the necessary information.

"Someone has already called for emergency services. They'll arrive shortly," the operator said.

Adam and B.J. grew up in the turbulent 1960s. The Vietnam war, unsettling riots across college campuses and unrest in just about every corner of America filled them with gloom. Even at home, they faced prejudice and poverty, but their community never let any of them forget that in this place dwelled an unconditional love. Adam and B.J. knew they had to seek a better life away from family and friends. Together? Why not? Out of a sense of hopelessness, they entered into a marriage of convenience. Was it a crazy idea? At the time, it felt like the only solution. But did they do the unthinkable? You decide…

ceed, until tragedy strikes and strips away the façade they have created, and they are reminded of the one thing that really counts—family. Filled with both unconditional love and unbearable heartbreak, *If Only for a Season* is a story that will break your heart as it warms it. Eye-opening and thought-provoking, it is a book that every-one, young and old, should read. *~ Regan Murphy, The Review Team of Taylor Jones & Regan Murphy*

ACKNOWLEDGMENTS

Thank you to my family for their continued encouragement and faith in me. And to all my friends who offered words of encouragement, too.

A very special thanks to my friend, Diane Thompson. She prayed for me and with me and called every day to help me stay focused. And then she overflowed my mailbox with cards of encouragement. I thank you.

If Only for a Season

Bertha Connally Abraham

A Black Opal Books Publication

DEDICATION

In loving memory of Nathan Bradley Abraham #21
3-24-2003

Author's Note

In rural Louisiana in the 1960s, like most small segregated towns across America, people survived on hope and a sense of community. The legacy of the community I grew up in sadly resembled many unnamed farming communities throughout the south.

On Easter Sunday, April 12, 1873, a group of Blacks forcefully took over the courthouse in the farming community of Colfax, in Grant Parish. Their act of defiance enraged the Whites who refused to acknowledge the rights guaranteed Blacks by the Fourteenth and Fifteenth Amendments. The recorded accounts and the accounts passed down from generation to generation differed, but both agreed the fight started because someone set fire to the courthouse. According to the history books, after the fighting ended, one hundred Blacks lay sprawled against the cold, red-soaked earth alongside three Whites. Later, a monument of eternal flames burned brightly in front of a newly erected courthouse in the center of town square marking this significant event.

Now, more than a century later, difficult times still lay ahead. Even though regarded as second-class citizens in our own homeland, our pride never faltered. I witnessed tremendous sacrifices and the courage to fight for change.

This fictional story draws from the shared experiences and stories of those who lived during the 1960s—some palatable and others not so much, but all the experiences shaped our lives. During those chaotic years, some people participated in non-violent marches while others chose a more violent approach. Regardless of their method, they challenged the world's view of its second-class citizens and substantive changes, although slow, eventually began to unfold. I often wonder how different my life would be had the 1960s not molded me.

If only for a Season, introduces Adam Mirabeau and Beatrice Johanna Marten who grew up in the south with limited opportunities, but the same goal. They believed education would lift them out of poverty and family would stabilize their existence. Theirs was a marriage of convenience.

During their nomadic wandering, B.J. and Adam learned many lessons about forgiveness, faith, and the power of God.

I lovingly recall the teachings of my soft spoken one-hundred-three-year-old grandmother. Watching her, I discovered a secret. I learned that complicated lives expend too much energy, and the most basic ingredient in a happy life comes from unselfish living.

The characters in this book learn and teach joyful and sometimes painful lessons while forging strong relationships. But always, the looming specter of segregation presented a constant challenge for them, just as it had for those of us who lived through the struggle.

Segregation spilled from the bowels of ungodly, greedy individuals. These small-minded men, with willful intent and malice, swallowed up the rights of decent, hard-working people. But because so many dared to challenge the hypocritical idea of "separate but equal," a much better nation began slowly emerging. It's imperative that we learn from those who challenged a few for a better way of life for all. Great and powerful leaders rose up, sometimes to their own amazement, as they pushed and prodded us to stand up for present *and* future generations, and, in the end, good will always triumph evil.

Chapter 1

The Struggle

Adam and I grew up in a rural community of sharecroppers. Our parents worked from sunrise until sunset day after day. Some cooked, some cleaned while others tilled the soil and brought in the crops. All week long they toiled, but on Sunday morning everyone dressed up and headed off to church. Our church and family instilled principles that shaped our self-worth and taught us that the color of our skin was a blessing and not a curse.

Adam and I attended Timothy Joseph, a Black segregated school in the heart of the South in Beauregard, Louisiana. The campus housed first through eighth and ninth through twelfth grades. Our proud community boasted a mighty allegiance to the school and to its sports activities, especially football and baseball. On Friday nights, like every red-blooded community in America, regardless of race, people lived and breathed sports. And although treated with disdain, the color of our skin didn't diminish our love for our country. We belonged here.

Adam didn't play any sports. We saw each other in

school and only on those rare occasions when he attended a school function. His family needed his help. Therefore, he spent most of his time after school working. His parents made their living off the land. They raised hogs, chickens and produced a large vegetable garden. Sharing seemed second nature to his family. Whatever they could spare, they shared with their neighbors.

Our paths crossed year after year where students from all grade levels at some point walked through the same hallways. In third grade, a tall, lanky Adam, with big glasses and a square head, sat directly behind me. One day, he pulled my pig tails and made me cry. Mrs. Miller sent him to the principal's office. "I hate you, Adam Mirabeau," I whispered under my breath.

Now in sixth grade, this skinny kid had outgrown those big glasses, and a more stylish pair rested on the bridge of his nose. During recess one day, he kicked a football squarely into my forehead. A huge bump rose up and, with it, the worst headache. Mrs. Sims sent Adam to the principal's office. *Maybe his lack of coordination kept him from playing sports.* I thought. By the eighth grade, my pig tails disappeared and, in their place, was a naturally curly Afro. Whenever I gazed into the mirror, I saw my mother's milk-chocolate skin staring back at me. She moved like a beautiful swan, gliding gracefully across a wintery pond, with her shoulders pushed back and her head held high. Except for Adam and a few of the athletes, I towered over the boys in my class.

Adam lived on the outskirts of town with his parents and younger sister in a tiny weathered farmhouse decorated with a tin roof. The special attention his mother gave to the inside clearly showed, and, although the rooms were small, everyone had a comfortable place to sleep. Compared to the cluttered space I shared with my mother, some of the rooms in his house looked quite appealing.

In the early 1960s, like every southern town in America, our community maintained "separate but equal" businesses, housing, and schools, but they weren't equal. Blacks in every small town understood that the railroad track, its demarcation line, upheld separatism. Blacks had a place, as long as they stayed on their side of the tracks. Teenagers had trouble finding fun events to fill their weekends. Sometimes, the school hosted sock hops, a school -sponsored dance on Friday nights. Almost everybody came. A few minutes before the magic hour of ten-thirty, the lights mysteriously went out, and the boys stole that forbidden kiss. The chaperones fumed, but Maggie and I found it amusing.

Warm memories still lingered of those late evening fun-filled hay rides with my friends. Adam, Maggie and a few of my other friends lived on farms. They always included me in their special outings and, especially, the late October hay ride. Somebody's father hitched up an old mule to a long flatbed trailer filled with bales of hay and drove down a bumpy dirt road, over the hill past the Johnsons' abandoned farmhouse, and through the woods. We ended up crouched around a campfire, listening to ghost stories. How fitting! After all, we grew up in the South, where campfires and hair-raising ghost stories were born. The rural South didn't offer much in the way of entertainment. The juke joint proudly symbolized the only place in town where we could purchase a hamburger. With the owner's permission, we entered, placed our order, and then waited across the street. He feared that if minors got caught on the premises, he'd lose his liquor license and his living.

Inside, thick smoke hung in the air like a threatening storm cloud. The stale smell of alcohol filled my nostrils, and an ever-present, caustic odor burned my eyes. It took every ounce of strength to keep from gagging. The smell clung to me, as if I'd welcomed it in. People drank and danced to the loud, bellowing sounds of the blues. One song after another told the same sad tale of hard times. The piercing sadness of the music filled me with gloom. When old Bubba Mac finished our order, he came to the door, gave us his toothless grin, and yelled, "Adam, B.J., you ordur readee."

We didn't need affirmation from anyone of our separate and unequal lives. We saw it play out every day in the faces of the people we knew and loved.

A Black owned corner store partially sustained our community. Whites owned the other two grocery stores where Blacks bought food on credit. The more they paid, the more they owed. These commissary stores allowed the sharecropper to buy supplies on credit and pay off his debt with crops from the next season. Quite often, the sharecropper couldn't catch a break when the next season's poor weather conditions destroyed all hope of profitability. These commissaries created another way for White farmers to keep their sharecroppers on the farms. Many Blacks gave up the dream of a better life.

The post office, bank, and general store looked like replicas from the old West, with their weather-worn store fronts. Our town had an earthy smell like fresh-plowed dirt on a rainy day. Stores sat on both sides of the street. In the middle of the square sat a pecan house where everyone came to pedal their wares. Though the town was not much to look at, we proudly came back on most weekends because of the homespun comfort it provided. I often wondered if a few open-minded city councilmen willing to embrace change could've shifted the tide and ushered in a new period of trust and united the community. What would've happened to our closely woven community had they welcomed big businesses rather than slamming the door in their faces? Perhaps better paid job opportunities for both Whites and Blacks would've made the search for an improved life away from home less attractive. But, certainly, the welfare of Black folks didn't concern them. Sadly, they forgot about the White folks who needed help, too. They protected their investments and continued lining their pockets. Slowly, our quiet little community died, and only vague reminders of her heritage remained behind.

When Senator John F. Kennedy took the office of president, uttering those now famous words, "Ask not what your country can do for you, but what you can do for your country," Blacks had hope that real change was on the way. But with his assassination on that warm sunny day in Dallas in 1963, hope died along with him. Our town and our nation went into mourning that day. When the news reached my home economics class, students and teachers wept openly. Tears stung my eyes, and a sick feeling rose from the pit of my stomach. Black people had fallen in love with the Kennedys, and now one of their favorite sons lay dead. That evening filled with total disbelief, everyone gathered around an open fire and talked.

The fear now that nothing would change caused more resentment and continued mistrust of Whites. And then, the signing of the Civil rights Act of 1964 sparked a small glimmer of renewed hope. I actually believed change would happen overnight and that White people would finally accept us as God created equals. Foolishly, I thought this Act would instantly erase the shame of going to the back door of the White restaurant or the humiliation of climbing the stairs at the local theater. A big surprise awaited those naive enough to think like me.

Change came slowly and, along with it, came much resistance.

In the summer of 1969, we graduated from high school. Adam and I, along with some of our classmates, got accepted into the same college only a few miles from home. Grant College sat on the banks of the Mississippi River in La Racine, Louisiana. When the wind blew, the big old southern magnolia trees filled the air with a heavenly fragrance. Huge oak trees stood majestically. For hundreds of years, those old trees waited patiently, as if they knew their place. On the banks of the Mississippi River, we relaxed and watched barges and ships pass by.

The money earned from various jobs back home made an enormous difference in the quality of our lives at school. We spent most Saturdays from September to December picking up pecans and sold them for extra money. In one whole day, I couldn't pick enough cotton to pay for my lunch. With that realization, someone always needed some ironing and housekeeping in town. Often, babysitting jobs presented themselves.

With heightened excitement, I looked forward to the beginning of my first college semester. The summer started out busier than normal with little time for anything other than work. Chores took up most of my time. My mother did her best. I applauded her effort, but the work study program and my partial scholarship covered the shortage. I took work and school in stride then settled into a routine. After a while, it was hard to determine which demanded more of my time.

Throughout high school, we shared lots of classes. From the moment he walked into my high school algebra class and our eyes locked, I knew my life would change. I understood from my mother's constant reminders that commitment to family meant more than good looks, although Adam certainly had both. My mother learned that lesson too late in life. It made her sad. Adam sat on a stool facing the open doorway of the biology class. Lucky for me, I took the seat right next to him. The thought of dissecting a frog made me more than a little uncomfortable, but not Adam. After the professor gave a brief demonstration in the art of dissecting frogs, Adam waved his assigned weapon of choice in the air. Armed, dangerous, and ready, he took aim. I closed my eyes. Finally, it was over. Then I breathed a sigh of relief.

Adam and I became best friends. He walked me to and from some of my classes or stopped over at my dorm sometimes on the pretense of saying hello. As always, he played it very cool. I knew he liked me, and I liked him, but he also hung out with Melissa Tate. The extent of their relationship seemed unclear. Besides, we were just friends. Of course, that's the lie I told myself. My classes demanded discipline. Thank goodness high school prepared me.

The semester ended right on schedule. Winter break for me only meant more work without any free time. Like always, we headed back to our place of refuge, the place where we felt most connected—home. Several of our high school classmates attended the same college. Therefore, transportation was never a problem. I slept late. The next morning, I rode my bicycle into town to get a few items my mother needed from the local grocery store.

I had my head down rummaging through my purse when I bumped into Adam. "Hello, what's up?" he asked.

Flustered, I think I said something strange along the lines of "Uh huh," which made no sense. I felt really foolish. My face turned a bruised red. Adam smiled. He'd changed over the years from a lanky little boy into a really cool, six-foot guy with broad shoulders. His looks first attracted me to him, but later his confidence and optimism captivated me. I'd never met anyone who knew exactly what they wanted and how they planned to achieve that goal. He understood that hard work paid off.

However, my mother's advice kept me focused. "Beatrice Johanna, family comes first."

"Yes, Anna." Growing up under the scrutiny of my mother, I understood that life brought with it uncertainty. Still, I dreamed.

Adam asked me out on a date that day. Word spread quickly that Melissa dumped him for her old high school boyfriend. Suddenly, Adam and I became an item. On our first date, we went to the movies in a neighboring town a few miles away and sat holding hands while eating buttered popcorn. We participated in a few worthwhile causes, volunteered at food and clothing drives for a nearby makeshift church shelter and once even marched in a peace rally.

Adam and I both understood the language of sacrifice and that our circumstances would only change when we embraced education. Clearly, success didn't happen just because we dreamed about it. Rather, it happened through persistence and hard work. When Dr. Martin Luther King, Jr. received the Nobel Peace Prize, it convinced me that education played a significant role in paving the way for his great honor. Every time Dr. King marched, my spirit marched, too while holding up the banner for peace. A couple of my classmates felt so strongly about his nonviolent approach to freedom that they left school to attend his marches. I knew my mother wouldn't approve, so I stayed in school. All too well she understood the fight for freedom. However, she opposed the idea of my leaving school. She'd seen the beatings, the hosing, and the arrests on television. These scenes alarmed her. "B.J., them Whites angry, and they'll do just about anything to keep us right where we at. I don't want you going near them marches, you hear?"

"Yes, Anna." I obeyed, but my spirit attended every march, despite the fact, that my mother had absolutely forbidden me from going.

Maybe it was hard to see or feel the difference in our small, isolated community, but change had spread like an unattended wildfire. Thurgood Marshall, the first Black Chief Justice, took office in the United States Supreme Court. A Black man now occupied a seat in the highest court in the land. None of us fully understood the importance of the office of Justice, but it made us proud that he'd sit in the same room with Whites and make important decisions. We'd come a long way, but not far enough.

In Beauregard, people continued to work on the farms for small wages and the word "equality" carried with it a certain element of hypocrisy, verging on a cruel joke. The Nobel Peace Prize held at best only a diluted meaning for us. We couldn't wrap our heads around how such a prestigious award could change our immediate circumstances. We'd already gleaned that education meant a much greater chance of finding a better job and establishing a decent life for ourselves. But, in our community, good jobs didn't come easy, and education had nothing to do with it. The good jobs never crossed over the tracks. Of course, someone always needed a sharecropper or a domestic worker, but never anything more than that.

I resented working all the time while some of my friends enjoyed their weekends and holidays. It didn't seem fair. Sometimes my resentment and anger spilled over into my comments to my mother. She lashed out at me. "Beatrice Johanna," she said in a stern voice as she raised her hand to me, "grow up. Life sho 'nuff ain't fair. I'd done work hard all my life, and for what? To see you act like an ungrateful little brat?" With my pride deflated,

I cried and shuffled off to my room. My mother never came to console me.

Tough times knocked at everyone's door. Life seemed gloomy for the entire community. Sometimes, Adam worked on the road, digging ditches, but when he wasn't in a ditch, he helped his parents bring in the crop for the next season. In between endless days of chores on the farm, Adam financed his schooling with odd jobs. He took honest work as long as it paid a decent wage. Keenly aware of his sacrifices, my mother said, "Beatrice Johanna, that boy knows responsibility."

The White city councilmen owned large farms in our parish. Unanimously, they voted to keep businesses and industry out. In many ways, our "separate but equal" apartness resembled apartheid in South Africa. Maybe not truly institutionalized, but many endorsed it. These councilmen worked against the community they represented for their own financial gain. At least with an education, we hoped to find teaching or secretarial jobs in the larger towns surrounding our small community. I hadn't planned on spending the rest of my life picking up and cleaning after strangers.

My mother spent countless hours washing and ironing for the smallest of wages. Many times, as a young girl, I tagged along with her. She let me sort the clothes and dust the expensive furniture that filled the oversized rooms. I don't ever remember hearing one person say to my mother how much they appreciated her. From that experience, I promised to carve out a better life for myself. Despite having to scrape by with meager wages, her dignity remained intact. She felt ensnared in her circumstances, but she honored her responsibility as a single parent. By observing, I learned from her that choices brought consequences. I feared I'd end up in an unappreciated job working for pennies, like my mother, for people who would never appreciate me and avoid any issue that forced them to recognize me as their equal.

Very few Whites saw the world through our lens. Those who understood assisted our family and provided good recommendations that brought my mother work. One summer, she became ill and was unable to work for about a month. Some of her employers made sure we had sufficient food and even loaned her enough money for our essentials. My proud mother wouldn't accept charity. She paid back every dime and showed her gratitude by working longer hours some days without extra compensation. "Beatrice Johanna, don't accept no charity. You poor; you ain't desperate." She gave me everything that she thought mattered. I had food, clothing, and shelter. My mother had seen to that.

Our tiny wooden, three-room shotgun shack sat on a small lot buried among rows of similar houses. I stood on the front porch and looked all the way through the back door without altering my position left or right. My mother's bed sat at one end of the living room, along with the sofa, chair, and all sorts of mismatched furniture that she'd acquired for a small price over the years.

This hard-working woman didn't believe in accepting anything that she couldn't pay for. Old newspapers, magazines, and books cluttered her room, sprawled against the backdrop of the rain-streaked wallpaper. The middle room was my retreat. A curtain separated my bed from the makeshift closet used to store extra pots and pans. My mother, the packrat kept everything. Too many things filled our already compact house. Regardless, I worked within the constraints of her world and with her things. When we first moved there, we had an outhouse like everyone else. Fortunately for us, the landlord decided we needed a proper bathroom, unlike the accommodations of many of our neighbors. Although we had an indoor toilet, we carried water for bathing. It wasn't an ideal situation, but it was still better than most. My mother longed for a traditional family in every sense of the word. She wanted a husband who would share the responsibility of parenting and providing for the family. No doubt, she would've gladly relinquished her role as head of household if she'd found the right person. Instead, she had Aunt Eva and me. Even though she found it troubling to say the words, "I love you," she tried hard to show me how she felt.

Finally, the day I'd waited for came. My mother had been the driving force behind everything I'd done in life. She'd missed out on so much that I wanted in some small way to please her, but it grew into much more. Deep down inside, I feared that, without an education, I'd end up like her—tired, miserable, and alone. Whenever I looked at her, I saw sadness. That scared me to death. I knew, upon graduating, my education would provide more. For that, I had my mother to thank.

On that day, our parents beamed with pride. Mama Joe and Mr. Mirabeau stood proudly next to Adam as his sister took pictures. By far, this day topped my mother's list of her happiest moments. For the first time that I could remember, she had a smile on her face and a gleam in eyes. The distance stare was gone. Sometimes parents live vicariously through their children. Perhaps, this day really belonged to her. That made me extremely happy. She'd earned it.

Shortly after graduation, Adam proposed without any romantic fanfare. The ring wasn't hidden in my dessert, nor did it arrive accompanied by a poem confessing his undying love for me. It followed a simple and honest question spoken from his heart. "B.J.," he said nervously, "will you marry me?" Then he reached into his pocket and pulled out a ring with a diamond so tiny it seemed almost invisible. Without thinking, I quickly grabbed his arm in an effort to steady his hand while he placed the ring on my finger.

My answer came back to him as simple as his question: "Yes, I'll marry you." Adam and I loved each other without falling in love. Our relationship resembled an arranged marriage, an agreement of convenience that suited our combined goals. I'd lived my whole life observing my mother mourn the loss of her youth and unable to establish the family life she dreamed of for herself. I decided I'd accomplish what my mother sought in her many efforts and failed.

Unlike me, Adam lived a coveted life with both his parents lovingly at his side. For him, the freedom of becoming his own person and making his own choices fueled the marriage proposal to someone he thought most like him.

I'd known Adam all my life and hadn't expected anything different than what he offered. In his no-nonsense sort of way, he viewed the world simply. The idea of falling in love with that "fireworks drama" seemed unimportant at the time. Only that he'd ask me to marry him mattered. We developed a very close friendship while playing a game of cat and mouse. Perhaps destiny presided over our births, but on the day that Adam proposed, it took charge of our lives, too.

Chapter 2

Uncharted Waters

We exchanged wedding vows in a small church on a gray and misty day. Instead of a typical sunny, warm June day, it felt characteristically cold and bleak, like the dog days of winter. Depression lurked nearby, and I couldn't escape feeling trapped without windows or doors inside a dark, dingy dungeon. Perhaps it felt strange because January always brought with it remnants of the holidays gone too soon. It rushed in with an air of festive gala only to dash out just as quickly.

Adam's family and close friends filled the church. My small gathering included my mother, Aunt Eva, and a few cousins. I stood under an uncovered portal fearing the sky would open up at any minute and rain down its fury on us. A sprinkle fell every once in a while. We survived. Adam stood at the front of the church, looking nervous and handsome in his black one size too small rented tuxedo. His long limp arms hung at his side as the sleeve of his jacket rested several noticeable inches above his wrist.

Mama Joe, Adam's mother, asked her friend to make

my wedding dress. She once worked in a factory up North as a seamstress but lost her job due to layoffs, so she returned home, hoping for steady work. But instead, she found a few odd jobs mending and repairing clothes for folks around town. She took up washing and ironing and sometimes worked at farming when she couldn't make ends meet. My dress didn't come out of the bride's Magazines that my mother brought home, but it was more beautiful than the dresses I envied in those magazines. The soft white satin A-line dress with its high regal neckline had tiny beads covering every inch. Mama Joe's friend, Ms. Elaine had sewn every one of those beads on by hand. The train created a continuous flow of lace that floated in the air as if caught up in an imaginary wind gust. We enjoyed an unforgettable wedding ceremony because of the support of many people.

The rain moved out. The reception was another grand and selfless gift presented to us by our families and friends. Today, held hostage by those memories, I thought about all who cared enough to impart to us wonderful words of wisdom. We moved into the church courtyard where years before my baptism ceremony took place. Lovely pink and white paper flowers, all handmade by friends decorated the chairs and tables. They didn't carry with them the sweet aroma of springtime but generated an ambiance just the same. Soft music played from somewhere in the distance. Tables stretched across the courtyard, lined with trays of home-cooked food. In the center of the table stood a perfectly round, two-tiered homemade chocolate wedding cake, dripping with white icing and topped with a cute little plastic bride and groom. At the far corner of the courtyard, a bar served rows of non-alcoholic beverages.

We walked into the courtyard in time for the introduction. The baritone voice of Adam's best man billowed, "Ladies and gentlemen, I present to you, Mr. and Mrs. Adam Mirabeau." Before today, my name belonged exclusively to me, but within a few short minutes following the words, "I do," it evaporated into the night air. Beatrice Johanna Marten was my given name. Except for my mother, everyone called me B.J. Suddenly, I felt disconnected.

We danced. Adam had two left feet. Thank goodness, the song finally ended. My feet hurt from the half dozen times he stepped on them. We mingled, shared hugs, and thanked our guests. We owed this evening to so many. That higher power that guided my life was pointing me in the direction of a master plan. When the evening drew nigh, I paused and reflected on this season of my life. It began with a first date, high school graduation, college graduation, and finally, my wedding day.

We felt safe together and loved each other from deep inside a secret place overflowing with mostly gratitude. We spent hours planning our life together, the children we would one day have, and the beautiful house with the white picket fence. Adam wanted lots of kids. I figured a little compromise wouldn't hurt. After all, we had plenty of time. We didn't think about financial stability. Of course, money mattered, but what really counted had nothing to do with money. We'd made a promise to God and man that we'd spend the rest of our lives in faithful companionship. Theirs wasn't a conventional kind of love even though whenever any genuine affection signs a contract with the heart, the mind stands as its witness.

Earlier that day Adam's remarkable parents presented us with a sacrifice of their love. The screened door slammed behind us as we entered the kitchen. Mama Joe called out from their bedroom. "Adam, B.J., y'all come on in here." Mama Joe sat on one side of the bed and René, Adam's sister sat on the other side. Mama Joe patted the edge of the bed. I walked over and sat down next to her. The old iron bed squeaked from our weight. Mr. Mirabeau looked up from his chair and smiled. Adam walked over and stood next to his dad. The years had been kind to this copper-colored beauty with deep, coffee-colored eyes and black woolly plaits that hung below her shoulders.

She pulled a handkerchief from somewhere deep inside her bosom. The faded handkerchief held the stains of the blood, sweat, and tears of their labors. Tightly twisted into the knots and folds of that handkerchief lay two hundred dollars that represented a lifetime of saving. She joined our hands together and pressed the handkerchief inside. "Y'all need this. It ain't much, but we want y'all to have it with our blessings." With the naked eyes her gesture seemed common, but when we looked with the heart, it surpassed ordinary.

We started out in the world with the blessings and generosity of our parents. We left that room happier than we thought possible. Their gift came from their hearts. My mother had nothing in the way of material wealth to bestow upon us. She gave us what she had--her blessing and her advice. "Beatrice Johanna, family the most important thing."

"Yes, Anna." Adam and I knew people who loved and wanted the best for us without condition, people like my mother, Aunt Eva, Mama Joe, Mr. Mirabeau, René, and a host of others.

We grew up in poverty, but on an equal footing with everyone around us. We never saw any differences. I remember that what we had, everyone else had and helping others was a way of life. We became a united front where and when it counted. Neighbors displayed the true meaning of community. They were not an independent, but rather an interdependent community helping and looking out for each other. Adam's hardworking and loving parents, Thomas and Josephine Mirabeau, had a strong sense of family and commitment to God. And like his parents, our lives started out the exact same way.

I kept wondering how I got from there to here. At times, I felt haunted by my past. After high school, a few guys joined the army and immediately found themselves in a combat zone. They left home young and idealistic but returned from the Vietnam War as frightened, disillusioned replicas of themselves. They'd seen and done too many things for what others told them was the right reason. Our friend, Charlie completely snapped one day while driving into town. Everything reversed in his mind. He thought a green light meant stop and a red light meant proceed. Fortunately, a friend who rode into town with him recognized he needed help. Night after night another classmate lay in the fetal position soaked in his own tears until the sun came up. At barely eighteen, what he witnessed and participated in tormented his nights more than his days. These young men saw in a short time more than any of us could ever imagine in a whole lifetime.

He was the class clown in high school. His notoriously funny jokes made us laugh even on our worst day. Now, when I looked into his eyes, his fun-loving soul, his laughter, and his smile had gone. His hollow stare pierced my heart. It took a long, long time, but once his parents checked him into the VA hospital, he could once again sleep throughout the night. That smile and jovial spirit we all loved so much slowly returned. Still, the war raged on claiming lives and maiming bodies.

My friend Maggie Paxton and I developed a deep appreciation for all kinds of music. We particularly loved music with powerful thought provoking words. Usually, we turned the music up loud and danced around the room holding hands and laughing until her mama yelled,

"Maggie Mae, turn dat music down." We loved Diana Ross and the Supremes' song, "Someday We'll Be Together." Our little town, like many other small towns nestled in the South, felt the effects of the Vietnam War. But, not until Marvin Gaye released "What's Going on, Brotha?" in protest of the war did we understand the impact of the war on our country. An old discarded newspaper, crumpled and resting in a heap in the corner of my mother's room, said the release date of the album changed due to controversy. The year of the release didn't matter. The feelings remained the same as the war raged on creating unrest here at home.

Maggie bought the album. We spent hours listening to the sound of Marvin Gaye's smooth, sexy voice. The song delivered a clear message about the plight of Black men fighting for a country that didn't love them and yet, expected and demanded their loyalty. They returned home to conditions worse than when they left. They couldn't find work—certainly nothing that resembled real jobs. No place had immunity from this unsettling feeling. Several months earlier at Kent State, four students died when a riot broke out at a block party. Some said the block party got out of hand due to excessive drinking, and some speculated that resentment to the war fueled the riot. All over America, across college campuses, similar protests played out. Our country was angry and restless.

It was a crisp, sunny November day, as I walked toward the administration building on my quiet campus. Suddenly, the sound of barking dogs got my attention. Then I saw students running in all directions. A young woman shouted as she ran toward me, "Watch out for the dogs!" Then she paused long enough to tell me that the police released their dogs then threw cans of tear gas into the crowd. People ran pass me with their faces covered, gasping for air. I looked on in shock as a dog chased after a student. Quickly, I turned and ran toward my dorm while thinking of the shocking display of force used at Kent State. Emergency calls for evacuation had already reached my dorm by the time I got there. When the disturbance ended, two students lay dead. We'd faced tough times before today, but the war, the riots, and the disturbances seemed insurmountable. "Stop it!" I whispered. Why dredge up those horrible memories on my wedding day? Sure, uncharted waters lay ahead for me, but hopefully not unfriendly ones.

Nine years into our marriage, while living in Suellen, Florida, Mama Joe died. She had the usual minor ailments brought on by old age, but on this day, she sat down in her old rocking chair that faced east and slipped away. When Renée called us with the sad news, we sat together and cried. She meant as much to me as she had to Adam. Renée and I handled the funeral arrangements. The loss of his mother proved difficult for Adam. She adored him. Whenever Mama Joe wanted to get his attention, she yelled out, "Come here, baby boy."

Mama Joe resisted the fact that Adam had grown up. He was forever her baby boy.

The day of the funeral, a crowd filled the small wood-framed church. A pillar of the community, a strong woman of faith, a loving wife, mother, and compassionate friend summed up the life of Josephine Cavanaugh Mirabeau. She always found time to visit the sick and bring them her famous homemade chicken soup for a speedy recovery. And she always found time to pray for her neighbors. Mr. Mirabeau looked absolutely lost that day. His head hung low, and when he spoke, his voice cracked like splintering wood. He'd lost his best friend in the whole world. In the many years they spent together as husband and wife, she handled all the day-to-day details of life. He'd surely feel her absence more than anyone.

Over the years, we corresponded through letters. Although smart and witty, she had only an eighth-grade education. But, she had the ability to weave a story so intriguing that her expressive words would leap from the pages and capture your very soul. They breathed and came alive. Her young grandchildren sat at her feet mesmerized, wide eyed, listening while she entertained them with her anecdotes. Everyone, young and old alike, found her stories captivating. Mama Joe knew very little about her family, except that her White grandfather and her full-blooded Cherokee grandmother came from a town west of the place she called home.

In her letters, she talked about important things, like what she called some of the dumb decisions made by our politicians. She also talked about some not-so-important things to me, like her summer or winter gardens and their preparation. She had an opinion on just about everything, including strong views on the world's affairs. She could've run this country with minimum effort. After all, what else could you expect from Josephine Mirabeau? Her letters gave her a platform without the label of opinionated, not that she really cared what anyone thought of her. She trusted God with every aspect of her life. She wrote, "B.J., honey, if you can't trust God, thens you might as well lays down and die. There ain't any hope for ya." I enjoyed reading her letters and looked forward to their arrival. Among the many letters I received, one stands out. She wrote, "B.J., honey—" She always called me 'B.J. honey,' as if 'B.J.' was my first name and 'honey' my middle name. "—trust yore instancts. Ain't no man worth losing your soul over, not even my baby boy?" That day she offered me her best advice, and I ignored it, but her letters remained among my most prized belongings. I planned to reread them someday and once again experience the magic of her pen.

I've often longed for the same closeness with my own mother. Mama Joe and René shared a real mother-daughter bond. I watched Mama Joe hug her and sometimes plant a big wet kiss on her cheek for no reason—just because. I envied their intimacy. The gap between my mother and me had grown much too wide. It needed too much mending time. We both had flaws and worked at a mother-daughter relationship the best that we could. A gradual change took place and the older I got; the more I realized I'd become my mother in some ways. In the earlier years, we certainly looked alike, although we saw the world differently. My mother wanted a safe place, and not let anyone in for fear she might get hurt again. Not me, I wanted to experience life despite the consequences. I wanted to see, feel, and touch the world I dreamed and read about in the books and magazines she brought home to me.

Mr. Mirabeau, a quiet, very shy man spent so much time at work, I barely got to know him. He worked from dawn to dusk providing for his family as if he'd found his true purpose in life. He never spoke a harsh word and smiled all the time. His fondness for alcohol was apparent on those occasions when he appeared much more outgoing than his usual demure self. Perhaps it helped him escape from the demands life placed upon him and from the quite spirited and controlling love of his life. Whatever the reasons, everyone pretended not to notice.

Adam looked like his mother and had many of her dominating qualities, especially her confidence and strong opinions on most topics. He denied it, of course, but I said, "Let's call it like we see it."

René was even more beautiful than her mom with the same copper skin and long thick, black woolly hair that hung down her back. But with her sweet, shy spirit and youth on her side, these qualities only enhanced her beauty.

As time passed, I finally understood that my mother really did love me. It was her inability to express her feelings that drove a wedge between us. It's funny what you refuse to remember in an effort to hide the truth. I can't remember her embrace, or if she ever said she loved me. However, I remembered the cold, distant person she'd become and felt her deep denial. When I got older, I realized she didn't intentionally make her only child the object of her rejection. For her, change took time. From the moment I uttered my first sound, not once did I ever call her mama or mom, only Anna. She didn't mind. My mother wore her pain openly for all to see. She met my father and fell in love with him so long ago she could hardly recall what it felt like to be in love. He was already in the army, and they were much too young.

Once I asked Aunt Eva to tell me about my father. She said, "Child, he wuz sho' nuff some kind of handsome, tall, wit them devilish brown eyes and smooth brown skin. Them gurls loved him, including your mama. He loved to play tricks on me 'cause he knows I wuz afraid of the dark. He would hides behind something and then jump out at me. He git a big laugh out of hearing me scream. He wuz my baby brotha, child and I sho' nuff loved him."

I listened and imagined my father and Aunt Eva playing together as kids. My Aunt Eva, my father's sister, told me he lied about his age so that he could join the army. He was much younger than the legal requirement. Perhaps she told me this wild story to impress upon me the importance of telling the truth, or just maybe it actually had merit. Unfortunately, he entered the service of his country a young man and returned a broken, discarded piece of rubble. My father was a prisoner of the forgotten war for thirty-two months almost the entire length of the Korean War that began in 1950 and ended in 1953.

Slowly, bits and pieces leaked out about the conditions in which he lived during his captivity. I blocked out what I could of the beatings, the days without food and water, the unclean living quarters, and the water tortures. However, every now and then a fragment broke loose and reminded me that under certain conditions some people are capable of committing unspeakable acts of inhumanity. When they released him, he returned to the home of his parents. As for my father, the war reduced my mother and me to total strangers. The young boy that left home eager to fight for his country came back a broken shell of a man. Did he come looking for his family? No, he did not. He needed more than what a tired, overworked young woman with a small child could offer him. My mother and father never married nor claimed common law status. Knowing my mother, she would rather live alone than claim a lie. Accepting what didn't belong to her didn't fit her character. None of that mattered now because what he needed she clearly couldn't give him. He had tremendous psychological issues and found comfort, not in his love for my mother, but in his daily consumption of alcohol and drugs. They became the constant companions he leaned heavily on to make it through each day.

I never met my father. Aunt Eva told me that the man who came home from the war resembled no one she knew—not my father, her brother, or my grandmother's son. His battered body returned, but his spirit remained behind in a small village on the other side of the world. Many nights I dreamed about traveling to this faraway place somewhere in North Korea to find my father's spirit and bring it home. I thought that perhaps I could return to him what he'd lost. And then, maybe, he'd return to me and fulfill his little girl's dream.

Chapter 3

In The Beginning

With no time or money for a honeymoon, we spent our wedding night in a small motel on the outskirts of town. The discovery of the most tender and romantic love filled the night. We promised to love and care for each other always. We repeated our vows, "for better or worse, in sickness and in health, as long as we both shall live," and drifted off into a deep sleep. Sunday morning, we rose early and headed north to our new beginning. As I adjusted the knobs on the radio, I heard the faint sound of the Temptations' hit song "Just My Imagination." Our move would take us to Baxter, Louisiana, a small college town approximately three hundred miles away. Excitement replaced tiredness as we looked ahead to all those promises we made to each other. Adam's college professor and mentor found us a little trailer that sat on a tiny lot directly behind their home. A small clump of trees sat to the rear and on both the east and west side of the trailer. Secluded, even though it was in the city, it was exactly what we needed to start saving for a house.

Mr. and Mrs. Smallwood took us under their wings. Mr. Smallwood, a man of short stature with a receding hairline, greeted us with a smile and invited us inside. Adam and Mr. Smallwood shook hands. I gave him a hug as I stepped past him and into the foyer. He always had a pipe clamped between his teeth, whether smoking it or just resting it in the corner of his mouth. He wore glasses and spoke in a deep, baritone voice, that sounded like rolling thunder. Mrs. Smallwood, a very slender woman and legally—but not completely—blind came out of the kitchen. She wore thick glasses that never sat straight on her face, always tilting off the bridge of her nose. Her job as a nurse in one of the poorest and most underfunded hospitals in the city kept her very busy. We greeted her with a warm hug.

We talked about the upcoming college football season, the weather, and the stock market. They didn't dabble much in small talk and today, neither did we. Every nerve in our tired bodies ached from the long drive. Sleep wasn't a priority the night before. We discussed our plans for the future. Adam believed in having a plan. We offered our apologies as we got up to leave. They smiled as if they understood. Their youth might've slipped away, but the memories had not. These wonderful people, Mr. and Mrs. Smallwood, grew up in the Mississippi Delta on farms. Mr. Smallwood's parents owned the land they worked. She was the daughter of educators. Mrs. Smallwood's parents taught school and lived on a farm passed down to them from their parents.

Educated, smart, and active in their community, church and school, they helped educate many children from their families and the community at large. Faithful alumni, they traveled with the school's football program and took along with them Max, their little terrier. They had no children of their own, but children and laughter filled their home and their hearts. Their home became a safe haven for many who needed it, and, many times, the need weighed all of us down. Some who sought shelter came from broken homes. Their parents experimented with drugs and sold their bodies on the streets always one step ahead of the law.

The Smallwoods offered these kids a place to sleep, plenty of food and a means of earning an honest living. Odd jobs kept the kids going and perhaps kept some of them alive. Adam stopped over frequently and busied himself with small jobs. He loved every minute that he spent with Mr. Smallwood. In his free time, Adam took charge of job assignments with the help of Adrian, one of the older boys. Under the guidance of the Smallwoods, Adrian thrived and took on the role of big brother to the other kids. Sometimes, Mr. Smallwood created jobs, so the kids would have some work. Adam adopted Mr. Smallwood out of genuine respect for a man equally as worthy of his love as his biological father.

On Monday morning we headed off to our new jobs. The marketing firm of Broadmoor and St. Charles hired me as their office manager. Adam took a county agent position assigned to parts of Louisiana and the Delta. The long hours didn't bother Adam, he loved his job. I enjoyed my job, too. The wacky escapades of some of my co-workers helped the time pass with amazing speed. As I glance back with fondness at the memories of some of the people that I met, I laugh out loud. Adam and I managed well starting out. Our combined salaries paid the bills and gave Adam an opportunity to enroll in a master's program working toward a degree in physics with a small amount left over for savings.

We decided to make our stay in the trailer a short one. It seemed this part of the South had a love affair with tornados and storms. Kind to us most times, they blew briskly by with little or no aftermath. Other times they left such damage and destruction in the wake of their visit that we couldn't help but feel in awe of their power. We worked hard; saved our money; cut out vacations, movies, and anything that interfered with our plans to someday own a house. On weekends, we went house hunting, in hopes of finding something affordable. We'd passed the one-year mark, and we still lived in the trailer.

One evening while visiting with the Smallwoods, the conversation turned to saving for a house. "Mrs. Smallwood, with increased prices, it has gotten tougher to save. Milk, eggs, and gasoline keep going up, but our salaries stay the same. Gasoline's up to thirty-nine cents a gallon, with eggs at seventy-eight cents a dozen, and now milk's a dollar and thirty-one cents a gallon. It's a real stretch for us to manage these things," I said.

"You know, B.J., I just thought of something. I heard from my friend the other day that she's trying to rent a duplex that she owns. It needs a lot of work, but it could be worth the effort. Virginia won't charge any rent for the first six months and will share in the cost of any repairs. She wants someone in the house to keep down vandalism." It sounded like the perfect opportunity.

"Mrs. Smallwood, would you contact your friend and let her know we might be interested?"

"Sure," The next day we drove to an address she left in our mailbox. Ms. Virginia hoped that Adam and I would see its potential and rent the duplex.

I'd never met a more perfect couple. Material things didn't impress the Smallwoods. They placed the highest value on people and education. Although they didn't care for material things, they had plenty. But they used their wealth to improve the lives of people. Some people accumulate things, they accumulated family. Mr. Smallwood sat every evening reading the stock market. He in-

vested in blue chips and kept a close eye on his investments. They taught us how to invest. Later, we developed
a healthy respect for the market. Mr. Smallwood believed
in utilizing the services and products of the companies
that he owned stock in. That pretty much became our
motto, too. We shopped carefully, researched products
and the companies that owned them, and paid close attention to the items we bought. Soon, this interesting pastime became a great lesson in the art of making money.
Our surrogate parents, Mr. and Mrs. Smallwood, were
held in high esteem, and even though we never called
them Mom or Dad or by their first names Robert and Ru-
by, we respectfully called them Mr. and Mrs. Smallwood.

We drove west on the loop toward the outskirts of
the city. Fifteen minutes later, we parked in front of a
small, wood-framed duplex. Paint peeled away from the
sides of the faded blue, washed out building. The small
overgrown yard had a chain link fence, missing more
than a few links. In some parts of the yard, the weeds appeared taller than the fence. Inside we saw small rooms in
need of paint and floors bare, right down to the concrete
foundation. The work didn't seem impossible until I saw
the ruins that once housed a kitchen. My heart sank as I
stared up into the clearest and bluest sky from a hole in
the ceiling the size of Texas. Hurt sprang forth. Tears
filled my eyes. Quickly, I turned away not wanting my
sadness and disappointment to compound his disappointment, too. The task before us seemed overwhelming
but, surprisingly, I regained my composure then turned to
Adam with confidence, "We can do this."

"Thanks," he said, as he held me close. We stood
there for a moment locked in each other's arms before he
made the call. We moved in the following week with lots
of work in our foreseeable future. The rewards of our labor took longer than we imagined. Things kept falling

apart. As soon as we fixed one thing, something else needed our attention and resources. Ms. Virginia split the cost of everything, but we still had to prioritize or deplete our savings. The roof was a major undertaking and too big of a job for Adam, so we hired a roofing company. The rooms got a fresh coat of paint and shiny, new, inexpensive flooring. A little bit of each check went into fixing up the place we christened home. Living rent-free, now going on three months was another gift from God.

The Smallwoods and Ms. Virginia dropped in one evening to see our progress. "Great Job, Adam," Mr. Smallwood said.

"Thank you, sir."

Things couldn't have been any better until I started to outgrow most of my clothes. I ate like a bear preparing for hibernation. *I've got to stop eating so much*, I thought. It never dawned on me that I was eating for two until I noticed my swollen ankles. Morning sickness, the obvious symptom took pity on me and stayed away. I made a doctor's appointment and waited restlessly all week long. When the day finally came, I dressed quickly and rushed out. Adam wanted to come with me, but I talked him out of it. Besides, he made me too nervous. Once in the office, I didn't wait long. The doctor checked me and sent me out into the waiting area. A few minutes later, he called me back into his office.

"Mrs. Mirabeau, you're indeed pregnant." I nodded, picked up my purse, and walked out of the door. Adam was so excited about the possibility of a new arrival that he made me feel guilty. I wanted children, too. In fact, I wanted them more than Adam—just not now or as many. *Here I go, sounding like my oldest and once inseparable friend from childhood, Maggie Mae Paxton. What would happen to our savings and plans to buy a house?* I wondered. Now wasn't the time for a baby. And besides, now

Adam had work and school. I called his office, left an urgent message, and went home. Within minutes, he pulled into the driveway. The news thrilled him, but it worried me. He thought timing was a foolish notion. How often had I heard Maggie say, timing's everything? Maggie and I still chatted every once in a while. Everything in her life still had to do with timing. Anyway, apart from what I considered bad timing, there was real change on the way.

Anticipating my baby's arrival gave me nightmares. My all-too-willing-to-help co-workers shared horror stories that kept me awake at night. Dannie, my beautiful baby boy came on schedule. He weighed eight pounds and seven ounces. It was an easy delivery. The most memorable moment happened the minute the nurse placed a soft bundle with coal black hair in my arms.

My heart overflowed with joy. We named him Daniel (Dannie) Marten Mirabeau. After Dannie came, saving became more difficult, but we managed.

But I knew Adam needed my help, so I went back to work. My income helped with all the extras like diapers and formula. I hadn't adjusted to one small baby when I discovered that another one would soon arrive. A year later, Nathaniel Marten Mirabeau, or Nate, came on May tenth, his brother's birthday. Adam appeared more joyful than ever with the birth of his second son. Nate had a head full of those curly black locks and wrinkles covering every inch of his tiny body. I'd never seen a baby so wrinkled before. I took it as a sign of wisdom. It was the right prediction. He had an old spirit for someone so young. As he grew up, he loved the elderly and enjoyed spending time with them. Perhaps, he saw their wrinkles as a gateway to wisdom, too. When he opened those hazel eyes and looked directly into mine, I knew we would love each other forever.

We finally met Mark and Barbara Clearwater, the couple who shared the other half of the duplex. At our first meeting, they seemed very warm and friendly, but I had a strange feeling about them. Mark's broad shoulders reminded me of a robust linebacker. Sophie, like her father, had the same fair-skin and sea foam green eyes. His petite wife, Barbara's round, plump face was the color of rich dark chocolate. Her wide hips and bowed legs made her appear dwarfed. Every evening we waved as we returned from our jobs dressed in business attire, with the smaller ones tucked gently under our arms. Dannie followed right behind me. Mark fished a lot. In fact, he fished all the time. He pulled out early in the mornings before we left for work with his boat in tow. Sometimes he stopped and offered us some of his catch of the day. Apparently, he chose fishing as his occupation.

A single wall divided the house into apartments, yet we never found time to develop a friendship. We inevitably found some lame excuse for not visiting. Adam disliked Mark because he didn't have a real job. Adam remarked, "Fishing isn't work, it's meant for pleasure. It doesn't provide a steady income for a man's family, and, besides, how can he let his wife support him?" I listened. Adam ranted. Despite his obvious dislike of Mark, he had a valid point. The less said, however, the quicker he'd move on to something else, like the amount of work piling up at his office.

In Mark's defense, I said, "His uniqueness makes him different."

"Different," Adam snapped and walked out. Whenever the kids played together in the backyard, Barbara and I chatted. On a few occasions I saw Mark in the yard with Sophie, but most of the time Barbara played with her.

Sometimes Barbara and I met in the grocery store

and started a conversation, always about the kids. Mark loved to barbecue, so they invited us over sometimes. Oddly, their backyard barbecue cookouts consisted of just their immediate family. We figured that with their schedules they had difficulty meeting people and that's why they kept asking us over, even though we declined all the time. The absence of friends didn't throw up any red flags for us. Besides, we seldom got visitors ourselves. Sometimes, Mr. and Mrs. Smallwood stopped over, and, occasionally, a co-worker of mine would show up unannounced. I got the feeling that she intentionally came over to see Adam. And even stranger that she found Adam's discussions on physics so interesting. Imagine that!

Mark had a heavy Creole accent like the people from the southernmost part of Cap le Rouge. We lived in close proximity to our neighbors, but we made up ridiculous excuses to keep from socializing with them. Except for the kids, we had nothing in common, even though we looked about the same age.

Three years later and I could recall only a few insignificant things about the couple who lived next door. Barbara worked for a department store in sales. Many, many years ago, Mark worked as a lineman for a local phone company until his on-the-job injury. *What did they really know about us?* I wondered. Had I told Barbara that Adam and I grew up together, attended the same high school and college? It was an odd feeling to live so close to someone and discover that you didn't know them. Sometimes it was the same with blood relatives who shared a connection only through genes with nothing else in common. I knew more about world news than my neighbors. We stayed focused on our goal of buying a house, but it seemed impossible now with Adam's tuition and two kids. One of them always needed something, including Adam, or somebody kept getting sick, including

Adam. We both worked long hours all week and looked forward to the weekends, but school and work jockeyed for Adam's time. It got harder for us to spend quality time together, so we made the best of the little free time we got.

Adam and I rushed home, dog-tired from a demanding week. We decided on pizza and an early bed time for everyone. *Perhaps tomorrow we could spend some family time together*, I thought. Adam had exams all week, and I endured a job performance review. After getting the kids tucked in, we fell into bed and into a deep sleep until a loud knock woke us. I looked over at the clock. It was after midnight. Adam jumped up. I followed. The knock sounded forceful and anxious. Before we reached the door, a voice called out, demanding that we open the door. Adam peered through the peek hole, unlocked the door, and stepped quickly back as it flung open. Six police officers in full body armor stared down at us with guns drawn. My scream jarred the kids from their sleep. They began to cry. Leaving Adam surrounded without any regard for his safety and forgetting about my own, I ran to comfort my frightened children. "We're looking for Mark Clearwater," one of the officers said. "We understand that he lives here."

Angrily Adam replied, "No, not here, Mark lives next door." They looked dumbfounded and embarrassed. Suddenly, they realized they'd mistakenly pounced like hungry lions on unsuspecting and innocent prey. They had the wrong address.

Apologies flew left and right and perhaps a few up to God, with thanks that this hadn't turned out any worse. Regardless, we found their apology lacking sincerity. We just wanted them to put away their guns and get the hell out of our home. When they finally entered Mark's side of the duplex, he'd gone. From my very brief conversations with Mark over the years, I recognized his street smarts. On a hunch, he packed up his family the day before, as we later learned from another neighbor, and disappeared into the night. Nothing remained to remind us that only a few days earlier Sophie and her family shared that tiny space next door.

Barbara told me once, as we watched the kids play that she named her daughter Sophia after her famous grandmother, an opera singer who lived in Europe. Everyone called this little beauty Sophie. She looked and sounded exactly like Mark, right down to his Creole accent. Her light brown ringlets hung down and around the sides of her face and her eyes danced when the light hit them. She had a sweet little giggle. What would become of Sophie? After discovering Mark's means of employment created some health hazards for them and for us, I regret not helping Barbara see she had other options. Adam had been right about Mark.

We got little sleep that night and in the many nights to come. We learned that Mark sold drugs and always eluded the police. This time they thought they had him, but to their chagrin, he escaped them again. "It looked as though Mark's daily fishing trips provided some income after all." I chuckled to myself. Adam had made a hasty but true judgment. Mark had a plan after all for taking care of his family, but it fell outside of the legal guidelines. The officers' apologies brought me little comfort. Right now, I certainly didn't care if they ever found Mark, especially after they barged into our home without any regard for our safety. I felt angry and insulted that somebody dropped the ball. They should've done a more thorough investigative job before scaring all of us half to death.

That encounter posed a danger to us, our community, and to the officers themselves. It worried me that they showed such a blatant disregard for checking the facts. This type of loose-cannon behavior could only lead to future disasters. Those who had sworn to uphold justice jeopardized the welfare of an innocent family. Different scenarios ran through my head. What if Adam, fearing for the safety of his family, had flung the door open armed? What if they thought they had enough probable cause to just break the door down? What if the slightest movement caused a scared rookie just out of basic training to discharge his weapon? From where we stood, we saw disorganization among the ranks. We couldn't tell if anyone held a position of authority that night. Next time, the homeowners might fear they're in imminent danger, and a gun battle could break out. Anything's possible when fear reigns supreme. Clearly, we saw why Mark stayed one step ahead of them. I laughed, imagining a whole bunch of tails without any heads standing around in my living room. We moved on from that dreadful night and didn't look back.

Chapter 4

A Perfect Place in Time

Obviously, Mark and Barbara moved on, so we decided the time had come for us to do the same. This place no longer felt like home. The night the police burst through our front door served as a constant reminder of how quickly life could change. It took us almost three months to find a house. Exactly three and a half months later, we packed our last box, loaded it onto a borrowed truck, and headed to our new residence. Packing took very little effort. We had very few material possessions.

Our nomadic journey had begun. We moved from the homes of our parents in Beauregard, to the trailer that sat at the southwest corner of a wooded lot, to the quaint little duplex that we adored. Now we looked forward to our first real home.

Our small, yet perfect, house worked for the four of us. With two boys under school age, we decided I should stay home, even though we still had to manage Adam's tuition. I took a leave of absence and hoped one day to return. Daycare for two small boys cost much more than we could afford. Together, our salaries barely covered our basic needs without us feeling the strain it put on our marriage and our finances. Despite a reduced household income, I loved being a stay-at-home mom.

For too many years, the small duplex created a comfortable, safe environment. The police charging through our door gave us the nudge we needed. We wasted valuable family time house-hunting without committing. Certainly, we needed the space and had outgrown the duplex after the kids came along. The time to move had come and gone many times, yet we remained indecisive. Why had we stayed? We still struggled financially, so Adam began a new job search. He'd long ago outgrown his current position. Now with a family and a freeze on promotions and raises, he couldn't move up, so he decided to move out. Prices steadily increased on everything. Like his father, Adam wanted to provide the best life possible for his family.

A friend of a friend told Adam that a research and development company called R&D had some openings. He knew Adam certainly had the credentials. The company needed a project manager with a background in math and science. Adam had his undergraduate degree in biology and now was working on his master's in physics. He went for a battery of interviews over a period of two weeks. "How do you think the interviews went?" I asked.

"Really well, I'm just waiting to hear from someone." At the end of the third week, the company made him an offer. We accepted. The job offered better benefits, more vacation time, better pay, and room for advancement. Two kids, and with only Adam employed, the opportunity came right on time. The Mirabeau's had a strict code of responsibility when it came to their family. Unfortunately, a thin line separated Adam's sense of right and wrong as it applied to some other areas of his conduct. That Mirabeau blood raced passionately through Adam's veins like so many of the men before him.

Within weeks of starting the new job, we settled into our first house. The house with its simple design and average size rooms had everything we wanted and needed. The boys had their own bedroom. The large fenced-in backyard gave the kids a safe playground. I enjoyed watching them grow. Most of our neighbors worked, with a few retired seniors sprinkled in here and there. No stay-at-home moms like me and no chats over coffee in the mornings. While they worked, I stayed home with the kids. But everyone freed up their weekends for family outings. We stopped and said hello if we met on the sidewalk or at the market on Saturdays. I knew a few of the families because our kids sometimes played together.

The Scotts, the youngest of the couples and married barely seven years, came from Atlanta, Georgia. They had one son, Paul, the same age as Nate. The Scotts both worked for a utility company.

The Clarks seemed close to our age, with twin girls the same age as Dannie. They transferred from California a year before we moved in and didn't like it here at all. They missed their sunny, warm California weather, and constantly reminded all of us just how much they missed it. We got tired of them complaining about our humidity and one-hundred-degree temperatures. Mattie Clark was a nurse, and her husband David worked as a computer salesman for a large conglomerate.

Only married a few years, Mattie told me they hadn't stayed in one place longer than six months.

We formed casual relationships with our new neighbors. The right chemistry wasn't there for anything more. We'd lived in the duplex three years before we moved to our first house. The week we left, Nate and Dannie celebrated one and two, respectively. Five years passed in our home, our longest stay anywhere with the boys in school and Adam's master's degree hanging on the wall in his office.

Three years after settling into our home, Kellee Josephine Marten Mirabeau came along. The delivery was difficult. Fourteen hours later, Kellee stubbornly made her arrival. My beautiful baby girl resembled my mother, Anna with her milk chocolate skin, but she had Mama Joe's black, woolly curls that looked as if each strand had been individually twisted.

From the moment she got here, she did everything in her own time. And as she grew, it became clear that she would always get things done in her own time, her own way. She was third in the succession, and God had shown her favor. As Kellee lay snugly in my arms, I thought about Mama Joe and my own mother and realized that they had a lot in common. Each struggled to find their place. My mother and I talked every month and during the holidays. She'd changed some in the years since I'd gone away. Perhaps, she felt relief from an overwhelming responsibility that absorbed most of her life. There was no longer any sadness in her voice. Although our conversations were brief, she always asked about our health.

"B.J., how them kids? You taking care yurself?" And then after that, she'd engage in mostly small talk about something insignificant to me, like the new dress she just finished.

As we said our goodbyes, I whispered softly, "I love you, Anna."

She simply said, "Okay," as she hung up. Even though I sent my mother money, she never spent it on herself. She equated asking for or receiving help to charity. We disguised the money we sent as holiday gifts and birthday presents. I knew she'd never accept it if she thought it represented anything other than a gift and as always, despite our efforts to conceal its intent on our birthdays and during the holidays, the money came right back to us. I expected this behavior because I understood my mother. *What price would I've paid to hear her say just once, I love you? What value would I've placed on those words had she spoken them?* I thought.

She died of a massive heart attack at the age of fifty-eight in late November several years later. Besides me, a few of the members of her church attended her funeral. Adam stayed with the kids. Anna didn't know how to show her love and didn't expect it in return. With the birth of each of the children she never offered to come, and I never asked. I always got a phone call. She lived her life cut off from most of the world, except for me and Aunt Eva. Now my mother, my grandparents, and Aunt Eva had all passed away. And Cole Parker, the man she fell in love with and mourned for most of her life—my father—died the year before she passed after living for a month in a drug-induced coma.

My mother called to tell me the day after his funeral that my father had died. It upset me when she told me. "Anna," I screamed in disbelief, "why did you wait until after the funeral to call me? I deserved a chance to say goodbye."

"Beatrice Johanna, I ain't want you mourning his death all over again. You said goodbye when he didn't come back from the war a long time ago." I never blamed her for trying to protect me. But, this time she'd gone too far. She took away my right to choose whether I wanted to say goodbye again. I cried the day my mother died and understood, for the first time, her existence through a revelation at the end of her life. I had many regrets. Among them, that I never got to hear her say "I love you" and would never feel the closeness that daughters share with their mothers. Then I remembered the day I graduated from college. She smiled, and, underneath that smile, I saw true happiness. In the time that God allotted her, she completed her assignment. She took care of me the best that she could, and, even without the spoken words, "I love you," her actions demonstrated her love for me. On a cold, wet, and dreary November morning, the earth took temporary possession of the spirit of Anna Louise Marten as another season passed on.

By now, Dannie, Nate, and Kellee ran the Mirabeau household. Plans for returning to work seemed an impossible idea with three kids. My ongoing assignment included raising my kids and catering to the needs of my husband, which meant putting my dreams and aspirations on hold. Some people saw all those transfers as a negative aspect of Adam's job. We thought of each move as an opportunity to explore new places and meet new friends. Preparing and then finally getting there took over the better part of our married life, but we didn't mind. At least, I didn't mind.

Lately, Adam seemed restless. All around us things began to change. Briefly, the company held a stagnant posture, faced with cutbacks and layoffs. Despite all the downsides, Adam's responsibilities expanded. The job required more travel, despite the company's fight to ward off adverse conditions. And just as we suspected, Adam received a call from his boss. "Adam," he said, "some important changes will take place, and we need your help, but, unfortunately, it means a transfer." Adam had had his suspicions long before the call came. For a while the company hadn't made any decisions, but then its financial future took a sharp upward swing, opening wide the field for transfers and promotions. By now, I'd become a skilled organizer, and if the movers had an available timeslot, we could disappear within a matter of days.

Occasionally, moving brought unexpected challenges, but none I couldn't handle.

Adam's assignment to Suellen, Florida, came within a week. His sister, Renée, came in on Friday morning to watch the kids. We needed housing fast, so we flew out late that same evening. Moving farther away from our small family didn't present a problem, since our parents, grandparents and Aunt Eva died many years ago.

Adam and his sister remained very close since the death of their parents. Renée called every other week. Adam established himself in the role of protector of his baby sister. She was single now and working as a nurse in a hospital thirty-miles outside of Beauregard. She'd gone through a bitter divorce, and starting a new relationship didn't interest her right now. On our last visit, six months before we moved from Suellen, I noticed that Mr. Mirabeau's steps had grown shorter and his breathing shallower. Surely, everyone saw what I saw. I leaned over and kissed him as we got ready to leave.

"B.J., I really miss Joe," he said.

I smiled and held his hand. "I miss her, too."

She'd blessed my life in so many ways that trying to explain her importance seemed futile. Certainly, she fed and nurtured that part of me missing a mother's touch. Mr. Mirabeau only lived a year after Mama Joe. The protector and provider of his family died quietly in his sleep. In a much quieter service, many friends and family came and said farewell to a man of few words. He died as he lived—quiet and unassuming.

Chapter 5

Deep In the Heart of Suellen

We got in late Friday night and headed straight to the hotel. I was hoping for a much simpler move. Adam never got involved in the process of moving. Actually, I'd gotten very good at organizing and reorganizing our lives. Just weeks before Adam got his new assignment, R&D transferred another family from Florida to the west coast. They sold their house to the company, and we hoped their home would fit our needs. After dinner, we turned in early. The next morning, we left the hotel around mid-morning, with the key and directions to the house.

At ten o'clock in the morning, the sun stuck its head out from behind the clouds and began a game of hide and seek. Despite a few clouds, the weather showered us with its warmth. We pulled into the driveway and walked up to the door of a grand looking house. The entrance had three large windows that swept in so much light it white-washed the rooms as the light bounced off the ceiling and then the floors. Custom drapes and lavish décor lovingly adorned the bedrooms. The owners had obviously spent an enormous amount of time, money and energy preparing this house to become their home. The backyard sat on the eighteenth hole of a perfectly manicured golf course. Adam played a little and encouraged me to learn. I kept saying maybe later. It looked like my lack of commitment and interest in the game had caught up with me.

We spent the rest of the week checking out our new city. The fresh and self-contained community was an innovative and unique concept. It placed playgrounds, grocery stores, dry cleaners, theaters, and beauty salons within minutes of its residents. I'd forgotten how much I enjoyed an afternoon matinee.

Jolene, one of the neighbors back in Baxter said the new movie; *Kramer vs. Kramer* would surely win the Oscar this year. "I already knew I'd end up going alone. Adam's time away from home always got in the way of family. We made the decision to buy the house. On Monday morning, early, we headed to the airport. The flight started off a little bumpy with lots of wind. The pilot climbed a little higher, and everything settled down again. I missed the kids. We arrived home early, and I spent the day catching up on Renee's week with them. "How did things go, I asked?"

"Uneventful," she said. Renée considered it a treat to spend time with them. However, knowing my kids, I didn't trust the word "uneventful." Short of burning down the house, whatever they'd done probably didn't faze her. She loved her niece and nephews. The next morning Renée left.

"B.J., you'll need to handle the move, I have a meeting in Denver," Adam said. *Why should that surprise me?* I thought. I packed his things for a week, and the following morning he walked out of the door. Many times, his leaving filled the house with a breath of fresh air. Sometimes, he acted like a tyrant.

Again, I took charge of organizing yet another move. How many times had I done this? Thank goodness a habit of acquiring things only out of necessity made the job of packing easier. My neighbor came over to offer her help. I eagerly accepted when I looked around at the mounds of clothing. With three kids moving began to get messy. I'd forgotten to factor the kids into the equation when I said this would be an easy move. My neighbor and I spent hours boxing up clothing and toys. I glanced around the room in shock—we had things to throw away.

By the end of the week, with the final check completed, the move had my seal of approval. We knew the drill. Like before we prepared to live out of boxes. Friday came. The movers briskly moved about, placing our tangible memories onto the truck. An hour later, they disappeared. Adam returned just as the workers loaded the last box onto the truck. We stayed in a hotel that night and got up early the next morning to start our trip. With Adam's busy schedule and my running a little boot camp, we searched for time to share our thoughts. Today, we got the chance. The kids slept most of the way, while we talked about his job, our new home and where we saw ourselves in the next ten years.

"Adam," I asked, "do you think we'll ever settle down in one place?"

He laughed, "Would you be happy in one place, B.J.?"

I thought for what seemed like a really long time, and then I said, "I don't know, my roots aren't planted in one place like most people. They spread out like the tap roots of a big oak tree across the terrains of time." He laughed again. I loved his laugh. Then we continued for a long time in silence before we reached our destination. We settled in quickly. The boys had school, which freed up some extra time, even though Kellee demanded more of me. I joined different clubs and charitable organizations and became an active member of the PTA. Some weekends the kids and I enjoyed a picnic in the park or a visit to the zoo. We found something to do all the time. Nate and Dannie had their sports. Adam spent very little time with his family these days. His new job took away our quality time, but the kids and I still enjoyed our times together. On those Saturday mornings when he carved out a moment, we sat and read the newspaper together. Today, as he sat across the table from me, I said, "Wow! Adam look at this article, can you believe our first black Miss America has lost her crown?"

The article said she posed for some provocative nude pictures before she won the crown. My mother always said that with choices come consequences. I stopped reading and sat there thinking, *Where did the time go?* Change was evident in everything and everyone. The kids, no longer babies grew faster than I could keep up with. And our community expanded, adding more shops and stores. The moment we stepped off the plane a little over a year ago we fell in love with Suellen, Florida and its beautiful weather.

I met a few of the ladies in the PTA and attended lunch with some, mostly stay-at-home moms. Joan Morris, an arrogant and bossy woman, held the office of PTA president. Most of the ladies, including me, just tolerated her. My gut said that she could kiss this position goodbye in the next election year. A very intelligent woman with great people skills, Jane Nelson, captured everyone's attention and seemed favored to take Joan's place in the next election. Sometimes I accepted an invitation to play doubles with some of the ladies. A group from my church begged me to join the women's tennis league, but with Kellee still young, I declined. The boys were at an age where I felt comfortable going off for a few hours, but

Kellee still needed me. Then shortly after my neighbor's daughter turned fifteen, I decided a few hours away from Kellee wouldn't hurt. It was great getting out occasionally, mingling with a bunch of women and enjoying grown up conversations. She watched the kids after school, on teacher in-service days, and in the summer months. I chose my outings carefully because I felt guilty leaving the kids, especially Kellee. Many days I went to the movies alone. Today, I finally saw the movie Jolene told me about and made a mental note to call her. The terrifically powerful story, *Kramer vs. Kramer*, touched my heart. It had my approval for the Oscar.

That old anxious feeling started nudging me, and I knew we should start preparing for a change. For several months anxiety hung over me like a dark rain cloud. I couldn't shake it. The kids loved their school, and we had the blessing of our health; what else could we ask for? Three short years ago a moving truck pulled up to our current residence. We loved it here. Like the Clarks, we fell in love with near perfect weather. It wasn't California, but it hosted cool breezes coming in off the ocean in the early mornings and again in the late evenings. The temperatures held in the low eighties most days, with little or no humidity and cooler nights. Finally, I now understood the Clarks' love of California. Mattie bragged all the time about the great weather and how much she missed it. Suellen began to feel the most like home of all the places we'd ever lived. Adam and I talked about buying another car. Every time we turned around, my old once prized possession needed some repairs. It was now a piece of junk. We bought this car the year we moved into the trailer. It served us well over the last nine or so years. At least we'd learned an important lesson of frugality from Mr. and Mrs. Smallwood.

I thought of the Smallwoods often. They died in a

head-on collision as they were returning from a weekend retreat. A drunk driver veered into their path, killing them instantly. Adrian called with the news. The phone rang as I turned the key and stepped inside.

Gasping, I shouted, "Hello?"

"B.J., it's Adrian."

"Oh, hello, Adrian, how are you? Is everything okay?"

"No," he said in a trembling voice, "Mr. and Mrs. Smallwood are dead." Emotionally, we both collapsed before he somehow managed to give me the details. I called Adam at the office. He rushed home. We cried and grieved deeply for the people who loved us as their own. Adam flew back for the services. Our beloved Mr. and Mrs. Smallwood devoted their lives to helping others. They left a beautiful legacy as an example for all of us to follow. In their will, they bequeathed to the three of us their earthly possessions, along with specific instructions that their home continue to provide a safe place for those in need. We honored their request.

"The Smallwood," as it's now called provides a shelter for kids seeking a refuge from difficult conditions.

Max found a new home with Adrian.

We needed a car. No, I needed a car, so I asked Adam to handle securing a loan. He agreed and later that day he met with the senior finance officer at the bank. Adam knew the finance officer's son, Jeff. He worked in human resources at R&D. They had met before. On his way back to the office, Jeff called Adam with a heads up about some upcoming promotions and transfers. That evening when Adam got home, I excitedly asked, "How did things go with the loan application?" I'd spent the day thinking about finally getting rid of that old crappy car along with wonderful memories of my friends, the Smallwoods.

He stared at me oddly. "I've decided to hold off on making a decision on the car. There're some changes coming down the pipeline. I should hear from the corporate office soon." Thinking about the what-ifs and possibilities drove us crazy. Had Adam's promotion been approved? He had an impeccable job performance ranking, and his reviews were stellar. For us, the timing seemed perfect.

With layoffs and cutbacks no longer threatening our livelihood, Adam knew it was just a matter of time. He'd worked hard, had an impressive track record, with numerous awards for his accomplishments in the cutting-edge field of research and development.

Just last year, he won the prestigious "Risk Taker Award" in his field and landed on the company's who's who list of influential people. We received invitations to fancy dinners with important and powerful top executives, as well as with community and state leaders. The movers and shakers at R&D sat around the old campfire and decided the fate of their top-performers. The wait, well worth the agony, came a week later when Adam received a call from the CEO himself. He offered Adam a job as head of a newly formed division responsible for lobbying and securing patents on top secret research. It was a groundbreaking assignment, but it meant another transfer. This move would take us to the small town of Cheyenne on the eastern shores of Pennsylvania. It sounded like the other side of the world, instead of northeast, and a few thousand miles from Suellen.

Chapter 6

Cheyenne

I began the grueling task of packing, deciding what should or shouldn't go, but knew I could handle the challenge. The movers came and immediately turned the house upside down. It reminded me of the war zones my veteran friends once described to me. With everything gone, the house stood devoid of all life. An eerie silence filed every room. The kids didn't remember much about the move to Suellen, but they saw this next move as an adventure. They couldn't wait to ride for the first time in a big airplane with its giant wings "flapping in the wind." Their excitement spilled over into every waking hour.

"How does it stay in the air?" Nate asked.

"Will it fall from the sky?" Kellee asked.

Dannie remained quiet and not bothered with such silly questions. Besides, as the big brother, he didn't want his anxiety exposed like that of his younger siblings.

We arrived at the airport on time, but not unusually early. Before Nine/Eleven, nobody ever rushed to the airport. With kids and baggage in tow, we checked in and settled down to wait for the boarding call. Suellen's beautiful, sunny weather set the standards for great weather. Even with a little humidity, it stole the show. The warmer-than-normal weather greeted the first day of September and bid us farewell as we boarded our plane. We'd heard from the foreman on our big renovation that our home was three weeks behind schedule. We came prepared to tackle whatever awaited us, although the challenge came sooner than any of us expected.

The sun shone brightly on a cool morning in early September as we stepped off the plane in Cheyenne. Airport workers, the cab driver, and even the hotel staff commented on how uncommonly nice the weather for this time of the year. Wow! I thought. Cheyenne, according to my research, had lots of snowy days, but they didn't usually start until around Mid-October. Today reminded me of the weather we left behind in Suellen, although a little on the cooler side. We checked into the hotel hoping for a little relaxation before feeding time at the Mirabeau zoo. Any minute, we expected one of our little pets to remind us of chow time.

Kellee looked out of the window just as snowflakes fell from the sky. "Look, look," she yelled.

We ran to the window and stared out in amazement. At first, the snowflakes fell slowly and deliberately, as if they wanted us to count each one of them. Then they picked up the pace, falling faster and more anxiously. Within hours, we'd moved across the country from warm, sunny weather to a winter wonderland, almost completely unprepared. Today, Mother Nature hadn't asked for our advice. The kids begged to go outside. Adam insisted they wait. He found his jacket packed in one of our many pieces of luggage and bravely walked across the street to get some soup and sandwiches for dinner.

We folded ourselves into the swiftly moving days

and nights. The kids fell in love with the weather. We'd never lived in a cold climate before, but the kids didn't mind the snow. All day, they ran in and out of the hotel room, shouting and cheering. And all day long, I yelled, "Dannie put your hat back on!" or "Nate, keep your gloves on!" or "Kellee, where did you leave your scarf?"

Immediately, I enrolled the boys in school. Adam left early in the mornings and returned late in the evenings. He never missed our evening dinner together, even if he had to return to the office later. My mornings began when I dropped off the kids at school, in the community that we'd eventually call home. I loved the small, comfortable neighborhood and the steady routine of the simple life. It gave me the same cozy feeling I got sitting by the fireplace wrapped snugly in a warm blanket on a winter day.

Only fifteen houses made up our community. The countdown had begun with renovation nearing completion. We started getting on one another's nerves, crammed into two tiny, adjoining rooms. Each afternoon, I fastened Kellee into her car seat and drove a few short blocks north and then left onto the freeway, heading toward the community. Then I picked the kids up at the bus stop, turned around and headed back. A snack waited then homework. After finishing homework, they played inside or outside, depending on the weather; they always preferred outside. Some days, our new neighbors invited us for snacks and conversation. The kids had a great time, and I enjoyed some grown up company. Then we loaded up again and headed back to our cramped quarters. My new friends offered their homes to us many times.

"B.J., just think about all the time you'll save each day!" they said. I wouldn't hear of it. I knew what they offered had nothing to do with charity.

Still, I couldn't accept it. After all, I was my mother's daughter. "We'll be fine."

Later in the evening, when Adam came in from work, we piled into the car and went out to our favorite diner. On lazy days, we ordered in. The staples on those cold winter nights consisted of sandwiches, minestrone soup or clam chowder. The same routine played out every day for weeks.

The week of our scheduled move, a terrible storm stalled over the Atlantic Ocean causing a shift in the weather pattern. A news reporter said that the year's storm season had been calm—only two tropical storms and two named hurricanes, and not one causing significant damage. But this storm looked awful severe. In this part of the country, the weather could change quickly. The phone rang. It was Lee.

Lee and I met one day at the bus stop. "Hello, I'm Lee," she said smiling as she extended her hand.

"I'm B.J." I extended my hand and smiled back at her. She introduced her kids, Alan and Mia, and kissed them goodbye as they boarded the bus. Dannie and Nate had already gotten on the bus. Kellee looked up at Lee as she clung lovingly to my leg. We chatted. I liked Lee right away. There was something unassuming about her.

"Have you seen the weather lately, B.J.?" Lee asked.

I preferred B.J., and not my given name, Beatrice Johanna, but my mother loved it.

When I asked her once why she gave me that name she pointed to a stack of newspapers she used for cutting patterns and said, "Well, just a few weeks 'fore you wuz born, I looked through them old newspapers over yonder in the corner, and I sees the name Beatrice Johanna. When I say them words out loud, they sound important. I knows then that's what I wuz gonna call you."

"What if I'd been a boy, then what?" I asked.

"I would've named you Bennie."

"Why Bennie?" She bent her head low and kept cutting out her pattern. Tears began to fill her eyes.

"Pays attention," she said sharply.

I knew that was the end of our conversation.

That moment lost in my mother's world quickly faded as Kellee's tiny hand grabbed hold of mine.

"Oh, I'm sorry, Lee," I said. "Sure, I watch every afternoon right before Kellee and I walk out the door."

"Well, there's a bad snow storm coming in this afternoon. Perhaps you should let the kids stay at my house," Lee said.

"No thanks, I'll call you if things look too bad." The weather seemed fine when Kellee and I left the hotel. Sure, it was snowing, but it looked and felt the same— just another Cheyenne day. By now, we'd grown accustomed to these snowy days. They'd become more of a nuisance than anything else.

We took our usual route. Within minutes, the weather quickly changed. Trees bowed under the weight of the falling snow. Flakes twirled and then drifted upward making weird patterns. It blew hard from left to right and then began spinning around and around until it formed a funnel. The road ahead was no longer visible, but I inched along and finally reached my exit. Carefully, I pulled off the main road onto a narrow street leading into our neighborhood and started up the hill. The wheels started spinning. I couldn't gain any traction. Anxiety swept over me. I hadn't noticed the other cars parked at the bottom of the hill. The image of my children stranded at the bus stop in a snowstorm kept flooding my thoughts. Of course, I knew my neighbors would take care of them, but I worried anyway.

I backed the car down slowly until it reached the foot of the hill then pulled in alongside all the other stranded cars parked at the deserted gas station. The snow fell faster and harder. I had to get to my kids, so I closed my eyes and asked God to keep us safe. Then I started walking up the sloped hill with Kellee wrapped tightly inside of my coat. Snow pounded our bodies. The freezing water cracked my lips. Little drops of blood dotted the white fallen snow. The wind-tossed snow chiseled our faces, as if cutting stone. Kellee cried out from the pain. I held her closer.

"Be brave, Kellee, it's just another adventure. What's mommy's favorite poem?" I asked.

She smiled. On those cold winter nights when Adam traveled, the kids climbed into our bed and, before drifting off to sleep, listened as I recited one of my favorite poems. I'd learned "Stopping by the Woods on a Snowy Evening" by Robert Frost in the sixth grade, what now seemed like a hundred years ago.

> *Whose woods these are I think I know.*
> *His house is in the village though;*
> *He will not see me stopping here*
> *To watch the woods fill up with snow.*
> *My little horse must think it queer*
> *To stop without a farmhouse near*
> *Between the woods and frozen lake*
> *The darkest evening of the year.*
> *He gives his harness bells a shake*
> *To ask if there is some mistake.*
> *The only other sound's the sweep*
> *Of easy wind and downy flake.*
> *The woods are lovely, dark, and deep.*
> *But I have promises to keep,*
> *And miles to go before I sleep,*
> *And miles to go before I sleep.*

Right before I finished the last line, a shiny silver truck pulled up next to us. The driver leaned over and opened the door. Inside sat a scrawny looking teenage boy with sandy blond hair that hung almost to his shoulders and piercing grayish-green eyes. I didn't question fate. I felt like God had heard my prayer, so I whispered, "Thank you," and jumped in. Those watching probably thought they'd witnessed the abduction of a mother and her child at gunpoint. The truck plowed through the snow on oversized tires that lifted it high off the ground. I held Kellee close to my breast. For the entire ride, the driver didn't say a word. Nervously, I talked about the weather's abrupt change. He trudged along and sometime later, he pulled up at the bus stop. I opened the door. "Thank you," I said and got out. No one waited there for me. As I looked back on that day, I don't remember ever telling the young driver where to drop me. The bus stop was his decision. Why, I'll never know. Maybe, he figured this was my starting point. I watched the truck turn around and head back up the same narrow, treacherous, icy road. My arms grew tired from holding Kellee so tightly. I shifted her weight and started walking toward Lynette's house. It sat facing the entrance of our community. When Kellee and I reached her house, we found the kids perched near the warm, cozy fireplace. Lee had dropped them off. She knew I wouldn't mind.

After I finished telling Lynette about our ordeal in the snowstorm, I asked her if she knew the young man driving the shiny silver truck. It was important to me that I repay his kindness. After all, I was my mother's daughter.

"I don't know him," she said, puzzled. Later, I discovered that none of my neighbors had ever seen him before. Every day I still think of my guardian angel sent by God to protect us that day.

A few hours later, Adam called. He had made it safely to the hotel. "Be safe, take care of the kids, and stay put until this thing blows over."

"Don't worry, I'm not about to get back out there right now." We waited out the storm for six hours, and, when it settled down, we slowly ventured back to our hotel.

No one thought to warn this southern girl to keep a blanket in her car in case of a snowstorm. Unaware of the frozen perils ahead, I could've used that bit of advice before Kellee and I started out that day. Looking back, I learned a lesson I'll never forget. It's something I repeat to myself often. "Always expect the unexpected."

Chapter 7

Joey

A week and one day later, we moved into our newly renovated home. Out came all things old and familiar from storage. It had taken only a month of house-hunting, before we finally found it. Although necessary, the improvements took longer than we expected. The big colonial-looking monster sat high upon a hillside folded into the backdrop of a barren half-acre tract of land. The house looked as if some freak accident of nature caused it to appear out of nowhere. Houses with land carried an expensive price tag and were hard to find. We'd looked at older neighborhoods, well-established homes, and at smaller communities like this one. We liked both the quietness and the diversity of this neighborhood, though mostly the diversity.

On our house-hunting visits, we rode through the neighborhood late in the evenings and saw lots of kids at play. The houses sat hidden from view among densely tree lined streets. It looked like a wonderful place to raise our children until the next move. However, a problem existed. In this established neighborhood, our lot lacked the one thing that made all the other houses look perfect. It had no trees. The absence of trees made it unattractive. I'd had an ongoing love affair with trees my entire life. While my mother worked, Aunt Eva took care of me. She tied a rope around an old tire and hung it from the large pecan tree that stood in the center of her backyard. I spent hours swinging, lost in thoughts of the faraway places in my books. Land void of trees seemed unnatural. Immediately, we got busy planting shrubs and trees that created a beautiful landscape.

All kinds of flowering and deciduous trees began to cover our yard. We planted hemlock, red maple and pin oak along with some dogwoods and redbuds. The neighbors watched admiringly, grateful for our efforts to populate our land with trees and improve our landscape. In our community, winning hands down the flowering dogwood seemed the favorite. We settled into our life and began to enjoy the season. The north winds blew in as a reminder that winter was here. The September snowstorm foretold the days and weeks that lay in wait. Born and raised in the South, the cold climate felt brutal. My body refused to adjust. I felt the cold, damp and gloomy days of winter more intensely than everyone else. Adam and the kids adjusted right away. In fact, they fell in love with the weather. But I longed for those mild summer days—and frankly would even welcome those hot and humid ones. I missed my old friend, warm weather.

We met the most incredible people. They understood the important issues of life without traveling the world. The Matthews, both educators, lived across the street. Larry taught math at the local high school. Lynette worked as a librarian at the public library in downtown Cheyenne. Larry's quick wit and funny sense of humor endeared him to us. Lynette kept us engaged with all kinds of trivial bits and pieces that she'd read. They made us feel welcome from the minute we said hello. As the movers unloaded the truck, the Matthews stood by our side offering their services. Lynette held a casserole dish in her hand as we exchanged greetings. Like always, I thought I had everything under control, but I couldn't resist their thoughtfulness and accepted their help. All the kids pitched in, too.

We kept getting into each other's way until Lynette finally yelled, "Time out."

I had a good feeling about the Matthews. The kids really hit it off, as if they'd known one another all their short lives. The older boys, Dannie and Ted, loved board games, especially chess. They loved to read and match wits when it came to sports stats. Ted had a skinny crane-like body with sandy hair and azure eyes the color of the ocean. Dannie looked like Adam as a young boy with his lanky body and coal black hair.

Sam, the Matthews' middle child, had dark brown hair and the same remarkably blue eyes just like their mother. Sometimes when I looked directly into Lynette's eyes, I could swear I heard the ocean. Although shorter than Sam by only a few inches, Nate, my handsome baby boy, made up for it with his muscular body and his adorably sweet smile. The athletic middle boys, Nate and Sam, played soccer, football, and baseball.

Right away, everyone got acclimated to the school and its sports programs. At times, keeping all the schedules straight had my head spinning. Nate and Sam, made their teammates look good. The plays they made on the field amazed all of us. Born champions, it didn't matter the sport, they dominated all of them. Every Saturday we packed up and headed to a football, soccer or baseball game. At least three evenings during the week, we camped out at a practice. I didn't mind the never-ending games. Adam seldom made the practices, but he made most home games.

The girls played with dolls and dressed up in some of our old clothes. Never sure where they wanted to play, they constantly moved back and forth between our two houses. I stood at the window and watched them walk hand in hand across the street. Sometimes, they wrapped their arms around each other's shoulders like a scene from the movie "Beaches." It made me smile. Although slightly chubbier than Kellee, Leah Ann had light brown hair and those same piercingly deep blue eyes. Kellee stood out with her boyish frame, milk chocolate skin, and long coarse pigtails. At the very end of the street, nestled between coves of trees, lay an enchanting little pond. This friend to every child in the neighborhood appealed to them sort of like a mall or ice cream shop where city kids hung out. Ice skating on the pond grew into the favorite pastime. Delaware bordered the frozen pond on one side and Pennsylvania on the other.

One beautiful day, long after we'd settled into our new surroundings, the unthinkable happened. It was cold outside. I sat at the kitchen table reading the morning paper with a second cup of coffee wedged between my hands. Whenever I thought seriously about seeking employment again, I felt anxious. It seemed a lifetime ago since I worked outside of the home. The headlines read "Berlin Wall Beginning to Come Down." I recalled a discussion in our history class back in college about a wall built to prevent the East Germans from escaping to the West in search of a better life. The East hadn't wanted to lose their skilled workers, so they put up a wall. Many people died seeking a better life. It doesn't matter what part of history we examine, we'll find someone hindering progress and someone else willing to die for a better life.

Suddenly, Dannie ran into the room. His wide eyes

held fear. His panting slowed as he caught his breath and shouted, "Mommy, Mommy, Joey fell in the pond!" Joey lived at the far end of the street nearest the pond.

All of a sudden, memories of a chubby little boy with reddish brown hair and a dazzling twinkle in his big brown eyes flashed through my mind. Younger than the other boys, he had one slightly shorter leg that caused him to limp when he walked. He loved sports. Although a little awkward, they allowed him to play anyway. Nate affectionately took on the role of Joey's big brother. I remembered Nate tossing him the football in our backyard. Joey reminded me of an angel with a broken wing. My own angel experience flooded my thoughts as I recalled that one icy day when God dispatched an angel to protect me. Joey always found some excuse to show up at our house around dinner time. He loved my cooking. I knew Rita, Joey's mom, but didn't know his father, Charlie. He attended a function every once in a while, but, for the most part, kept to himself.

Five years into their marriage, Rita gave birth to Joey. "The doctor told us that we would never have children, but then Joey came. Charlie's heart exploded with pride at the birth of his son." Rita said.

Then I thought of something Joey said once as we sat together at the kitchen table snapping peas for dinner. He looked up at me with those adorable brown eyes, "My daddy hit my mommy," then he leaned his head against my shoulder. My heart ached for Joey. Our tiny community had no secrets. Everyone knew Charlie had lost his job and started spending more time in bars. His drinking got worse. We also suspected that he let his temper get out of hand on occasion. Yet each of us stood by and waited for someone else to act first on our suspicions. As Joey and I grew closer, my guilt eased. Joey had chosen my house as his sanctuary. Dannie's tug at my arm snapped me back to the present. Startled and gripped with fear, I dialed nine-one-one and provided the emergency personnel the necessary information.

"Someone has already called for emergency services. They'll arrive shortly," the operator said.

I ran as fast as I could, my legs heavy, with Dannie right behind me. When we got within reach of the pond, I gasped. The outline of a lifeless body lay on the cold ground covered with a white sheet. It flapped in the wind as the breeze danced across the pond. I couldn't see Joey's face, and yet I knew. My heart pounded against my chest, and I wiped away the tears. A wave of nausea gripped me as I held tightly to my own kids and watched in horror as Rita collapsed onto the icy ground beneath her. Tears streamed down the faces of my children. With heavy hearts, parents stood anchored, visibly shaken as they comforted their own children. Joey fell through a weak crack and drowned that day in the cold, icy waters of his favorite pond. I couldn't remember ever feeling as sad or helpless. My kids stood next to me, safe. *How do I help Rita? I wondered.* For weeks, I couldn't eat or sleep. I lost weight. Adam kept saying, "B.J., you've got to pull yourself together. You're not to blame for Joey's death. That unfortunate accident could've happened to any one of those kids." Guilt haunted me. When Joey needed me, I wasn't there. I believed God assigned me as his protector or maybe, I decided on my own without consulting God. I wasn't sure anymore. Why couldn't I pull myself together? The thought of losing someone so young and so soon scared me. I had young children, too.

I wrestled with my thoughts and asked myself, "Who am I that I should question a divine power?"

In time, I accepted that it's God and God alone who determines how soon. I tucked my needs away and focused on helping my own children deal with their grief. I wanted them to move past this tragedy without any emotional scars. The process began a long hard journey with months of ongoing counseling. Every night, I prayed. When the nightmares finally stopped, and the kids slept through the night, life returned to an almost normal state.

Many years later, as I look back, remnants of that day have given me pause. Even now, I still hear Rita's scream bursting forth from her lips and see Joey's body lying motionless on the ground. I hear Dannie's loud and uncontrollable sobs. And I'll never forget the anguish on Nate's face. But guilt no longer tormented me. Like Mama Joe, I'd found the same unwavering faith. Much later, I found the courage to visit Rita. She came to the door wearing an old discolored pink robe. Her skin was so fragile and pale I couldn't tell where the robe stopped, and her flesh began. She looked much older than her years. Instinctively, I walked toward the kitchen and sat down at a round breakfast table that sat in the middle of the room. She poured up two cups of coffee, and we began to talk. Many days, I sat in that same spot drinking coffee with Rita and talking about Joey, our travels, family, and all sorts of things. She had the most amazing collection of funny stories and jokes. Sometimes, I laughed until my side hurt.

"Stop it, Rita," I said. I always told her she missed calling. "You would've made a terrific stand-up comedian."

She laughed. "I'm glad you came."

"I am, too." We shared stories about Joey and how much we loved him. She smiled when she spoke of him. I knew in my spirit that she would eventually be all right.

The moment I saw him sitting with his mother on that bench at the edge of the pond, I loved him.

They walked over to me. "Hello, I'm Rita Maxwell, and this is my son, Joey."

I bent down and hugged this adorable little boy, "I'm Ms. B.J." That day, I learned that Rita grew up in Iowa and her husband Charlie lived most of his life in Baltimore, although not a native. They lived in Chicago for a few years before they moved here. The young boy with the reddish-brown hair and big brown eyes stole a small corner of my heart that day. Rita and I liked each other, but Joey ignited a spark.

Kids no longer came to the pond to play unsupervised, and, even when they came, it wasn't the same. We took shifts monitoring their time, but fewer and fewer kids came. When summer arrived, all activities again resumed outdoors. The ice melted along with the pond's ability to excite. It became a sad reminder of a place that had stolen a friend and would never return him to this life. The kids spent their days in summer mode, filled with everything fun. A constant barrage of kids, noise, and pets filled our house. We acquired two dogs and a cat. Nate named our cat Beau and the two cocker spaniels Kit and Carter. Our family grew from five to eight.

Even the adults got into the spirit of summer fun. Our neighbors, the Steins, came up with a great idea of a progressive dinner and, after polling everyone, we got an overwhelmingly positive response. We drew names and assigned the various dishes; desserts, the main course, trimmings, beverages, and cocktails. Lee got desserts. I got cocktails. Not so bad, I thought, until I realized that everyone would linger at our house much longer on a Sunday night, with the ever-dreaded Monday ahead. Why hadn't we decided on a Friday night or Saturday night? Oh well, when the time came to move to our house, we'd make the best of it. Besides, everyone attending had to face the workday except for me and of course Lee.

The evening turned out great. Everyone participated. Nothing compared to the absolutely wonderful food and desserts. A few of the neighbors came that we hadn't met, and several others that we seldom got the chance to see. We especially wanted to meet the St. Claires, friends of Larry and Lynette, who lived farther out in the countryside. Unfortunately, they had a prior engagement. Lynette, Lee, and I worked our butts off making sure that the evening was successful. After finishing the main course and dessert, everyone headed to our house for cocktails.

Adam was the perfect bartender mixing all kinds of concoctions with the various kinds of alcoholic beverages he kept stocked. He looked right at home behind that bar. *Something else I didn't know about Adam.* I thought.

When eleven o'clock came, everyone said goodnight and walked in the direction of their homes. The evening turned out amazingly well, thanks to my friends.

Chapter 8

"Whatever Lola Wants Lola Gets"

Edmond and Lee Stein became our very close friends. We liked each other perhaps because of our differences. Edmond loved the indoors and spent most of his time studying and working on important briefs. He told me that as a young boy he never played outside. Instead, he sat at his desk and read. "I love to read," he said. "In my world of books, I'm captain of a pirate ship searching for sunken treasure one minute, and only hours later I'm off on a safari hunting big game in Africa."

He never knew the feeling of throwing or catching a football, kicking a soccer ball or playing one on one basketball. He had no childhood memories of attending a baseball game—America's favorite pastime. I think he had some regrets. There was sadness in his eyes as he talked about watching from his window as the kids tossed a ball around.

I liked Edmond. He had this ability to make you feel very comfortable in his presence, and his good looks only helped. It made me sad when I thought of him missing out on simple childhood games.

Unlike Edmond, Adam loved the outdoors. He enjoyed fishing, hunting and camping, and just the slightest mention of the word sports excited him. He loved every kind of sport and knew every football and baseball team, its players and their stats. Like his dad, Dannie loved sports, too. Those days that Adam made time to spend with the boys, hours passed as they sat at his feet, watching television and yelling loudly at the players and coaches, as if they could change the plays. The whole house shook under the powerful quake of noise that roared through our home during football and baseball season. Our families spent a lot of time in each other's homes getting, acquainted and watching sports, while the younger kids played. Edmond enjoyed hanging out with the guys more that he did watching the games. However, if the truth ever surfaced, everyone would discover he naturally preferred a good book. Regardless, Adam and Edmond really enjoyed each other's company. The liberal Democrat and his newly acquired staunch Republican adversary found time to talk about everything from politics to religion, always finding some common ground. Perhaps equally as odd to them, their wives also demonstrated that opposites really attract. We enjoyed the theater, traveling, a good book, and loved dining out. Edmond and Lee had two children. Alan, the older sibling with that jet-black hair and dark complexion, could pass for his father's younger brother. Mia, his strikingly beautiful baby sister, had her mother's genes.

In a few short months, we'd met the Matthews gang, Rita and Charlie Maxwell, their son, Joey, and of course the Steins. Already I sensed the right chemistry. Edmond and Lee Stein came from New York. Lee's Jewish background began in Brooklyn. Edmond grew up in a wealthy family in upstate New York where he later worked in the well-established law firm that his grandfather founded. He made partner before his thirtieth birthday, but his dad died before they could carry on the family tradition. Now Edmond shared the same law firm with a law school colleague. Lee said when Edmond's mother wasn't working as a nurse, she volunteered. Both of his parents died long before we met Edmond and Lee.

Lee met Edmond while working as a dental assistant for one of his clients. They got married. After a few years, Lee quit her job, and, before too long, Alan came. Edmond had already made partner. The way Lee talked, I got the feeling that Edmond's family never really cared for her. We shared so many secrets I knew that at the right time, she'd confide in me. I didn't press the issue. She had a right to her privacy. Then one day, she dropped a clue. It sounded like Edmond's mom resented her because she quit her job. In many ways, Lee led a complicated life. She saw the world as black and white with very few shades of gray. She, like Adam, loved the outdoors. This avid outdoors buff loved tennis and played an average of three to four times a week. Until I met Lee, I considered myself a pretty good tennis player. We played together at least twice a week. She beat me unmercifully while playing hard and calling it playing for fun. I just played for the love of the game.

Once a week we dropped in at the Steins for drinks. The kids headed straight to the game room as always. Tonight, we needed soda for the bourbon, so Lee took me down into the basement to help her bring up some water and sodas. I couldn't believe my eyes. Every kind of food and beverage filled the basement from top to bottom, along the sides of each wall, and crammed everywhere in between. It resembled a small mom and pop grocery store. My mouth opened wide as I stood taking it all in.

Lee saw my expression and laughed so loudly I laughed, too. Then she shared a very unhappy story taken from the vault of a little girl's memory. "Growing up in Brooklyn, my family had very little," she said. "My father died young and left my mother with three young children and a run-down boarding house. Every day my mother, with the help of a friend, prepared meals for the guests. Sometimes, my brothers and I sat and watched. The smells permeated the house and filled us with hope. Most days, my mother barely saved enough for one of us. But, no matter how small the portion, we shared with each other. Literally, we waited for the leftovers lovingly saved from our own table. I vowed I'd never go hungry again." The overwhelming contents of her basement shocked me. At that moment, we connected, and, for some strange reason, I felt compelled to share the haunting memory of my peculiar relationship with my mother.

A strange feeling stirred inside me. Although I couldn't relate to never having enough food, I could identify with the painful, choking sound in her voice and the tears that filled her eyes. That feeling I knew too well. I also knew that we made snap judgments based on a person's outer appearance long before we took the time to know them. Looks didn't always line up with reality. That certainly appeared true looking at Lee. Somehow it seemed impossible that Lee ever went without or needed anything. She epitomized success. The Lee from long ago no longer existed. She carefully orchestrated her life from the moment she walked away from their boarding house. The past became a well-guarded secret. Her brothers also built successful and happy lives, and, together, they provided for their mother.

My mother and I had owned very little, but, strangely for me, it never seemed a life of deprivation. Everyone around us faced the same dilemma. What constituted a difficult life depended upon your perspective. I grew up an only child in the home of a single parent. She turned her back on welfare and worked every day of her life to provide for me. My father had long ago become a memory. Some nights, I lay awake wondering if we looked alike or if we had anything in common. My mother never talked about him. When I found the courage to ask her about him, she said, "Beatrice Johanna, you ask too many questions." After a few minutes, she turned to me and said, "He wuz handsome and smart." And then Anna, as I affectionately called my mother, sat quietly lost in her thoughts. My mother felt abandoned and had grown resentful of a man who left her behind. She never made a lot of money as a domestic, but we always had enough food to eat and warm shelter. She realized, early on, the importance of education, and, in her own quiet way, helped me see it, too. She brought me books and magazines from her various jobs. The pictures of these incredibly stunning places held me spellbound and rendered me a slave to the possibilities. Sometimes, I read her stories from one of the *LIFE Magazines*, but, clearly, I saw that she found refuge in her private thoughts. In her gaze, I saw emptiness and a longing for something or someone. Maybe she wondered how different her life would've been had she stayed in school. As a teenage mom, her parents offered no moral or financial support. They forced her to bear the shame and humiliation of her mistake. So, whatever she dreamed or wished for in her life remained hidden. She guarded her thoughts and dedicated her life to me. *Obligation, rather than love for me united us*, I thought. Much too late, I finally understood.

I needed to let go of some of those painful experiences and had found the right audience. For the first time, I shared the story of my first real shopping experience. The summer before I entered the eleventh grade, my Aunt

Eva took me to a big department store. My mother had saved a little extra from each week's paycheck so I could get something special for the upcoming school year. My wardrobe consisted of hand-me-downs from the daughters of the people my mother worked for, and those things she made herself on her old sewing machine. Although she only completed the ninth grade, she read all those old faded newspapers. When she finished reading them, she used them to cut out patterns for a new dress, skirt or blouse for me.

My mother enlisted Aunt Eva to take me shopping. Time off from work meant a short paycheck, and we couldn't afford that. I wanted my mother to know how much I appreciated her. When we got ready to leave, I wrapped my arms around her waist and hugged her tightly.

"Thank you, Anna," I whispered.

She patted the top of my head gently. "You's welcome."

I couldn't bring myself to say the words "I love you," because I knew those words wouldn't return to me. We arrived a half hour later and stood in front of a tall building on the corner of its main street in the heart of the city. The building's large picture windows looked out toward the street. Inside each window, the most beautiful clothes adorned mannequins. I walked around the store staring up at incredible displays of the latest fashions. Beautiful clothes hung everywhere, and the smell of the newness like spring filled my nostrils. Sales people busied themselves helping customers. Only in the books and magazines my mother brought home to me had I seen so many beautiful things. My aunt helped me pick out two pastel skirts, one blue and one pink, and two very pristine white blouses. That day remains one of the fondest memories of unspoken love shown to me by my mother.

"I swore that, one day, when I got a real job, I wouldn't ever wear anything homemade or hand-me-down again. I've kept that promise." We both laughed. I recall asking my mother to teach me to sew, but she never got around to it.

"Beatrice Johanna," she said, "best you learn them books, you hear?"

"Yes, Anna." Born out of different experiences, what Lee and I shared that evening solidified our friendship and created a sincere awareness and appreciation for each other.

After that moment of sharing, we stood around talking about something unimportant when Adam shouted, "Ladies, do you need help?"

We laughed and yelled back, "Not really," then we picked up the drinks and headed back upstairs. We never spoke of that evening ever again.

Chapter 9

Can This Be Heaven?

When the new school year began, I had plenty of quiet time during the day. We enrolled Kellee and her friend Leah Ann in a private school. Always together, they reminded me of Siamese twins. Suddenly, an old urge returned. Every day, I browsed through the help wanted ads. Occasionally, on Saturday mornings, Adam sat and read the paper with me. This morning as he started reading, an article caught his attention. He turned to me, "B.J. you should read this article about this woman who started her consulting firm only a few short years ago. Ironically, her career parallels yours almost to the very day."

I grabbed the paper. I had a relatively short career with two kids coming so soon. However, during the years that I worked, my job experience matched hers exactly. It seemed like we'd lived each other's lives but in different parts of the country. Adam remarked, "How odd? Give her a call if you're serious about working and see if you can get an interview."

"Maybe I will," and continued to browse the want ads.

Monday morning, at nine thirty, I picked up the phone. A receptionist answered and transferred my call. Ms. Lacee Lewiston sounded excited and asked if I'd come in that very day. I arrived at the interview shortly after lunch. We talked and shared our experiences and compared notes on our careers like long-time colleagues. The energetic and driven woman hired me that same day. Her small company handled special billing for large corporations and required visits to the site of our clients every quarter to inventory their equipment. At first, Adam opposed my overnight trips.

"B.J., what if something happens to the kids while you're away?"

"You'll be there."

And as quickly as it began, the opposition ended. Sometimes we needed hardhats while crawling around on floors peering into unsightly crevices in the outside plant areas.

I loved this job, for the adventure more than the money. The company grew fast and hired more employees. Expansion happened right before my eyes, and knowing I contributed to its success gave me chills. Lacee promoted me to a human resource manager position shortly, and, with the promotion, came more responsibility. She gave me the platform to stand on. The rest was up to me. I'd worked as an office manager before and understood, somewhat, the job requirements, but Lacee sent me to training.

The kids got busy with their lives, and Adam spent less time traveling. Things improved, but I missed the tiny town of Suellen, Florida, with that almost perfect year-round weather. The kids loved their schools. One day Dannie came in from school excited about a new friend. "Mom, Kyle invited me to spend the weekend at his house."

"I don't know Kyle or his family. You can't spend the night or weekend." He stormed out as if I'd banned him from the tennis court for life. Well, guess what? Dannie went to school and told his new friend Kyle that his mother wouldn't let him stay with strange people. Not strangers, but strange people. Then Kyle went home and told his mother what I supposedly said. Kyle's mother didn't respond, and, as it turned out, I'm glad she didn't. Things have a way of working out."

R&D, Adam's company, employed most of the people in our small community, the surrounding townships, and probably a third of the state. Several days later, a young man came by Adam's office and introduced himself. "Mr. Mirabeau, I'm Martin Jones. My sister's name is Ellie St. Claire." Martin couldn't resist sharing the saga of a weekend sleepover invitation that his nephew told him about. Adam felt the blood rush to his cheeks.

As Martin got up to leave Adam's office, he said, "You know, Mr. Mirabeau, my sister is a really nice lady. Their home's a safe place—that I can promise." They laughed and shook hands.

Adam couldn't wait to call me. I felt very small.

We hadn't met the St. Claires yet, but their son Kyle, and Dannie became fast friends. Kyle had another sleepover, and, this time, with my blessing, Dannie accepted the invitation. Ellen and Winston St. Claire, the most down-to-earth people, became our friends, too. Winston, upon first inspection, appeared just another old unimpressive country boy, but behind that rough exterior was a brilliant scholar who graduated from college by age nineteen and taught math at the university most of his life. On weekends, we found him taking apart just about anything he got his hands on, from a lawn mower to a car. Like an inquisitive child, it got harder and harder to keep things out of his reach. He couldn't help himself. How things worked intrigued him. In order of what he loved most, Ellie and Kyle, hands down came first, but his love for tinkering followed closely behind.

The beautiful, well-read, and charming Ellen St. Claire owned a very successful real estate company. Our families got together occasionally for barbecues and drinks and like us they loved the outdoors. Their massive ranch house sat deep in the woods of their three-acre tract of land. In an especially breathtaking view from her breakfast window, Ellie watched snow land gently upon the treetops, capping them with the splendor of its beauty. As the sunlight shone through the trees, the leaves glistened. Winston and his dad worked the entire summer building a deck that would co-exist with nature. Everyone including the wildlife felt right at home on that enormous deck, and we'd found another terrific couple to call our friends.

Work settled into a routine, as the newness wore off and yet, I couldn't think of a better job, ever. Fatigue, my constant companion came and, along with it, no dull moments, no slow days, just a fast and demanding pace. Applications for new hires, employment placement, testing, compensation, benefits, training, and development covered the top of my desk most days. The list kept growing, and, of course, every day I had a fire to put out, either at home or work. The kids got more active in school, and again Adam's hours changed and got longer. Summer moved out, fall approached with winter on its heels. Oh, how I dreaded the winter months. And before I could finish moaning and groaning, winter stormed in.

With each passing cold and blustery day, I thought of home, and, occasionally, I thought of the place of my birth. My head and my heart overflowed with memories.

Unfortunately, I knew nothing about my mother's parents. I'd never met them. They died, to my mother, long before they took their final breath. My grandfather died from a stroke, and my grandmother died in her sleep some years later. My mother didn't attend her father's funeral. However, she did attend her mother's burial. Everyone had left by the time Anna and I got there. Looking back, I think she planned it that way. I'd never forget that day. The sky opened, and the raindrops fell in rapid succession as we stood holding hands. The hard downpour ran down our faces then soaked our hair and our clothes. I took the back of my hand and wiped my face. My mother lifted her hand and wiped the water from her face, too. Refusing to cry, rain and not tears stained her cheeks. I gripped her hand, and we walked away. But, on the day Aunt Eva died, my mother cried. Aunt Eva was my father's sister, my mother's only real family, and her best friend.

One evening in early November, while I watched the news, a report flashed across the screen about a terrible plane crash that claimed the lives of over 200 passengers and crew. It was an awful sight. The giant Boeing 747 split into several pieces and scattered debris for miles. With the holidays approaching, I thought of the families of the passengers and crew, then of Joey, and Lynette. It made me very sad. A long time ago, Lynette lived through a similar tragedy. I sat there for a long time and prayed for all those families and for Rita. I hadn't spoken to her in some time. When Adam came home, we talked about the plane crash and the impact on the families during the holiday season. I think he sensed that I missed home, but he said nothing.

The next day, Adam came home excited. He said Louie and his family offered us the use of their country home for the holidays while they toured Europe. I didn't know that Adam and his old college frat buddy and classmate, Louis Morgan, had kept in touch. Back in the day, we affectionately called him "Big Louie." Louis, a gentle and loving teddy bear, loved to eat, and it showed. As hard as I tried to find an excuse, my only reason had no real merit. What if the kids broke something was a very lame excuse. I missed the warmer weather, and, besides, the kids had a holiday week off from school. Then it struck me. We had to fly. Until I turned my focus to the only one with power over life and death, the recent plane crash unnerved me.

The following week, we stepped into the most beautiful place on earth. What I'd imagined paled in comparison. Their property looked like a little slice of heaven had fallen from the sky and landed in this remote corner of the world. And the weather, oh my goodness! Lush green grass carpeted an unbelievable landscape, and manicured grounds played host to tall trees that swayed in the breeze, as if bowing down before a majestic God himself. Vines wrapped themselves protectively around the back walls of the house. And flowers of every shade of the rainbow blanketed the flower beds. A lake curved its way around the back of the house and then flowed off beyond a forest of trees. In the center of the backyard was an Olympic-sized pool with water the color of the sky. A large grand entrance with slate floors and tall ceilings welcomed us. Everywhere we looked, glass flowed from ceiling to floor and around the perimeter of the entire living room. Light and life merged then spilled through the windows from every direction. Sometimes big houses seemed cold, but not this house. In the corner of the room sat a warm and inviting fireplace. The mantle held pictures of Louis's family. Mortar and stone made it a house, but the love I felt made it a home, as each room flowed over into another, like streams running into a river.

About an hour away from Louis's family home sat the town of Suellen, close enough to visit, but far enough to make us feel like stowaways on our own little private island. Right away, we jumped into the week and prepared for a great time. The kids loved the pool. They spent every minute diving and splashing around. Just walking the grounds and admiring its beauty made me giddy. Adam enjoyed its seclusion. Their place offered something for everyone. We pulled ourselves away long enough to enjoy Thanksgiving dinner with some of our old friends. When the week ended, we packed our bags, headed back up north for the winter, and arrived in Cheyenne around midnight on Saturday. Our short vacation came with its share of complications. The non-stop flight that normally took a few short hours ended up taking much longer. Anyway, we arrived home safely, and that was all that mattered, although the penny pincher in me had a hard time embracing the fact that we spent way too much. Air fare for the five of us was darn expensive. Normally, on Sunday, we attended worship services. Today, we slept in.

Chapter 10

The Moon's Filled with Honey

Our family enjoyed Thanksgiving in paradise. Now, back home with friends singing Christmas carols around the fireplace, we were experiencing the joy of another season. Santa's toys brought cheers of jubilation to everyone, whether they still believed or not. The boys got brand new shiny bicycles. Dannie got a football, and Nate, a baseball glove. Kellee got her favorite doll and a dollhouse. Adam and I didn't want anything special.

Later that night alone in bed, Adam turned to me. "You've never had a honeymoon B.J., where would you like to go?"

Surprised, I sat up in bed. I couldn't believe what I heard. I didn't answer.

"So where do you want to go?" he repeated, smiling.

I stared off into the distance for a moment then turned to him. "Let me think about it, and, by the way, I love you."

"Back at you," he said. I smiled and then he turned out the lights.

All week I thought about where I'd like to spend my honeymoon. During the years when we scraped by, many places filled my dreams. Now the opportunity to visit any place in the world made it a tough decision. I wanted to find the perfect place, memorable for both of us. Adam didn't enjoy swimming. I loved it. He loved playing golf. I didn't. He always said, "B.J., you had every opportunity to learn." He had a point—I just disliked the game. Over the years, his game improved. We loved the outdoors and warm weather, but some of us adapted to the cold climate. Anywhere on earth with Adam would've made me happy.

When Adam got home that evening, we had dinner, tucked the kids in, and sat down to talk. Without delay, I said, "Adam, I've found it." He looked at me waiting with anticipation. "I want to honeymoon in Alaska."

He smiled and kissed my forehead. "Great job, B.J.," he said as he headed for the shower. Adam knew me better than anyone else in the world except for Lee and Ellie. He knew I'd done my homework. In our family, I handled all the planning, whether for fun or business. Adam left things up to me to make them happen. Imposing on our friends to watch the kids for ten days seemed too much of an imposition. The brochure touted summer as the best time of year because temperatures ranged from the high eighties in the day to the sixties at night from about May to September. *My kind of weather,* I thought. The brochure also footnoted longer daylight hours between May and July. I don't know why I ignored that bit of information.

School was out, and, right away, I thought about the Matthews. We always dropped our kids off on each other's doorsteps for extended stays. One summer Lynette and Larry left their kids with us and took a seven-day cruise around the islands of St. Maarten and St. Croix.

We had a great time. During the day, the kids played every imaginable outdoor game. When it got too hot, we packed up and went swimming. Board games filled the evenings. "What's the difference," I said to Lynette, "three kids or six? It's all relative."

A couple of days later we asked Lynette and Larry if we could unload three kids on their doorstep in early July. "We've never had a honeymoon," I said. Lynette loved the idea. An Alaskan honeymoon sounded romantic and exciting for these outdoor-lovers. Larry chuckled. He had confidence in his friend's ability to bring home some salmon.

I booked our trip, and, according to our itinerary, we would fly into Anchorage and, from there, take a shuttle to a small town about an hour's drive south. The tour package included salmon and other fishing excursions, sightseeing, and a day cruise to the glaciers. I hoped to glean a lifetime of wonderful memories. The middle of June arrived with plenty of time left. Most of the planning started right after I chose the location. Now with time winding down, I checked and rechecked the list of necessary items to bring along. The thought of returning to a mountain of work forced me to double down on my duties.

After weeks of preparation, the checklist had my approval. My assistant had things running smoothly at the office, so I took off a few extra days.

Finally, as we stared ahead at ten whole days, I could hardly wait. The kids didn't want us to go, but time with their friends seemed equally as exciting. They began looking at our departure as their adventure. From an early age, the kids saw our travels as treasure hunts packed with loads of fun and surprises. Obviously, Larry and Lynette had a wild ride ahead with six kids under foot. We boarded the pets, and I prepared a week of meals for her entire family—spaghetti, lasagna, and a chicken and rice casserole. I didn't want Lynette and Larry to be out of anything, and I knew she didn't enjoy cooking. Surprisingly, she was a very good cook. A crease formed across her forehead when she saw all the food. She looked worried.

"I hope you didn't wear yourself out trying to get everything done."

"No, I'm fine." On my last and final trip to their door, we hugged, kissed and said our goodbyes to the kids.

Lynette turned to me, "For goodness sake, get some rest while you're away." I smiled, kissed her goodbye and said that I would. Then I called Lee and Ellie to say goodbye, also. The way they carried on, I started to wonder if they had some premonition that I wouldn't return. Everyone had words of wisdom. "Be safe," Lee said.

"Don't worry and have fun," Ellie said. I took all their advice with plans to do just that.

An hour later, we boarded the plane for Anchorage. For months, I planned our trip. Unless I counted the many trips that we took house-hunting and moving across the country, we'd never spent any real alone time together. I brought along my camera. With work behind us, Adam looked relaxed. In the last few years, stuff got in the way, we started drifting apart, and a disconnect set in. That worried me. He looked more self-assured as he stared at the newspaper he'd picked up at the airport newsstand. Still very handsome, he was a mere five pounds overweight with just a tinge of gray around the edges of his coal black hair and fierceness in his eyes. The long flight provided plenty of time to nap. I woke in time to finish watching the end of an old movie. Lee and I had watched this love story a couple of times and cried each time over the breakup scene. We absolutely loved steamy romance movies.

Adam read the paper and then dozed off for a while. The flight attendant offered us a light lunch and beverages. In an effort to take care of everyone else before I left, the growling noise coming from my stomach reminded me that I forgot to eat. We ate those sandwiches like hungry castaways stranded on a deserted island without food or water for weeks. Looking out of the window, I thought of the very first plane ride we took with the kids. That day the airplane appeared to float upon the clouds. A scripture danced its way into my thoughts, found in the book of Isaiah: "In the year that King Uzziah died, I saw also the Lord sitting upon a throne, high and lifted up, and his train filled the temple." I didn't see the Lord up there, but I sure felt his peace.

Hours later, the landing gear came down as we approached the Anchorage airport. The pilot announced great weather with bright sunshine, temperatures in the low eighties and zero humidity. We headed straight to baggage claim, along with the other passengers, and waited for the arrival of our luggage. Within minutes, the luggage slid down and around the carousel. We picked up our luggage and walked toward the south entrance where we spotted a driver holding a card announcing our destination. Several couples sat waiting. Another flight encountered bad weather. It caused those passengers a twenty-minute delay, so the driver suggested we get off and stretch our legs. Adam stayed behind with the other passengers, while I wandered off in search of a restroom. About twenty-five minutes later, the remaining passengers arrived, and we headed off to a lodge on the far southern shores of Alaska.

Adam got a chance to meet the three couples that arrived early. Formal introductions followed once everyone took their seats. Boarding that day was Charlie and Rachel Normans, Jack and Carla Roth, Sam and Juliet Moore, Mitch and Allison Longfellow and Jack and Kate Beaumont. Charlie was as a surgeon at Washington University Hospital where his wife Rachel also worked as a receptionist. Jack Roth, the musician, and his wife Carla, a real estate agent, grew up together in Los Angeles. Sam and Juliet were both retired teachers from the Maryland school system. The wide-open range belonged to Jack Beaumont, the rancher from Texas, and Kate, his wife, a stay-at-home mom. Mitch Longfellow, the artist, with his wife Allison, who wrote for a local newspaper came from New Mexico and were friends with the owners of the lodge. Each year they came back to rekindle old friendships and to create new ones.

Already these interesting and diverse personalities began unfolding. We arrived at the lodge in time for lunch. The staff greeted us and unloaded what looked like a mountain of baggage. Jonathan and Rebecca Tomlin, host and hostess of the lodge, rushed out to greet us. The massive architectural masterpiece called "The Tomlin" stood three stories high with twelve separate bedrooms on both the first and second floors each with their own private on-suite bathrooms. The entire third floor housed the private living quarters of Rebecca and Jonathan. Everywhere elegant paintings hung gracefully from the walls, and beautiful oriental rugs adorned the floors. Adam and I were the only first-time guests in our group. The owners assigned our group the second floor, closest to their quarters, and dedicated the first floor to an entire group of first timers.

The moment the Tomlins arrived in Alaska, they fell madly fell in love with its beauty. These young entrepreneurs, with no children and only a dream, went home, sold everything, and moved back. The Tomlins owned and operated the lodge now for almost twenty years.

"When your gut tells you its right, you go for it," Jonathan said.

"With the best years still ahead, I've never looked back," Rebecca said.

If I'd asked Jonathan, I'm sure he would've agreed with his wife.

"Other than our guest, it's just the two of us most of the time. Lots of family members show up and get free room and board along with the adventure of a lifetime," Rebecca said. Our group dined at one of the three long tables made from a natural wood, perhaps native to the area. The strikingly beautiful table sitting alone in the room managed to fill not only the space, but my thoughts. A lifetime ago, I'd seen beautiful furniture in the homes my mother and I cleaned, but not on this scale.

With no official plans, we sat around, got better acquainted and explained why we chose to visit this magnificent country. Initially, everyone agreed they came for the salmon fishing and stunning glaciers. For those who kept coming back, they admitted to falling in love with its simplistic beautiful and graceful wildlife scenes.

We engaged in very enlightening conversation and discovered that our new acquaintances led extremely enthralling lives. Jack Beaumont appeared larger than life, especially when he talked about himself in the third person as his white ten-gallon hat straddled his small head proudly. Sometimes it fell just below his brow and covered his eyes. His deep, rustic southern drawl was in stark contrast to his wife's soft whisper. The polished Kate looked like a southern belle standing comfortably next to her cowpoke husband. They owned a ranch somewhere in south Texas with hundreds of cattle.

A blackboard noting the name of our guides and each upcoming adventure hung on a wall just outside the entrance of the lodge. All tours started out very early in the mornings. Naturally, everyone turned in around eleven that evening. It was an incredible sight witnessing the sun sitting high in the sky and shining nearly as bright as noonday at midnight. Now, I understood. The footnotes in the brochure talked about the long days.

I pulled down the shades in the room and covered my head with my pillow to shut out the sun. Somehow, shutting out the light didn't seem possible. The brightness filling the room didn't bother Adam. He turned his face to the wall and fell fast asleep. It took a little more effort for me. Finally, sleep came, and then the morning. We grabbed a quick breakfast and took off with our guides. The host and hostess had one rule—everyone dined together each evening promptly at seven o'clock. After dinner, Charlie, the prominent surgeon turned standup comic, told jokes, and Jack played incredible music on his guitar.

Jack started a band in college. Unfortunately, the lean years outweighed the prosperous ones. "Life is good now, and we have solid bookings for the entire year," he said. Mitch's paintings hung throughout the lodge and in many local art galleries in his home state. Several other guests quickly joined our after-dinner fun.

This fantastic week changed my life, and I understood why many guests chose to come back year after year. The next day, we took a helicopter ride over to a remote stream. Fish swam back and forth, gliding past our feet in crystal clear water. Big brown bears stood in the shadows and watched. Keenly aware of their presence, we didn't stray from the group. We fished in streams and later ventured far out into the lakes for salmon. By midweek with the help of our guides, we had an amazing catch. With my camera always at my side, I captured a herd of caribou as they crossed the plains. This was better than anything I'd dreamed or read about in a book. We climbed rugged hillsides, took in the most beautiful sights and smells of summer, and seized every moment, not only for us, but for our kids and family back in Cheyenne.

But we had to return to the life we left behind. Our Alaskan honeymoon was magical. On our last night, we exchanged physical as well as email addresses and phone numbers with our new friends and promised to meet here again one day.

"I had the time of my life; thanks for a great honeymoon." Adam laughed. "Now that the honeymoon's over, maybe one day we can see Africa."

"Perhaps. I'll certainly never forget this honeymoon," he said.

I couldn't wait to see the kids and hoped they hadn't caused Larry and Lynette too much trouble. The couple of times we chatted, Lynette sounded like she had everything under control. "Stop worrying," she said. I wasn't worried. I knew they could handle them, especially Larry, the strict disciplinarian. They earned the respect they demanded. We got in early and grabbed a cab. As the cab pulled up, the kids raced out to greet us with wet kisses and lots of hugs. The rest of the gang followed.

"Thank you so much," I said and gave Lynette a big hug.

Adam shook Larry's hand. "Man, we owe you big time."

"No problem, we loved every minute of it," Larry said looking at Lynette. She agreed. I scooped Kellee up into my arms and started across the street. The sound of metal scraping the pavement pierced my ears as Adam and the boys dragged our luggage behind them.

I turned around to Lynette and said, "We should get together this weekend."

"Sounds good," she said. On Saturday evening, we hosted a cookout in our backyard. Everyone came, including Rita. Our prized salmon arrived just in time. We put some on the grill and handed out a package to each of our very thrilled guests. Then we proudly showed off pictures and shared amazing stories of our adventures while sitting around a warm fireplace somewhere on the southern shores of Alaska, miles from home with new friends.

Chapter 11

Home Plate

We resumed our everyday lives with Alaska a beautiful memory. Summer was over with school starting soon. Lately, Adam's eyes held a familiar look that I knew all too well. We hoped our final move would take us back South. Now, Cheyenne felt most like home, but as the years passed, home became any place we shared together.

I really loved my job. I remember the day Lacee called me into her office and offered me the promotion.

I sat across the desk from her. "When you walked into my office that Monday morning years ago, I knew we would work well together. I appreciate your commitment and loyalty. A position as head of the HR department opened last week, and I would like you to fill that slot. You're smart. The pay's great, but the hours are long. I know with kids you might need to flex your hours. I don't want your relationship with your kids to suffer," she said.

That kind of consideration made me feel really good.

"Will you take it?" she asked.

I knew I would, but I told her I needed to talk it over with Adam.

"Thank you for the confidence in me." I left her office excited and proud of myself. When Adam got home, I told him about my promotion. He congratulated me and said he'd support me one hundred percent. Coming from Adam, I gladly took the compliment. He always supported me, especially when he thought it was his idea. The next morning, I walked right into Lacee's office and accepted the position. *If only my mother could see me now.* I thought. I had a job that I really loved, and it paid me my worth, almost. Everything evolved so quickly, I didn't notice that the swift passing of time had started to rearrange my life.

Adam got home late. I'd already said goodnight to the kids. As they got older, he often came home before their bedtime, usually, to chat with them about their day at school. He kept his back turned and, rather casually, said, "B.J., two transfer slots just opened up. There's no guarantee of a promotion this time, only a transfer."

My mouth felt dry, but suddenly I found my voice and asked, "Where?"

"One's in California and the other in Florida."

I turned around as if I'd heard the answer to my prayer, and said, "Florida, of course." I couldn't believe it. Almost eight years had gone by. I kept hoping, and now the opportunity stared us in the face. In spite of my excitement at returning to Suellen, I'd fallen in love with Cheyenne and my new family here.

The first snow of the season didn't excite me anymore. Typically, it started out clean and beautiful, but, after weeks and months of piling up like a molehill, it lost its appeal. With lightning speed, the beautiful white flakes turned into dirty clumps of ice. It was delightful to experience the different seasons as the leaves changed to shades of red, yellow, and orange. The cherry blossoms stunned the imagination. Adam rushed back to work and submitted his request. We didn't care about a promotion anymore. We just wanted to go home. Why had this happened now? Dannie was entering his senior year. Waiting on the answer tested my patience, and it waned fast. On a Monday morning, several weeks and many restless nights later, the news came. We got the transfer.

The next morning around six-thirty a.m., I walked into the office of my boss and my friend. "Good morning Lacee."

"Good morning, B.J. Ready for another busy day?"

"Of course." Then I paused. "Lacee, I have some happy and sad news. Adam got a transfer. We're going back to Florida."

"I'm very happy for you, but sad, too. I'll really miss you."

Immediately, I started grooming my assistant to replace me. Edith worked hard and earned my praise. "Lacee, I'm sure Edith will do a good job. Her work's exceptional." Lacee trusted my judgment and accepted my recommendation. The weeks passed quickly. On that very last day, I picked up my boxes and walked toward the door. Lacee and I hugged and promised to stay in touch.

Although Adam and I thought of Suellen, Florida, as home, it played a less significant part in the lives of our children. They'd never lived in one place long enough to form a bond, except here in Cheyenne. We expected the move to cause some conflict. Adam and I had a few friends in Suellen, but it had nothing to do with friendships. Our circle of friends in Cheyenne became such an important part of our lives until we no longer saw them as friends. How did you say goodbye to people who felt closer than blood relatives? Friendship and loyalty withstood hardships and prevailed. We endured lost jobs, broken wedding vows, and the death of a friend's child. How could we turn our back on the best parts of our lives to start again in what would seem like a foreign land to our children? Being in Cheyenne for so long made it harder to imagine any place else feeling like home. But we loved the warm weather in Suellen and thought we should take advantage of a climate that, during our golden age, would treat us kinder. Unlike the "snowbirds," we hoped this trip would be our final voyage.

I dreaded the task ahead, and it brought on an anxiety attack. I imagined the looks on their faces and the unspoken words. Lee and I had a sisterly bond. We dedicated an evening every month for our special "GNO" (Girls Night Out.) We had the most enjoyable evenings hanging out. Sometimes we cried and laughed while watching movies and eating a tub of buttered popcorn. We never forgot the butter. What we loved, we loved, and that included our food. We adored our serious and often too complicated husbands, but we loved our time together. The idea of saying goodbye pierced my heart. We found common ground held together by the experiences of our past. With distance a part of the equation, I worried that the bond wouldn't hold. I hated saying goodbye. Each in their very own way played a significant role in our lives.

Lee's fire engine red hair matched her temper. This outspoken defender of the poor had a wild streak. The old song, "Whatever Lola wants Lola gets," summed her up perfectly. What she wanted, she got. Although physically different in many ways, commonalities existed between us. We strutted like models onto a New York runway, heads in the air and our attitudes not far behind. It was not arrogance, but confidence—what a combination! Whenever we entered a room, people turned and stared. We enjoyed the same movies, loved the outdoors and had a healthy appetite for politics and religion, but only discussed those topics during our GNO. Perhaps we feared the guys would feel threatened or intimidated by our strong opinions.

Lynette and I never formed the kind of bond worthy of that kind of sisterhood. Our children provided the common denominator in our remarkable and loving relationship. Years before Lynette and I met, her parents had died in a plane crash en route to Japan to celebrate their fortieth wedding anniversary.

"At least you and I can still talk when a crisis arrives or when we just need to hear each other's voice," Lynette said. We shared some good times, and as our children grew closer, we grew closer. Our shopping trips became epic. We loved shopping and sometimes spent hours just checking out the latest trends. Eventually, we made a purchase and incorporated it into our already stuffed closets. Friends via proxy, we accepted that our kids kept our lives tightly interwoven. This arrangement worked for us. The relationships our children cultivated taught all of us lessons about life. We learned that love's color blind and that the heart's a much better teacher of compassion. Their wisdom helped us grow into better humanitarians. I'm grateful for the times we shared in fun and folly. Lynette and I enjoyed Broadway plays, and whenever the chance presented itself, we went into the city. We couldn't stop talking about the play "Cats" based on a collection of poems written by T.S. Eliot and on one of our trips to New York City, we brought the guys along.

They acted nonchalant, and, with very little coaxing, they agreed to come with us to the play. When the curtains opened, Lynette and I sat there in absolute awe of everything. We shut out the world around us and drifted into the world of the costume-clad actors meowing and scratching like big cats on that incredible stage. The music held us spellbound. Adam hated the play, and Larry couldn't quite decide what to make of it but said, "I'll let you know in a year or so." Then he laughed and said jokingly, "Who knows? It might still be running in a year." Lynette and I looked at each other and laughed. It certainly met all our expectations. I thought I'd tell Larry later that Andrew Lloyd Webber's production of *Cats* had already smashed Broadway records.

Over the years, we also developed a close friendship with the St. Claires. Adam and Winston had a lot in common. Their likes and dislikes bounced back like mirror images of each other. Both smart and opinionated, they had the same views on just about everything. On very, very rare occasions, they displayed some humor and lightheartedness. The epitome of soul mates, Ellie and I confided in each other about the most personal things in our lives, especially about the mistakes and regrets embedded in the grain of who we'd become. We trusted each other. Whenever we felt the least bit lonely or sad that sixth sense kicked in and we could intuitively count on a visit or a phone call.

At the beginning of the year, Ellie discovered she had breast cancer. While doing a self-examination in the shower, she found a lump. As soon as she found out, she confided in me. She knew Winston and Kyle would need our support. Ellie and I spent those days leading up to her treatment praying together and sharing our thoughts and our dreams—new dreams and some old dreams, but dreams just the same. Ellie always dreamed of climbing to the top of the Eiffel Tower. Lately, her more localized dream was simply getting through her brutal treatment with as little discomfort as possible. The chemo and radiation rendered her so weak she could barely stand. After a treatment, it took almost the remainder of the week for her to recover, only to start the process all over again.

Some days seemed better than others, and despite that ray of hope, she grew increasingly fragile. Unfortunately, like so many others, she didn't tolerate the treatments very well. They made her violently ill. Usually, a warm shower helped wash away the tiredness of the day. As she slowly massaged the shampoo into her hair, she felt the loose strands between her fingers. She began to cry. Her beautiful curly hair fell out in clumps. She called me crying. I rushed right over. We cried together, and then we laughed. The next day I bought her a beautiful yellow scarf, her favorite color, and tied it around her head to hide what she had lost. "Yellow reminds me of happier times," Ellie said. That old sun and I stayed right there by Ellie's side.

I couldn't let my friend go through such an ordeal alone. Winston and Kyle needed a shoulder to lean on. Some days I sat by Ellie's bedside and read her favorite stories, and other times I made up stories that made her laugh. Again, and again, she teased me about Dannie and Kyle's weekend sleepover. Thank goodness, God had a plan.

"I had a feeling you came into my life for a reason," Ellie said. Sometimes I stared out of the window as her hope and strength faded and wondered what I'd do without her. The old twinkle in her eyes grew dim. Despite all of it, her troopers, Winston and Kyle stayed strong. Larry, Lynette, Adam, and I never left them alone. We made a great team. Days turned into weeks, and weeks turned into months. And then gradually, we noticed Ellie started showing amazing progress. The doctor admittedly confessed his shock because of her earlier bleak prognosis. But Ellie and I knew that a power greater than modern medicine had shown up. The incredible power of faith changed her circumstances. Our faith and teamwork brought Ellie back to us. In remission for over a year now, she works as tirelessly as ever in her real estate office.

One day, Winston stopped over. "I'd love to take Ellie to Paris in the spring," he said.

"I've heard that it's lovely in the springtime," I said.

When I think of my friend, Ellie, I think of springtime, and I smile. And I thank God every day for His blessing. We shared a tough year, as one sister to another.

Now, a simple goodbye wouldn't do. Should I call them up like casual strangers or perhaps just stop by and say, "Guys, guess what? We've gotten our transfer!" I pondered for several days the best way to tell our friends. Handling important news like this would take more than a phone call. Close friends deserved better than that. Not concerned with my unrest, Adam thought it foolish to enlist so much time and energy worrying over a simple move. To me, nothing about this move made it simple. And besides, how would Adam know—he'd never once orchestrated one. I had to prepare myself to let go of the people I'd come to love, so for me saying goodbye took strength. I decided we'd invite everyone over to our home and break the news. No doubt, Ellie and I needed some time alone, but someone else needed a private moment with me, too.

This last year taught me that love mattered and that it was not defined by gender, race, or bloodline, but rose up out of the earthly trials of life. I made the phone calls, and they cleared their calendars. All week I prepared to share news that would bring out mixed emotions, especially for the kids. My mind raced freely. Our friends would celebrate our happiness, but most definitely would regret our leaving. Everyone came, including Rita, although I hadn't expected to see her. In two days, Rita would sit alone and remember Joey's birthday. I understood the courage it took for her to come. The Winstons arrived late, but as soon as everyone exchanged greetings, we gathered in the kitchen and made the announcement.

Suddenly, a hush came over the room. I literally heard our breathing. Then, as expected, the younger kids began to cry. Lynette and I found ourselves consoling them and promising they could spend a holiday together. I had no idea the kids would reunite much sooner than later. They settled down, and we walked back into the kitchen with the others. The adults handled the news slightly better, but not by much, especially Ellie. I was sure the memories of the last year we spent together came rushing back. We shared some painful moments and lived to recount them. For sure, Ellie and I would see each other again since she grew up in Bentley, a small town less than thirty miles from Suellen. But before moving here, we'd never met. Ellie, Lynette, and Lee vowed, on our friendship, that we'd always remain close. Unfortunately, distance became our greatest enemy. They openly expressed their joy and happiness for us. We hugged with tears in our eyes and kissed each other. Today, marked the end of an era. With the others, we made the same promise but knew it would take some work to pull off. Exhausted from the heaviness of the news delivered that day, we ended the evening early. Yes, the evening went well, but we exerted a lot of energy reassuring ourselves that we'd be there for each other across the miles. And at the end of the day, the door closed on another season in the lives of Adam and B.J. Mirabeau.

Chaotic weeks followed. The deadline gave us barely enough time to transact all our business which included putting the house on the market. So many things required our time. Initially, our energy level soared, but as the days wore on, it dropped to an all-time low. Overwhelmed by the deadline and the move, I fretted over every detail and couldn't remember the last time I'd had a solid night of rest. As always, predictable Adam left everything up to me. Fortunately, our neighbors came to my rescue. They devoted hours of labor and many casseroles to help get the job done. Not a cross word passed between us—some swearing maybe—but nothing more. The frustrating task of moving eventually takes its toll on the body and the mind. In amazement, I looked around at all the stuff and wondered should it go with us, to Goodwill, or to a trash dumpster? Not an easy job. Again, boxes lined the hallway and covered most of the square footage of our home, leaving hardly any room to walk. Every corner of the room had a pile. The same scenario played out. Trash goes in that pile. This pile goes to Goodwill. That pile goes with us. What a mess!

Within a few short weeks, we had everything boxed up, packed up, and ready. The movers came early in the morning and didn't waste any time. With expedience, they moved everything out and into their truck. Our neighbors stood outside and watched as the movers loaded the last box onto the truck. With a stroke of divine luck at the eleventh hour, the company bought our house. What a relief! We hugged, and the kids cried. My body sagged under the weight of our departure. Still, I had one more private goodbye left.

I walked down the street alone and crossed over onto the sidewalk until I reached a house that sat at the farthest end of the street. The unimpressive, yet pretty, red brick house had black shutters that framed the windows. Its freshly mowed and edged lawn and neat flowerbeds reflected the pride of Mr. Jones, the yard man. The newspaper lay on the sidewalk, damp from the early morning dew. I picked it up and walked slowly up the long driveway and rang the doorbell. The door opened. Rita just stood there. Suddenly, dread seized me, stifling my courage and a wave of guilt followed. I felt like I was deserting a comrade. She looked pale and much too thin, but those were the same big brown eyes that haunted my dreams. Then Rita invited me in. After Joey's death, her world changed overnight. Charlie blamed Rita for Joey's death, and, of course, Rita blamed herself. They fought even more now, and his drinking didn't help. At least once a week, we counted on seeing a patrol car parked outside their home.

All of us felt guilty because we turned a blind eye to what we suspected went on at their home. Then one day, Charlie packed a bag and just walked away. She was now alone. The door opened wide, and she gestured for me to come inside. The house remained much like the last time I visited and yet something appeared to be missing. I placed the newspaper down on the kitchen table. We talked for a while about the weather and the new recipes we tried—nothing serious, just chit-chat—and laughed out loud a few times. Rita's deep, rich, laugh made you feel warm all over. Then we talked and laughed some more. She reached out and held my hand tightly, and then it came to me as clearly as daylight rises from darkness. I missed Joey. Never again would he run through that door. I saw his face smeared with cookie crumbs clinging to the corners of his mouth and heard his laughter as he ran in and out of the door. Then he'd stop and cover his ears as Rita yelled loudly only moments before the door banged shut behind him. "Joey! Don't slam that door!"

Finally, I got up and walked to the door. Then I hugged her again and closed the door behind me. Tears formed in the corners of my eyes. Quickly, I brushed them away and continued back down the street. We kissed our friends, said goodbye for the last time, then drove away.

Chapter 12

Unfamiliar and Safe

We rode in silence for a long time. I thought about all the good times. On weekends, when not tied up with sports, we took off to see other parts of the East Coast. Awake but almost in a dream state, my mind drifted in and out. On those leisurely weekends, we traveled up and down the interstate corridor and wandered along the back roads from Pennsylvania to Maine then down to Baltimore, and then back up the Eastern Seaboard. We ate at out-of-the-way Ma and Pa restaurants that delivered the best seafood ever. Nothing came close to the fresh and flavorful crabs, lobster, and clams prepared at those tiny off-the-beaten-path restaurants. Those less stressful winter schedules freed up some time and allowed us to travel. One summer, I recalled Nate changing clothes in the parking lot of one sports event so that he could make it to the next game on time.

The kids didn't share our quest for good food. Every sweet and savory morsel demanded our undivided attention. Good food for them consisted of fried shrimp and

French fries. Adam and I enjoyed watching the fall colors. However, the kids loved visiting the Smithsonian in Washington, DC. The museums along this stretch of turf housed everything from American and natural history to air and space and much, much more. The Smithsonian had something for everyone. The kids fell in love with the Air and Space Museum and never grew tired of the exhibits and the space simulation. We always had all kinds of snacks and goodies sufficiently supplied from Lee's storehouse. At times, the snacks passed their expiration, but not the love that came with them.

Today we headed back home to Suellen, a small town on the southeastern end of the state. I turned and looked at the kids asleep in the back seat, now teenagers, and wondered what lay ahead for them. Would they keep in touch with any of the kids they played with or attended school with? In their new schools, would they have a hard time fitting in? Each had become their very own person. Dannie, a smart young man with strong convictions and his father's confidence, would start his senior year in a brand new high school. Sometimes, tough decisions especially this one, left us guessing as to whether we made the right call.

Dannie hated to leave his friends, and I think, deep down, he resented us for taking him away. "Mom, Dad, can I stay? I could live with Aunt Lynette," he said. Lynette had already offered. Lee and Ellie also offered, but we declined.

"It's best that we go back as a family," Adam said. "We came here as a family, and we will leave the same way."

Dannie walked briskly from the room, not uttering a sound. Coolness radiated from him, and, later when we asked him questions, he gave short answers. This gregarious young man withdrew. Perhaps, he viewed us as the enemy. After all, we'd forced him to leave behind the friends and things he loved. We moved here when they were very young. They knew no other place. Cheyenne was home to them. I prayed that we'd made the right choice and wondered if other people saw our decision as selfish.

Of course, our decision appeared unfair, especially to Dannie. Since he wasn't in a steady relationship, I didn't worry that we might destroy a blazing love affair. However, I worried he might resent us forever and hoped one day he would understand. Not as athletic as his brother, but a very good athlete, Dannie mastered the game of tennis, but had no desire to play professionally. His decision lined up with what we wanted for his future—college and a steady job. We didn't stand in total opposition to the sport, we simply desired the best for him. Unlike his dad and brother, he wasn't a dream chaser. He loved the game, but his passion for the game didn't foster a lifelong career choice. When Dannie could hold a tennis racket unassisted, I taught him the art of the game. The day his serve became more forceful than mine, I introduced him to a coach. After countless private tennis lessons, and hundreds of tennis matches and victories, Dannie decided he wanted out.

"I hate the constant pressure to win," he said. That chapter closed, and, soon, we needed to sit down and talk about plans for college. Today, I didn't want to fight that battle. He'd made it clear that, from this point on, he wanted to make his own choices. Dannie, like his dad, let nothing stand in the way of what he wanted. The word "impossible" meant nothing to either of them. I had to believe that we'd done our job.

Nate, our middle child, didn't mind leaving. The one thing he loved most would go with him. He said very little when we told him about the transfer. Baseball scouts paid close attention to him now. I think he felt like an insect under a microscope. Wherever he played, people noticed. This handsome, shy, and gifted athlete had a passion for all sports and life, and it spilled over into everything. His hazel eyes twinkled when he smiled and, when he laughed, it sounded more like a soft chuckle—magical and truly charismatic. He felt life so deeply sometimes, it frightened me. I sensed his fervor for life would someday bring him much suffering.

One day during one of my deeply philosophical sharings, I said, "Nate, you'll meet two kinds of people in this world." Whenever he tilted his head slightly to the right, he also shifted his focus. "Some will take, and some will give," I continued. "Those who take will never quench their thirst because, for them, enough is never enough."

"I know," he said, as if he'd already had that experience. He was never smart enough or quit-witted enough to compete with his siblings but possessed a natural ability to play sports. He could play anything and play it well, especially baseball, even though he loved football and soccer, too. He'd found his niche and played the game with an innate passion and vigor. Nate looked happy, and his life became a joy to watch. In only one more year, Nate, too, would enter college.

"When you love what you do, it will love you back."

"Thanks, Mom," he said, smiling back at me.

Kellee threw a tantrum. She had two best friends she thought she couldn't live without. We spent hours discussing the pros and cons of our decision, and, after much debate, she came around. She learned early in life to choose her battles, living in a house with two boys and her dad. Her beauty sometimes overshadowed her intelligence, but not her strong opinions. When she batted those big brown eyes at them, it helped her case. She had a ferocious appetite for the written word and tackled issues beyond her years. She played volleyball and was a member of the debate team. Within a few months, she'd already started adding new friends to her list of old ones. The school year moved quickly. Already the holiday season teased us with the thought of great food and Santa's surprises. We honored our promise for our kids to stay in touch. They talked every weekend with their friends back East. Two weeks before Thanksgiving, Lynette called. "The kids want to come out for Thanksgiving. Is that okay?" she asked.

"That's wonderful."

We missed everyone and knew how much the kids missed their friends, too, so this odd request sounded like a great idea. I promised to call Lynette back the next day. That evening Adam and I talked and agreed that the trip could do everybody some good. The kids bubbled with excitement. They couldn't wait to see their friends again. As agreed, I called Lynette the next day. Lynette had a tough decision to make. The trip would force her to face issues she still struggled with because of a plane crash that killed her parents. For years, she blamed God for taking them. Counseling and prayer helped. When her faith grew stronger, she recognized the omnipotence of God and accepted the death of her parents as His will. Later, she said, "My parents believed in their vows: "till death do us part. Their death now seems fitting."

Anyway, she thought she'd give God a little help and arrange for the kids to travel in shifts. She planned for them to arrive on the same day, but on different airlines. Ted, the older child, would travel alone. Sam and Leah Ann would travel together. In this crazy scenario, Lynette felt the odds of them losing all their children slim to impossible. Even after working everything out down to the last detail, things didn't work out exactly the way she planned.

Ted's flight arrived on time without any problem. But the flight carrying Leah Ann and her brother Sam ran into bad weather and ended up not just a few minutes, but hours late. In fact, it got rerouted to avoid more intense weather. I called Lynette to say Ted made it, but I had to tell her that the flight carrying Leah Ann and Sam wouldn't arrive until much later. The panic in her voice revealed her thoughts, even though she tried to remain calm. "I'll call as soon as they arrive," I said. Two hours came and went, and still no flight. Three hours later, the plane approached the runway. I heard a sigh of relief when I told her Sam and Leah Ann arrived safely. I knew she'd been praying and so had we. The kids had lots of things planned for the week. Besides, no one came to Florida without a trip to Disney World. We spent two days at the theme park. Unless hidden under a rock, the boys rode every ride in sight. The girls rode some, but the sounds and sights fascinated them more. And when the evening came, the nightly parade closed the day with the most spectacular light show on earth.

Excitement and fun filled the week. Adam had to work, but that didn't stop the fun. Leah Ann ate so much she got sick. Too much funnel cake, I supposed. Their visit brought back warm memories of these remarkable people, the Matthews, who saw us simply as kindred souls. They taught their children to judge the worth of a person from the inside and not the outside. The week came to an end, and the kids returned home on their separate flights. This time they arrived safely and on time. Their visit ended an unforgettable holiday week.

Ellie and I kept in touch. We wrote sometimes but called more often. I needed to hear the wellness in her voice. She sounded strong and healthy. We made plans to see each other the next time they came home. Kyle was doing very well in his college studies and planned to teach math like his dad. Winston still tinkered with all his boy toys. What a terrific guy! Ellie, Lynette, Lee, and I joked about finding the last great catches in the sea. I missed all those philosophical evenings we shared, deep in some discussion that ultimately resulted in a draw. Ellie and I shared more than an occasional cup of coffee. We developed a genuine love for one another because of the battle scars from a fight for survival. I've moved on and no longer dwell on those bad days.

Often, I think of Rita, and tears fill my eyes. We loved someone so very special. Everything got said the day I walked out of her door. Now we sit in the wings of our separate theaters of life and trust that we'll see many more curtain calls. Ellie tells me that Rita sold her home and has since remarried. Occasionally, she'll ask about me, I'm told. Not knowing how to manage the pain, regrettably, Rita and I shut the door on what little we had left and, over time, the thread unraveled.

We only saw the constant reminder of what we'd lost and failed to see the beacon of hope he gave each of us.

I heard from Lee only twice last year. That first year, we chatted every weekend, and then less frequently. The last time we spoke, they'd bought a house in a small township outside of Cheyenne. The phone rang. "B.J.," she shouted, unable to contain her joy, "Edmond won. He won," she repeated." Her happiness was contagious.

Excitedly I said, "Congratulations! Give the mayor my love."

"I will," she said. We talked a few minutes longer, and then she hung up. They had a good life and were doing extremely well. She got involved in a few charities and still found time to play tennis. Alan completed his first year of college and Mia had plans to enter in the fall. Alan decided he'd become a lawyer and one day enter into a partnership with his dad. Mia had yet to decide her career choice. During those years, when Lee and I bonded, we discussed uncomfortable and sometimes painful topics in our lives.

Gradually, things began to change. Every now and then, a card arrived in the mail announcing one success after another in the lives of Lee, Edmond, and the kids. These polite notes signified a causal friendship, and not reflective of what we once meant to each other. The next year, I learned from Lee that Edmond won a senate seat, beating the incumbent by a large margin. The once - popular candidate became entangled in a sex scandal that dashed his political career and made it easy for a relative unknown to beat him. She'd made it, reaching the apex of her life. I knew all too well what this meant to her, so I stepped aside. Without any words spoken between us, I knew I'd never hear from her again. Shortly after Edmond won his senate seat, Adam and I went to DC on business. Ellie and Lynette kept me posted on the events in the lives of Senator and Mrs. Edmond Stein.

"We're less than a half hour's drive away from each other, and we never get together anymore," Lynette said.

"Lee has forgotten about us," Ellie said. Eventually, according to them, they stopped calling her.

Adam had gone to a meeting, so I lay sprawled across the bed in our hotel room reading the newspaper and contemplating whether to call Lee and say hello. I missed her and wanted to sit down and catch up on all those lost years. I turned the pages and came across an interesting article about Nelson Mandela's release from prison. The article said he'd spent twenty-seven years locked up for his strong opposition to Apartheid. I finished the story. I couldn't help but admire this man who fought so passionately for the good of his people and his country. With apprehension building, I mustered up some courage and made the call. Lee answered in a pleasant but distant tone as if talking to a telemarketer offering her a sales pitch. And yet, I heard the surprise in her voice. We talked as if time had stood still, and then I said, "Let's get together for lunch or dinner tomorrow. We leave on Thursday on one of those red-eye flights."

"That sounds great. Let me check Edmond's itinerary."

After a few minutes, she returned and offered her regrets. "B.J., I'm sorry, but we have an engagement out of town in the morning. I hate that we won't get to spend any time together. Edmond will hate that he missed you and Adam."

"I understand." Then I asked about Edmond and the kids.

"Everyone's doing great." Lee went on and on telling me about their busy lives. She named off half a dozen charities she worked with and reconfirmed that Edmond had his hands full with important legislative issues.

She didn't ask about my family. As she hung up, she promised to do a better job of keeping in touch. I knew it was a lie. That evening, I mentioned the phone call to Adam. He shrugged.

He was unforgiving of Lee's attitude toward me. "How could she turn her back on her very best friend?" Adam asked.

How could I expect him to understand why I still cared for Lee? He hadn't known her as intimately. Two days later, as we packed to leave, I glanced up at the television to see Senator Stein and his beautiful wife, Lee, at a luncheon for some charitable organization. "Goodbye, Lee," I said as I turned off the television and continued packing. In her mind, she'd climbed up out of her private hell and tucked me neatly away in the archives of her past life. Lee finally defeated the demons in her head that said she'd never be good enough. *I'm glad she conquered the demons, but at what cost?* I wondered. This time, I got off the sidelines where I waited, a little wounded for Lee to remember our friendship before I walked away.

Dannie graduated and got a job as an accountant. He lived a quiet and unassuming life in a home he purchased a short time ago and had done a wonderful job making it fit his personality. Sometimes, Dannie got restless. Unfortunately, or fortunately, depending on how you looked at it, he'd inherited that nomadic spirit from the Mirabeau and Marten bloodlines. But he'd met someone, and it seemed the relationship was serious. It kept him grounded. She balanced Dannie, and, most importantly, Amy loved him. She made him happy. In her last year of residency at a big hospital in the medical center downtown, she accepted an offer to work in their pediatrics department.

Coming back to Suellen, Florida, felt good. Our birthplace that held us together and kept us connected in our youth could never serve as home again. Many things had changed since we moved away. Adam's parents, my mother, Aunt Eva, and many others passed on, severing those ties that once bound us so tightly. We realized that nothing ever stayed the same—not the people or places. Even attitudes and perspectives changed.

We bought an old farm about five miles out of town, the homestead of five generations of the Jenkin's clan. The family once produced an orange crop on over two hundred acres of fertile land. Their land dated back to slavery. Only five acres of densely wooded land remained now, with the old homestead sitting on approximately a half acre. Almost all the family had died or moved away. Those left behind didn't want anything to do with the place. It reminded them of unpleasant times. They'd tried for a long time to sell the farm, with no prospects. It desperately needed repairs. When we lived here, we rode pass the farm sometimes and wondered what it looked and felt like to live there in better days. I could still see its hidden beauty under that rough exterior. It reminded me of the duplex back in Baxter. Now, most of the kids had left home. We asked ourselves why not, and, without hesitating, we bought the place. Nate's school was only a half hour drive away, and Dannie lived a few minutes away in town.

Amy and Dannie stopped over after church on Sundays for dinner and conversation. Nate came home some weekends as Kellee prepared to enter college, too. I held out hope that Dannie and Amy would get engaged soon. Nate hadn't committed to a serious relationship yet but dated off and on. Sometimes I thought I knew everything about Nate, and, other times, he felt like a stranger to me. On one of his weekend visits, we sat and talked for hours, as if never formally introduced. Those rare times when he talked, I couldn't shut him up. Other times, silence hung over him like the calm before the storm. Today, we talked. He had a lot to say and, this time, I shut up and listened. I remembered this little boy rushing home from school to tell me about his day. Recalling some of his antics made me smile. As he got older, the conversations grew less frequent with him having a lot less to say. He seemed always in a hurry. It was difficult to gauge his thoughts.

Chapter 13

Fear No Evil

Kellee graduated from high school in the summer of 2001. She checked out several schools but fixed her heart on just one, NYU in the heart of New York City. It lured her with its possibilities each time we visited. Still, it came as a surprise to all of us, including our friends, that Kellee wanted to go so far away from home. Once she made up her mind, we needed compelling arguments to sway her. Her only obvious character flaw besides being opinionated was her stubborn streak. Dannie and Kellee inherited that trait from their dad. Kindred spirits, Nate and I possessed the same quiet spirit and passive-aggressive nature. We hated confrontation and did our best to avoid it. We fought back if pushed, but affectionately wore the title of peacemakers. Finally, the day came. We arrived in New York with a ton of luggage, it seemed, and a bright-eyed, barely eighteen-year-old ready to take on the world. Adam and I knew we had to let her go, but we were unsure of how to do that.

Not a cloud in the sky among all the skyscrapers, just

this spectacular sunny day. The cab dropped us off in front of the school. The long line stretched around the block as we waited to get into the dorm. Surprisingly, it moved rather smoothly. The school's organized staff made every effort to accommodate everyone. Perhaps they wanted to impress upon these nervous parents that their kids were in good hands. We walked over to the appropriate line, picked up our instructions, grabbed our luggage, and went inside of the freshmen class dorm. It was a big apartment complex looking building. Students and their parents got on and off elevators. Some walked up and down stairs. The noise and crowds filled the city. Crowded dorm elevators, streets, and restaurants all added to an already overwhelmingly crowded city. We had to admit that the day turned out more unbelievable and exciting than we expected.

We spent several days getting her settled. Confident in her choice of schools, nothing we could've said or done would've made a difference. Adam kissed her goodbye. Kellee and I stood on the sidewalk outside her dorm and hugged, with tears in our eyes. At that moment, time didn't move. "I love you, Mom," she said.

"We love you, too," I said. Adam then hailed a cab. We left there, a little nervous, but proud of her courage to stand on her own. We flew back in silence, except for an occasional comment about our workloads, our thoughts and our prayers stayed with a brave young girl who was now miles away from home. As soon as we got home, I called to say we loved her, and that we would pray her studies went well. Once she settled in, we talked almost daily. I discussed my volunteer work and the family, and she kept us posted on her classes, her life, and the happenings in the "Big Apple."

Less than two weeks after we dropped her off, our world, along with the world of so many others, flipped upside down. I spent most of the morning quenching fires about some major policy changes. The day started out far from ordinary. Early September usually brought great weather, a little warm, but cooling off nicely, particularly in the mornings and late evenings. I sat slumped over a pile of contracts on my desk when Audrey, one of the secretaries, ran into my office. "Mrs. Mirabeau, doesn't your daughter attend school in New York City?"

I answered proudly, "Yes."

She looked directly at me with fear in her eyes. "An airplane flew right into one of the big towers."

What she said made no sense to me. I stared back at her thinking there must be some miscommunication happening here and asked, "What did you say?"

Eyes wide and misty, she repeated, "A plane just flew into one of the Trade Center towers."

Slowly, I rose from my chair, still unable to comprehend what she'd said. In the history of our country, no enemy fire ever touched American soil except for December 7, 1941, the day the Japanese bombed Pearl Harbor.

When I reached the doorway of the lounge, I heard the blaring sound coming from the television. Then I heard someone scream loudly, "Look! That plane just hit the other tower." I couldn't believe what I heard. People gathered around the television with expressions of shock and bewilderment on their faces. Disbelief etched age lines on our faces as we watched in horror. Surely, this wasn't happening here, not in our beloved America. Fear held me in its grip. Right then, I prayed for the people, especially for those trapped in the towers and their families. I felt disconnected from the reality of it all, until, suddenly, it hit me with such force my knees buckled beneath me. I stumbled backward.

I cried out, "Oh God, my daughter! With no family

or friends in the city, what will she do?" I ran to my office and dialed her number. No answer. Then my cell phone rang.

"B.J., have you seen the news, have you heard from Kellee?" Adam shouted all in one continuous breath.

"No," I said in a high-pitched voice." Even as a little girl, when frightened, my voice usually moved up an octave. In my current state of mind, fear escalated to hysteria. I felt my blood pressure rising.

"Calm down," he said in that soothing voice of his, "I know she's okay."

"I know." I tried her cell phone over and over for hours. Co-workers stopped in my office to offer words of comfort and to see if I'd heard any news. Hours passed. Adam checked in with me every fifteen minutes or so. Reports of school evacuations started pouring in. Where would she go? The only thing I could do, I did. I cried out to God and waited. Another time in my life, God had heard my cry for help and sent me an angel. I'm convinced that God hears every prayer, and, in his time, answers them all.

Three hours later, she called, visibly shaken and distraught, but all right. With air transportation halted, pretty much nothing ran the way it should. The city was literally cut off from the world. Kellee couldn't leave, and we couldn't get to her. She struggled to understand why someone would deliberately commit such a horrible act. She'd just arrived at her first class. She said, "We heard a loud booming noise. The professor said the maintenance crew probably hit something and continued his lecture. Then a classmate looked out the window, and shouted, 'The tower is on fire!'

"Everyone ran to the window, including the professor who then said, 'Class dismissed,' in a choked whisper. But before the words left his lips, students rushed out of the door in all directions, not fully aware of the extent of the devastation. I ran in the direction of my dorm. Along the way, people lined up at a payphone for a city block. I coughed and gasped as a thick, white, powdery dust filled the air around me. I reached down and pulled my sweater up over my nose. My glasses provided partial protection for my eyes. When I reached my dorm, I found more chaos and confusion.

"Dust and panic, these unlikely companions, filled the air in unison. With the evacuation under way, the dorm took on the appearance of an abandoned building. I sat down on the bed and tried to calm down. My body shook. Alone in a strange place with no visible means of escape scared me. *What if I'm the only one left in the dorm?* My thoughts gave way to fear and sheer panic took control. Then Lissie walked in. Her room sat at the end of the corridor facing the elevators. Elizabeth and I met in the elevator one morning on our way to class. Lissie's teary eyes revealed her fear too, but we tried to comfort each other. With no other options, we decided to stay put. 'I think it's safer in here,' Lissie said.

"I agreed. We formed our own search party, hoping to find other stranded souls, and we did. Just a few short weeks ago, this band of young men and women from diverse backgrounds and cultures thought only of pursuing their dreams. Today our priorities shifted, with survival now at the top of our list.

"By the time we finished our search, a group of twenty weary souls huddled together on the same floor for safety reasons. We gathered battery operated radios, a television, flashlights, located first aid kits, and placed all food and water in a centrally located area. For now, we had everything we needed. A few of the guys decided to venture outside. 'Everywhere we looked, men and women stared back at us like zombies had taken possession of their souls,' they said.

"Everything we heard and saw before school eventually resumed taught us the meaning of patriotism. Stranded, and isolated, we witnessed strength and courage from every walk of life playing out during those days and nights. None of us would ever look at life the same again."

It was a relief to hear Kellee's voice. We rejoiced like so many others who waited to hear from their loved ones. Most of the attempts to reach her, due to the volume of calls, resulted in jammed or busy signals. Very frustrated, I agonized over the entire ordeal. As the days found order, people stopped by my office and offered unsolicited words of advice. "I wouldn't let my child go back there," some said. My daughter, the survivor, stayed. She refused to let an intolerable act against humanity render her afraid to live her life. She survived some of the worst hours in our country's history and, in the process, discovered a young woman she never knew existed. How many of us get that chance and walk away proud of what we discovered about ourselves? I listened politely to their advice and tucked it away with all the other useless advice dropped on my doorstep in the days that followed. Witnessing my mother's shallow existence helped me to see the tragedy of living in fear. My mother allowed fear of rejection and fear of living to make her a prisoner in her own small world. Kellee faced her fear.

Chapter 14

The Trail Leads South

Nate transferred from one school to another, unable or unwilling to adjust. After the second move, we decided to help him locate a school or help him find a job. He continued to play the sport he loved, but problems started to crop up. He'd wasted valuable time, even though he still played with the same passion as that scrawny little kid on the playgrounds of Cheyenne. Baseball scouts, according to Adam, now searched for younger guys. I heard this comment for the very first time only after we left Cheyenne, and it made me question our decision. Nate commanded the sport of baseball. Cocky and self-assured—Wow! How could someone excel and fail miserably all in the same span of time? I didn't see his frustration. He was close enough to see the prize, but too far away to touch it. I saw what he wanted me to see: a young man having the time of his life.

We hadn't seen the Lloyds since we returned to Suellen. Most of the people we knew moved away, except for our college classmates, Frank and Lena Lloyd. They taught in the same high school our children once attended. Frank coached football and taught physical education and Lena taught English. We once had a solid relationship, but the years diminished it. Sometimes we got together for dinner and traveled into the city to see a play. Vicki Jordan, the only other person we knew, still lived here. She married Colin, her high school sweetheart, but it didn't work out. When we first moved here, the Lloyds introduced us to Vicki and Colin. "In high school, Vicki had it all—looks, popularity, a high school cheerleader, and voted most likely to succeed," Lena once said.

She and Colin divorced after ten years together. Small town gossip said Colin was the one that wanted out of the marriage. Anyway, Vicki moved on with her life and was working at the post office. For some strange reason, Vicki and I didn't like each other. Maybe it was the way she hung on Adam's every word, as if he spoke the gospel. It annoyed me.

From the first day we met in elementary school, Maggie Paxton remained my closest hometown friend. She made up her own rules, and all of us fell in line right behind this energetic and daring tomboy. Popular, smart, and thicker than thieves, nothing happened without our knowledge. Then we grew up, got married, and went our separate ways. Over the years, we kept in touch and shared stories about our families and, in Maggie's case, her career. She married and divorced three times. "Maggie," I said, "didn't you ever hear that three's a charm?"

"Yeah!" she said laughing, "But for whom?" We both laughed.

Then her voice softened. "B.J., just between friends, I need to confess my biggest regret."

"What's that?" I asked.

"I regret not having kids."

"Not to worry, you can have mine."

Maggie laughed.

We wrote often, and during the holidays we picked up the phone. Always chasing a story, she traveled mostly for business, and seldom for pleasure. For Maggie, everything evolved around finding the right time. She became a successful anchor for a syndicated television station. The magic of television made it possible for me to see her often. Time remained kind to Maggie, leaving little evidence of the defining lines of age on her soft brown skin. Her hair color changed from black to a lighter shade of auburn and although no longer overweight, this strikingly pretty woman, with those high cheekbones, looked like the school girl of our youth. Her maternal great grandmother, a full-blooded Choctaw Indian, lived in a tribe along the Mississippi River, although other members of her grandmother's tribe migrated to southern Alabama. Maggie never met any of them. She recounted what her mother and grandmother shared with her about her ancestors. Their farm passed through several generations of non-sharecroppers. Maggie said an old Indian burial ground lay hidden in the hills behind their farmhouse and one day we'd go there together. I'm not sure I believed her, but many of the stories she wrote later reflected her earlier beliefs. Visiting an old Indian burial ground didn't sound like such a good idea to me. Thank goodness she never dared me. Maggie boasted of her American Indian bloodline, although not uncommon in our part of the country. My great grandmother, a full-blooded Cherokee Indian, returned to her tribe after her husband died. I think Maggie believed that in our small community only her family had roots in the American Indian culture. We've all descended from some tribe, race or group. I never got why this seemed such a big deal to her.

Maggie worked hard and received constant recognition for her work. She'd done a terrific story on crime in the rural communities. Her special, "Crime Croppers" aired on television. The well-written story won all kinds of acclaim. Maggie and I loved to write. While the other girls played with dolls, we wrote and acted out our stories. Maggie knew me better than anyone growing up back then, but now Lynette and Ellie shared center stage. Still, I think Maggie really knew me best because of our humble beginnings. She now resided in Chelsea, some two hundred miles to the west of me. We talked frequently and promised to get together, but we had yet to do so.

Our family began migrating from one place to another, pretty much from the day Adam and I got married. Now the kids had grown up and established their own turfs. We respected that. It was time to do something wonderful again for ourselves so, we decided to embark upon another adventure, or maybe just a vacation.

Adam liked the idea but left the details to me. He always left the details to me. The following evening as he sat reading the paper, I said. "What about Biloxi? I've heard about an enchanting resort located there."

"Biloxi, what kind of resort?" I'd misplaced the brochure but remembered that it boasted of fishing from a pier, jogging along the beach, bike trails, swimming, golf—the list went on and on.

"I'll think about it," he said.

Later that evening, I found the brochure and took it to his office. On top of his cluttered desk, I spotted his itinerary, along with puzzling details of a recent business trip. The brief note read: *Wednesday night, Donnelly's Hotel, New York City*, and signed, *MT*.

Perhaps I misunderstood. Adam told me he stayed at the Rochester Hotel in New York last month. Oh, well! I got so busy some days it was hard to keep track but, Mama Joe's words *'Trust yore instancts,'* echoed in my head. I got busy with arrangements for our vacation and, when Adam got home, we discussed our plans to leave on Friday.

We no longer enjoyed taking those long drives anywhere anymore and no longer had to endure kids tagging along or fighting and complaining from the back seat. The flight arrived without incident and on time. We took a shuttle to the resort. The brochure captured its oh-so-southern charm. It looked like something out of the antebellum South and inside, it resembled a very ornate and grand looking palace reserved for royalty. Dazzling crystal chandeliers hung gracefully from the ceiling, and, in the corner, a gigantic fireplace stood boldly by, guarding the space. A lavish red and black rug lay comfortably on the floor in the entrance, with splashes of gold threads shining through. An older black gentleman greeted us as we entered the door. He took pride in explaining the history of a place he'd known his entire life. Later, we learned that he shared the title of historian and greeter with his father, his grandfather and his great-grandfather before him. We checked in, and a few minutes later the porter knocked on the door with our baggage stacked neatly on his cart. Instead of unpacking, we walked the shoreline for about a mile, passing old southern mansions that stood proud and defenseless against the Mississippi River, as the waves splashed about. We returned to the resort in time to enjoy a romantic dinner with soft music, candlelight, wine and even dancing. Couples danced gracefully around the floor. Adam never learned to dance. The kids and I tried to teach him, but we discovered that he had two left feet. Sadly, I thought, *What a shame! No dancing tonight.*

Adam got up and extended his hand. I don't remember if I responded, or if I sat there in shock before I rose from my chair. He held me tightly in his arms and began moving a little unsteadily around the floor at first, and then his steps became more fluid. Adam looked at the shock on my face and laughed. I loved his laugh. It reminded me of Nate's, not a laugh at all, but a chuckle. "Dannie and Amy taught me to dance. It started out as a joke between siblings. Then I thought why not? Dannie bet Kellee that he and Amy could teach me to dance." He looked at me and said, "Dannie and Amy won, wouldn't you agree? Besides, I wanted to see the look on your face, and you know what, you didn't disappoint me." We both laughed. As he held me tightly, I remembered our wedding dance, thinking how different from that clumsy first dance. Tonight, my storybook evening began with romance and ended late into the night the same way.

Adam got to play lots of golf. I jogged in the mornings and swam around midday. Late in the afternoons, we fished off the pier. Sometimes we jogged together before he hurried off to play golf. I didn't mind. I enjoyed my solitude. Some mornings, I sat on the balcony and listened to the waves as they crashed against the protective wall that guarded the resort. I always loved the sound of the river. One minute mighty and vicious and, within a few minutes, it turned calm and tranquil. The week rushed by.

We returned home more relaxed and appreciative of the unique people we'd become. We'd known each other forever it seemed, but every day revealed new and exciting components of him aside from father and husband.

We refocused and looked ahead to the empty nest stage of life—a full circle. Our children had their own lives and careers. It got harder for the nurturing mom in me to let go. An intricate part of my life revolved around the kids. Cutting the apron strings meant letting go. Mama Joe used to say, "Them kids tied to us out of a mothering instinct, but as they grows up, they attach themself to the strangs of our hearts and hold on tight." How true, I thought. No matter where they went, our prayers and our thoughts journeyed with them.

More and more, Adam and I started enjoying each other's company, again. Those little ones competing for our affection had grown up. Of course, now our jobs kept us busy and competed for our time. My nonprofit job supported and created all sorts of ways to collect contributions to help those in need. As the months rolled by, we devoted lots of time and money to the renovation of our farmhouse. Adam's workload shifted along with his hours.

One day after returning home from the city, I voiced my frustration at the lack of "me time" in my life. I loved my volunteer work, but I wanted some peace and quiet at the end of the day. "Why don't you call the county agent office, I'm sure they'll have some worthwhile programs available?" *For certain, worthwhile to him meant a class on canning or preserving.* I thought.

Even though no audible sound came from my lips, in my head, I heard a voice saying, '*No way, that will not happen.*' I had all the household duties I could handle. I wanted something that would nurture my soul.

Then he said something really dumb. "Maybe, I should attend the class with you." Another bad idea, but I stayed silent. Spending months in competition with my expert-in-everything husband wouldn't work. While I truly valued his advice, sometimes I wondered if he knew me at all. Anyway, I took his advice and called the county agent office the very next day. I enrolled two weeks later in Gardening 101. The class rewarded me with months of valuable hands-on experience. Each day I rushed off to class and walked away with more knowledge than I dreamed possible. If I lived one hundred years, I would never use it all, especially botany— although I discovered it had many, many uses. Somewhere along the way, nature and I developed this amazing romance.

The knowledge I gained helped me cultivate the most beautiful surroundings. I created a rose garden, a peaceful haven where I went to meditate and feel closer to God. In this place, when I talked to God, He listened. Sometimes he answered right away, and, other times, he waited until he knew I could handle his answer. I expressed my love and gratitude and thanked him for guiding me through some choppy waters. Who else, but God created such beauty or healed my dear friend Ellie? An immediate transformation took place in my heart and out flowed contentment. My pastor always said that only three types of people exist in this world; those in a storm, those coming out of a storm, and those heading into a storm.

Thank goodness most of our tropical disturbances never amounted to much.

In those very early years, Adam worked Louisiana and parts of Mississippi as a county agent traveling from one rural community to another. He inspected crops and set out tests throughout the parishes and counties of the south. Adam enjoyed meeting farmers and sharecroppers, just ordinary folks who struggled with the ups and downs of life. While traveling the dusty back roads, meeting people who shared their fascinating stories of perseverance further shaped the character of this wonderful man.

Adam and I decided to drive up to see Nate over the weekend. I called his cell phone. He didn't pick up, so I left him a message. His dad and I wanted to stop by this weekend. Later that evening, he called and reminded me to bring him some of my homemade lasagna. Nate and Joey loved my cooking, but Nate preferred my pasta dishes. We drove up to see him Saturday morning. He stood outside of his apartment and waited eagerly to help us bring in the goodies I'd spent hours preparing for him. We talked about his big day approaching. Surprisingly, he poured out ideas and plans for his future. Finally, the light bulb came on, and it shone brighter than ever. We spent several hours listening, talking, and offering advice. When we said goodbye that evening, we walked away with our spirits high.

Finally, the curse of the middle child was over. We got home late because Adam just had to stop at a golf shop and buy a new putter. Later that night in bed he turned to me, "Nate made me proud today."

"Me, too." I turned off the lights and fell asleep. Dannie came by on Sunday. Amy had to work. "Dannie, I said, "have you talked with your brother or sister this week?"

"Yes, I talked with Kellee earlier in the week. Nate and I spoke just yesterday." Dannie's closeness to his brother and sister was always evident in his defense of them. Dannie loved Nate and Kellee, though he didn't share their deep love for pets. When you loved Nate and Kellee, you got a package deal which included their pets. Only a year older than Nate and a few years older than Kellee, Dannie thought of himself as their protector. Without a doubt, our children represented God's greatest gift to me.

My children much like the sun, the moon, and the stars showcased their differences. Over time, they developed a sense of loyalty to one another. Granted, in their early childhood years, they fought like true siblings. Our family outings brought out the beast in them and unraveled my last nerves. The song of the day would eventually go on and on forever. "Mommy, he's touching me," or "Mommy, he's looking at me." And then there's my favorite: "Are we there yet?"

My children taught me numerous difficult and painstakingly challenging lessons. They taught me patience to handle a tomorrow filled with sorrows and disappointments. And yes, the pure joys and heart wrenching pleasures they gave me simply took my breath away. My faith, while tested, taught me to let go and live in the moment.

When the kids were younger, all their friends hung out at our house. I kept a watchful eye on all of them. Nate collected all living things, turtles, dogs, frogs, gerbils, and once he even tried to sneak a snake onto the premises.

That was when I drew a line in the sand.

Nate loved Kit and Carter, his two cocker spaniels. One afternoon Nate rushed home from school to pick up his practice gear. When he opened the gate, Carter dashed right past him into the street. In that split second, a speeding car hit Carter and kept on going. Carter died in a pool of blood in the middle of the street. Nate wrapped him in his arms with tears in his eyes and carried him into the backyard. I saw the compassion and heartbreak on the face of my son and discovered that what he loved, he really loved. We buried Carter that day in our pet cemetery alongside a few of his other close friends.

On another occasion, as surrogate parents of a kitten too young to be away from its mother, we rose to a piercing scream coming from the vicinity of Kellee's room. Adam and I ran upstairs and down the hall to her room. Dannie and Nate stood in her doorway. She screamed hysterically as she stared down at the kitten's stiff body stretched out across the edge of her bed with its feet extending upward. Adam picked up the lifeless kitten and carried it downstairs. Kellee cried as we stood in the drenching rain while Adam buried the kitten. "She's gone to kitten heaven," Adam said. Kellee sighed as if she knew what he said was the truth. As the years rolled by, all our beloved pets found a resting place in our backyard under the big oak tree that leaned against the weathered fence. Love for creatures great and small filled the hearts of our children.

Ellie and I shared many conversations while she fought the war on breast cancer. She worried about what would happen to Kyle if she didn't make it. "Ellie," I said, "our incredible children, regardless of our perception of them, over time will develop enormous fortitude and strength. Don't worry about Kyle, he'll be just fine. You know Winston will take good care of him, and I'll hover over them. Besides, you'll be around for a long time." She smiled, and then just from hearing those words, a peace came over her that illuminated her face. "Ellie, our kids, without question, will make mistakes, despite our teachings, but if we've done our jobs, they'll handle whatever comes. We can't protect them from everything. Sometimes, even with the best preparation, life will still spin out of control. We can only pray daily that life will remain their ally. We weathered the South and the sixties, and we turned out okay, right?"

"Yeah, I guess we did, at that."

Continuing, I said, "We wandered without focus on occasion confused, bewildered, struggling and trying to find our way. When we got to our destination, somebody else had beaten us there, because they'd had the same vision. What we came to understand most about our journey was that the people who loved us stood by waiting to pick us up if we fell. We must make sure our children know we'll wait tolerantly in the wings to help them if they should ever need us. Trust that Kyle will rely on your teachings."

That weekend after visiting with Nate, we left reassured that he would be okay. In a few days, he'd celebrate his birthday and then his graduation. Dannie and Kellee wanted to find the perfect gifts for him. I wanted to give him something both practical and useful but got lost in the material trappings of his accomplishment. I made reservations at one of his favorite restaurants. He seemed seriously involved with a young woman we'd not met, and I thought that perhaps I should invite her.

Lately, he talked about Lora—his new girlfriend—in almost all his conversations. I sensed without asking that he was in love. Curiosity got the best of me, so I called Dannie. I wanted to know just how serious was this relationship between Nate and Lora. If anyone knew the extent of their relationship, Dannie would know. There was one certainty. Dannie, his brother, and his sister had a very close relationship.

"Hello, Dannie."

"Hi, Mom!" he said cheerfully.

We talked briefly, before I jumped right in.

"Dannie, tell me about Nate's new girlfriend. What's she like, do you know her parents, where did he meet her? Should we get excited about this relationship?"

"Mom, if you want to know all of these things, ask Nate. It's his business, not mine." His response shocked me. It didn't sound at all like the Dannie I knew. He usually enjoyed meddling in his brother and sister's business, but I didn't press him and didn't mention it anymore.

I laughed and said, "All right, I will," and hung up. But, his tone disturbed me, the way he said it was Nate's business. So, I did the next best thing, I called Nate. The phone rang for a long time.

"Hello, Mom, how are you?"

"Fine. What about you?"

"I'm great."

I got straight to the point. "Nate honey, when will we get to meet Lora? Is it serious?"

He paused for a moment and then said, "Soon, Mom."

"I want to know all about her. Should I invite her to the celebration dinner?"

"Sure. I'll give you her phone number later."

"Okay, great. I love you," I'll talk with you later.

Nate came home the next day. I walked outside to talk with him while he washed his car. The warm spring weather lifted my spirits and reminded me of the two most important days in Nate's life: his birthday and his upcoming graduation day.

"Nate, don't forget to leave Lora's number for me."

"I won't." He'd long ago found the courage to relinquish his dream of playing professional baseball. He learned much too early the pain associated with letting go of the people and things he loved. The day Nate told me that he wouldn't play the game he loved anymore, it hurt me as much as it hurt him.

"Time's no longer on my side, Mom."

I saw the pain in his eyes as he fought back the tears.

"I take full responsibility for the outcome. It took me a long time to accept that I allowed my poor choices to steal my dream." Nate had many regrets, I know, because he told me that day. I tried to change the subject, but he kept right on talking. For him, this mood was rare, so I listened. "You know, Mom, I regret more than anything that I let you and Dad down. I wouldn't listen when you tried so hard to get me to see the important things. I allowed my friends to make my decisions. You used to tell all of us, including my friends, that consequences follow choices. I should've heard the wisdom coming from you and my own heart. Anyway, that's behind me, I have a job interview lined up already, and it looks promising."

"You didn't let us down, Nate. We only wanted for you what you wanted for yourself. It's oaky. Sometimes, life has its own agenda. We love you. Then I gave him a big hug and walked back inside. He'd finally faced his bad decisions. He would survive. An hour later he came inside to say goodbye, as he headed back to school. "Tell Dad I'll call him."

I stood at the kitchen window looking out trying to hold on to all those memories. Nate had lots of fond memories that he'd carry with him the rest of his life. He'd played in two Junior College World Series games and received the Most Valuable Player award twice. The second time, he received this honor was on a hot, sunny day. It was most definitely perfect baseball weather. Everyone expected the final game to be a tough one. Our team would play against a team that had the best pitcher in the league. Of course, all our boys knew it and let this knowledge shake them up. They fell into a slump, and their hitting suffered. The coach called a timeout and rallied them for a pep talk. I don't know what he said to them, but they bounced back by the fourth inning. Even the weakest hitter tagged the ball, and suddenly things turned around. And now with the bases loaded, Nate walked to the plate.

Everyone stood to their feet, confident that he'd get a hit. I couldn't imagine the pressure he felt right then. But he'd stood in the same spot many times before in his dreams and lived for this moment. The pitcher threw the first pitch, and the umpire called out loudly, "Ball!" The second pitch came across the plate, and the umpire again yelled, "Ball!" I sat eating sunflower seeds and biting my nails. Then the third pitch came toward Nate with such force, I held my breath as the umpire yelled even louder, "Ball!"

The crowd moaned.

Adam leaned over to me, "Nate has the advantage with a three-ball count. They don't want to take a chance on him hitting. They'll walk him." But Nate didn't care about their plans. He had his own plan as he stood in the box composed and ready. The pitch came right down the middle. He leaned into it and swung the bat. The ball flew high over the centerfielder's head and across the fence. I heard the crowd shouting, "It's gone, it's gone, its' a grand slam!" We jumped to our feet yelling and screaming, along with the hundreds of other people who witnessed his superb athletic ability. Proudly, we watched in amazement his awesome God-given talent. Another great performance happened. On that day he received the honor of MVP for the second year. I stood at the window a few minutes longer lost in my thoughts. Then I filled the dishwasher and headed off to the shower. Tomorrow we'd celebrate his birthday. "Lora's number?!" I said out loud. "Oh well, I'll get it later."

The next morning Adam called Nate.

"Happy birthday, son."

"Thanks, Dad." They talked a few minutes and then Adam passed the phone to me.

"Nate, I've loved you all of my life, and I'll love you the rest of my life, happy birthday!"

He laughed. "Thanks, Mom. I'll see you guys on Sunday for dinner and birthday cake. Oh! By the way, Kellee called earlier to wish me a happy birthday, too."

"Will you bring Lora on Sunday?" I asked.

"Perhaps," he said.

I spent Saturday morning at the grocery store and the rest of the day preparing several of Nate's favorite dishes. The menu included all his favorite pasta dishes and a German chocolate cake. We made a big deal over everyone's birthday in our family, and our children knew without question that we loved them.

Sunday morning Adam and I went to morning worship and returned home just as Dannie and Amy pulled into the driveway. Within minutes of their arrival, Nate pulled in behind them, alone. "Lora sends her regrets. She had to work today." Out of the corner of my eye, I noticed an odd exchange between the boys but just shrugged it off. We exchanged hugs and kisses and walked into the house. Later, I learned from Amy that Lora, a few years older than Nate, worked as a nurse in the local hospital. A few minutes later, as Amy and I set the table, the phone rang.

Adam answered, "Hello, Kellee."

"Hello, Dad," she said.

I heard the excitement in Adam's voice. They talked for a while, then I heard him call Nate. Nate and his sister talked for about ten minutes. Apparently, Kellee mentioned Lora because I heard him whisper to her, "Don't worry about Lora, I can handle it."

Finally, Nate hung up, and everyone followed me into the dining room where Adam offered up a prayer before we sat down to our Sunday tradition. Time got away from us, and, before long, everyone packed up the leftovers to take with them. I hugged my boys and kissed them goodbye. When I hugged Nate a strange urge to hold on forever came over me. Finally, I took a deep breath and let go. They got into their cars and drove off.

After everyone left, we went for a walk across the open pasture and down to the edge of the woods. On our way back, I stopped to visit my rose garden.

Adam walked back toward the house. "Don't be too long!" he shouted as he headed up the road.

"I'll be just a few minutes." The evening felt right for getting lost in my private thoughts. I couldn't remember the last time I spent time out here. Long ago, this refuge helped me escape the busyness of my life. Things kept getting added to my day until I lost myself in the madness of it all. But now, no longer frantic, my days felt well spent and unrehearsed. Finally, I had time to sit and inhale the fragrance of the season.

I looked closely as if to take inventory of my life and had to ask myself several questions. Had I demonstrated good parenting skills? Had I handled the challenges of life with courage and not just any old daunting spirit? I remembered how candidly Nate spoke about his bad decisions. He had regrets—too many parties, too much alcohol, and a few friends who didn't care about improving the quality of their lives. He thought he could save everyone. In the end, he refused to wallow in self-pity. His conscious decision to move on with his life touched my heart. As parents, we wanted to know that our children could handle the downside of life on their own, and that was what I tried to convey to Ellie.

My children's childhood seasons brought back poignant memories. Nobody rushed through a season to get to the next. We accepted every season at face value with the philosophy that if it were meant for us, it would wait for us. Cultivated and planted fields waited with anticipation for the birth of a new crop as all things new jump-started the beginning of spring. Trees took on new leaves, flowers blossomed, while the grass pushed up and out to embrace a brand-new day. We learned to live in the moment knowing that within seconds our contentment could change. Kellee's terrifying experience in New York City shaped her life forever.

The hour grew late. A few minutes turned into a half hour. Again, unable to stop the influx of memories, I paused and wondered what had my life's journey revealed about me? Hopefully, my purposeful choices benefited those I loved, and I hope as I evolved, they benefited me, too. I'd relied on the promise of every sunrise and every sunset to move me closer to a sense of serenity. In my quest, I'd learned that peace started on the inside. It had no extravagant price tag, nor would it bow to the clever bartering of men. It didn't ask for, but would grant, solace upon request. In my valley experience, the silence whispered louder than the wind. I thought about all my dreams, some realized, some unfulfilled, and of Adam as I walked back toward the house. In every one of our seasons together, I thanked God for the grace not earned. And each day awakened the consciousness of an opportunity to fix things left unsaid. Did I really need to say those things that I thought needed saying? The voice in my head told me to do it quickly before the chance slipped away. I sensed something was about to happen that would shake our foundation and fretted over getting Adam to heed my advice with only my intuition as the reason. When it came to our relationship, he lived in the land of make believe. Adam Mirabeau had a way of shutting out the world when it suited him. Therefore, I ignored my feelings and walked inside.

The important role my friends played in my life gave it new meaning. No question about it, God's grace and mercy covered me. When I finished thanking him, I was standing inside my house. I walked past Adam and said goodnight as he sat reading the Sunday paper. After a long and exhausting weekend, I showered and climbed into bed. Sometime later that night, I remember Adam crawling into bed. Monday mornings always came too early. Adam had already left for work when I got up. I walked into the kitchen, poured a cup of coffee, and sat for a moment locked in my thoughts. Nate stayed on my mind all weekend. I told myself it had to do with his upcoming graduation day. After a second cup of coffee, I dressed for work and walked out the door. Adam worked extra hours on Monday's. He now enjoyed a four-day work week which freed up his Friday's for yard work and odd jobs around the house.

Those reduced volunteer days created nice long weekends for us to get away. A flicker had taken the place of that steady spark, but I kept trying to start a blaze.

Chapter 15

Nate's Song

I got home around six-thirty Monday evening and pulled together a quick meal from what was left of Sunday's leftovers. I'd forgotten that the kids packed up before they left. Adam arrived much later, and we sat down to a quiet dinner. Tired and absorbed in our own thoughts, we asked the polite questions.

"How was your day?"

"Very good," he said.

After dinner, Adam turned in early while I sat watching the news. Much later, I crawled into bed. I tossed and turned most of the night. Somewhere in the dawn hours, the phone rang. It jolted me from my sleep.

"Oh, God," I whispered. I felt this moment would change my life forever.

Adam got up, half-dazed.

Suddenly, I heard a low moan, and then he turned around and cried out: "B.J., Nate's dead."

I jumped up and ran toward him. He reached for me as I collapsed to the floor. We fell together holding each other and sobbing. Pain filled my chest cavity. It felt like my heart had exploded. Once the bleeding started, I knew it would never completely stop.

First, I thought, "Surely this is a bad dream, and, any minute, I'll wake up." But, it didn't feel like a dream. Salty tears fell and then rolled down my cheeks into my open mouth. Adam didn't recognize the voice of the woman caller. Between sobs and fits of hysteria, she explained that Nate had been shot. Incoherent at times, she gave sketchy details and directions. Adam hung up. We dressed hurriedly and drove twenty agonizing minutes to a deserted street across town.

When we arrived, police cars and spectators lined the street. We jumped from the car and ran toward Nate's truck. The driver's door stood ajar filled with visible sprays of bullet holes. Before we reached the car, a police officer grabbed my arm. "Come with me, ma'am."

I jerked away and kept walking while waving my hands to keep the officer at bay. "That's my son's car," I yelled.

He placed his body between us and the bullet-riddled car and corralled us toward his patrol car. "Where's my son?" I shouted.

The officer calmly replied, "Ma'am, he didn't make it." Perhaps he could see that what he said hadn't registered, so he said it again. "I'm sorry," he said, this time with compassion in his voice, "The young man died."

I screamed so loudly it seemed like the earth moved beneath my feet. This wasn't happening. Eight days ago, Nate had a birthday. Why would this officer lie? Why would anyone play such a cruel joke on us? I heard Adam gasp as if the horrible news suddenly sucked up the surrounding air. Crowds gathered, watching as we held each other and sobbed. The officer said, "I'll lead you to the hospital." We got in our car and followed flashing lights, crying and praying that someone had made a terrible mistake. I even tried to barter with God, and, at the time, it didn't seem foolish. Now as I looked back, I saw the foolishness in my feeble attempt to barter with God for one of his own children. I think I said something like, "God, if you let my son live, I'll serve you more faithfully." Or perhaps I said, "God, take me." For a moment, I forgot whose hands held the power of life and death.

Within minutes, we stood at the front desk asking for our son. A young woman came from behind a closed door and escorted us to a waiting area. They reserved this room—I later discovered—for people not waiting on the living, but for those waiting for confirmation of the dead. We sat there frozen in fear and prayed. Minutes later, the same young woman returned and asked that we follow her. With compassion in her voice, she said, "Mr. and Mrs. Mirabeau, I need you to identify the body." I didn't understand what she meant. Why did we need to identify our own son, we knew him? We walked down the long hallway, turned left and then right, until we reached a cold and dimly lit room. It took a minute for my eyes to adjust and focus. The room was empty, except for a long metal table. When I looked closely, I saw the body of my son stretched out in front of me. Treading softly, I tiptoed over to the table so as not to wake him then rubbed his forehead gently. I kissed his cheek. His body felt warm, and he looked as if he was resting. He's asleep I told myself, but my heart knew better. I cried so hard my eyes hurt and then, as suddenly as the tears began, they stopped. I shut them off, prayed for my son, and walked out of that room. My baby boy was dead. Feeling empty and abandoned, I shouted out to God, "Why did you take my son?"

And in the faintest whisper, I heard, "Because he belonged to me first—I only loaned him to you for a little while."

Nate and I looked at the world the same way. Today part of me died, leaving a hole in my heart I knew would never heal. Things got a little fuzzy for me after Nate's death and some events, I still can't recall. I barely remember Adam with me at the hospital, returning to our farmhouse together, or the phone calls we made to our family and friends. To get through the days that followed, I forced myself not to feel or think. I knew that, if I did, the wound would reopen and blood would flow nonstop until death took me, too. At the time, death seemed easier than living with the emptiness. I hid the pain from my family and friends and cried only in private. But in my private world, I mourned as if I'd lost my soul.

The phone rang constantly. People stopped by with food, cards, and well wishes. A telegram came from Maggie. My friends gathered around, and because of them, we got through this dreadful ordeal. They propped me up so that I wouldn't fall, and they prayed for our family. Nate's death brought back memories of a cold, misty day when I stood on the edge of a pond far from here. Now in my strange reoccurring dream, Joey waited with a smile on his face, just as he waited to play catch with Nate in our back yard many times.

The dreams woke me up at night and invaded my thoughts during the day. Usually, I woke with my eyes swollen shut and my cheeks stained with my own tears.

Again, I felt helpless, just like I felt the day Joey died.

I repeatedly relived the scenarios that got us here. Why had I not seen that he needed me? What kind of parents couldn't protect their children? Why had this happened? In that very rose garden, I sensed a major change about to happen in our lives but could do nothing. Day after day, I sat around blaming myself for Nate's death. Whenever I closed my eyes and tilted my head back against the sofa, I heard his voice and saw him standing there smiling down at me. Sometimes hours passed before I realized how long I sat there.

I prayed and watched God take charge of my life. Who else saw in me enough value to save me? Sometime later, I decided to seek help. I found a grief counselor who helped me put the pieces back together with her patience, compassion, and experience. In the many sessions that followed, I began to not only recognize, but deal with my grief.

"We experience the common stages of grief differently," she said, "but eventually we'll face some, if not all, of them."

For me, anger came first and held it me hostage for months. I placed blame on everyone and everything: myself for not seeing he needed me, Adam for not protecting him, Nate for making such a stupid decision, and the world for the injustice. The intensity of my mourning brought on severe migraines. Sometimes I refused to mourn for fear of losing my mind and then felt guilty when I didn't. And yes, I hated myself for the misery that surrounded all of us. I'd denied the problem for too long. It got harder to get out of bed some days. I didn't see any reason to get up only to remember the child I loved died because of me. Other days I walked around in a trance. I stopped eating, lost weight and shut out the world and all its noise. Then I fell into a deep depression. *Such a terrible tragedy wouldn't happen to good parents.* I thought. I resented Adam for spending more time at his office than with his son. He treated Nate differently because he believed Nate let his dream die. Adam couldn't accept Nate's decision. Over time, I began to feel slightly better and even forgave Nate and myself, but, I couldn't let go of my resentment toward Adam. I held onto that blame for other reasons. Once I remembered saying Adam and I needed to discuss those things left unsaid, and if we didn't, we wouldn't recover.

The day of the funeral my entire body felt numb. If someone had held an automatic weapon at my temple, I wouldn't have reacted. Our friends and family came to show their support, and, for that, we owed them a debt of gratitude. When that moment came, I walked to the podium and stood. Seconds ticked away. I just stood there. Then I looked out at Nate's friends and read what I knew he wanted me to share with them.

"In life, you said you loved him, in death you weep at his passing. If the truth lies beneath your words, then change whatever casts suspicion upon your life and walk away. He would want you to learn from his mistakes."

Some of them wiped awkwardly at the tears that fell as the words tugged at their souls. They knew I spoke his truth. His death ended an unselfish life, and perhaps his loyalty to someone he loved, no doubt brought us here today. There was a mystery surrounding the woman who called us that night, and, for me, unanswered questions remained concerning his death. The trip to the cemetery remains a blur, but we made it through the day.

Our extended family, Lynette and Larry, Winston and Ellie, Lee, Edmond and all the kids came. Of all the people who came, Rita offered me what none of the others could give. Together, she and I once walked through this same valley. She understood that I could manage today with family and friends near, but the struggle lay ahead. We slipped away and spent a quiet moment alone in my garden. She looked older than her years, but her wisdom helped me focus on the important things. "B.J.," she said "remember that you've got two other children and a husband who needs you. They're experiencing the same pain. Your children are too young to cope on their own, and your husband doesn't want you to see his vulnerability."

Rita's words of wisdom cut through all the stuff I'd let cloud my view. My family needed me. Dannie lived in torment. Nate's self-appointed protector felt he'd failed his brother. Amy stayed at his side and consoled him every step of the way. She and Dannie genuinely loved each other.

Kellee cried so uncontrollably that it broke my heart. Her face turned a deep, bruised red almost as if the blood vessels in her face had broken. Her swollen and puffy eyes looked old and tired. Closer than a baby brother, he was her best friend. They talked all the time, always plotting against their big brother. Kellee pushed him to excel in his studies, and she finally got through to him. Adam struggled with his grief, and for the first time, I saw a crack in his armor. I grabbed Dannie by the hand and then motioned to Adam. Amy followed. We walked into the bedroom, and I closed the door. Kellee sat down on the edge of the bed. I pulled her to me while holding onto Dannie. Adam and I told them we loved them and then we prayed for our family's recovery. "Our love for Nate in life will not change our love for him in death," I said. They looked comforted. The rest of the evening and into the night, the memories our dearest friends shared gave us comfort. We laughed at some of the funnier things and cried over some of the sadder ones. When I looked into the eyes of my children, I knew they would be okay.

Several years had passed since Lee and I spent any time together. Still strikingly beautiful with that fire-engine-red hair, the years had shown her favor. Edmond looked more distinguished with a little gray around the edges. Today, we didn't dwell on politics or our lost years. Lynette aged well, too and had lost weight. She said she worked out every day. Larry suffered health issues and recently underwent major surgery, but he looked great. Winston hadn't changed from the first time we met. Ellie remained as beautiful as ever and healthy, with her cancer still in remission. They felt our loss as deeply but tried to help us cope with Nate's death. Our families had grown up together. I watched the kids temporarily shift Dannie and Kellie's focus. They made them laugh. Alan could always make Kellee laugh. Back when she was younger, Kellee had a serious school girl crush on him. I wonder if he ever knew. Secretly, I held out hope.

In the company of my girlfriends, it seemed like old times. My friends took charge and organized the house, from the kitchen to the bedrooms. They put away food and assigned the sleeping arrangements. I wouldn't hear of them going to a hotel. Tonight, I needed them close to me. Late into the night, we talked, and then one by one they crashed. Everyone got up early the next morning. Their lives back home awaited their return. My heart overflowed with joy because they came. They said their goodbyes and made the usual promises to stay in touch, and then they got in their rented cars and headed for the airport. Rita left the day of the funeral because of a prior engagement. Dannie and Amy went home too, and in a few days, Kellee would leave Adam and me to face our new existence together. Except for the hum of the refrigerator, the house felt oddly quiet. We moved about our humdrum lives and pretended everything was okay so Kellee wouldn't worry. No doubt, some dark days lay ahead for her, too, but I knew she'd work through them. She had that tough Mirabeau skin. She'd survived another tough ordeal and came out mostly unscathed. Friday came, and Kellee left for school. She planned to graduate next year and go on to medical school. For weeks, I had this eerie feeling that Dannie wanted to tell me something, but he had a hard time finding the words. I could wait, I thought. Seeing the anguish on his face every time he tried, I certainly didn't want to cause him anymore pain.

Chapter 16

Shattered Dreams

After Nate died, life changed for us. Adam and I hardly spent any time together, and when we did, we argued over the smallest things. "Who left a half empty carton of milk in the refrigerator?" It didn't take much to throw me into a tizzy. I seethed with anger, and, when I spit it out, Adam paid the price. We found fault in everything the other did. I remembered how Rita and Charlie drifted apart after Joey died, and finally Charlie gave up. Back then, I never understood how two people who loved each other could become so intolerant of one another. And surprisingly when Charlie walked out, I still didn't understand. But now I finally got it. The guilt becomes too much. Adam blamed me for Nate's death. I blamed me, but I blamed Adam more. Fault fell at both our feet. I played the blame game all the time, with so much more than enough to go around that I couldn't keep it all straight. We could no longer occupy the same space and grew more and more hostile toward each other.

Adam traveled more and spent every waking hour at

the office, while trying to escape me and our problems. It got harder for me to concentrate on work. Finally, I quit my volunteer work and stayed home. At first, I had a cocktail in the evening, then I needed one to get the day started, another at lunch and at dinner, after dinner and every minute of the day. Sometimes I was so drunk, I didn't even know my own name. My daily hygiene suffered. I walked the track at the local high school in a daze. Other times, I sat on the bleachers and watched an imaginary baseball game, trapped in my mind. My destructive behavior went on for months. I screened my phone calls and only accepted calls from the kids if coherent enough to hide my drunkenness so they wouldn't worry about me. Jokingly, I used to say that I lost my identity when Nate became a baseball player. Everyone referred to me as Nate's mom. I would've given anything to hear someone call out, "Hey, Nate's mom," just one more time.

I cried all the time now, and sometimes in my drunken stupor, I couldn't even remember why.

But the voice inside my head pushed and nudged me to pull up out of the hell into which I had fallen. And, finally, I obeyed, and again sought counseling to help me deal with my desire to hide my troubles in a bottle.

"Recovery is an ongoing process that takes one day at a time. "I am an alcoholic."

I no longer visited the place where hope once resided, and I stopped talking to God. I figured that he didn't care for me anymore. Instead of sitting in my rose garden, I walked pass it. When we started out a long time ago, I believed Adam and I would love each other forever. We still shared the same house, but no longer the same bed. He moved to the guest room shortly after the funeral, and we became more like strangers than partners. I thought about all the moves we'd made together and all the people we'd met along the way. Adam worked all the time while I kept things organized and running smoothly at home. I thought about the man who'd shared all my dreams for the last several decades until the doorbell rang.

"Hi, Dannie."

"Mom," he said, "you look so tired, are you getting enough sleep?"

"Yes," I said and changed the subject.

"How's Amy?"

"She's great."

"Mom, get some rest. You look really beat."

"I will. Maybe I'm coming down with a cold."

Did he suspect that alcohol had almost taken my soul? I didn't know, and he never said. He stayed long enough to make a sandwich, and then he left. My life blurred pass me. Saturday came and, with it, Kellee's phone call.

"Hello, Mom, how do you feel?"

"Great! And how're you?"

"I'm wonderful. Dannie said you looked ill."

"I'm much better, thank you."

"How's my daddy?"

"Very well. He's out playing a game of golf." Honestly, I didn't really know where Adam spent his time these days. Kellee and I talked for a while. She still struggled with her brother's death, but she laughed, anyway, at some of my silly remarks. She promised to call on Sunday and hung up. Then I walked into the kitchen, poured myself a drink, and sat down. I sat there, palming the glass in my hand for a minute or two, then got up, walked over to the sink, and poured it down the drain. There was a note on the counter from Adam that had probably sat there all day. I picked it up and read the note.

Dear B.J.,

I've made a decision, and I thought that, today when I get home, we could sit down and talk. I'll see you around six.

Adam

Before I got up from the table, I heard his key in the door. He walked into the kitchen and sat down across from me. "Hello B.J."

"Hello, Adam." He looked tired and much older. *I don't remember him looking so old.* I thought.

"B.J., I can't live like this, so I'm moving out today. I came by to get the rest of my things. I regret we couldn't work out our problems. At least you tried grief and alcohol counseling. I'm not there yet. I made a weak gesture with little luck. Every day I struggle with Nate's death, and I question if you're right to blame me." I let him finish and said nothing. We'd left most of the problems unsaid. Why should now be any different? He got up, went into the bedroom, and packed. A half hour later, he stood in the doorway. Blinded by my loss, I let him go. "Goodbye, B.J.," he said, and then he turned and closed the door behind him. Just eight short months ago, our son died. In the few sessions he showed up for, certain issues rose to the surface that Adam didn't want to face. Grief forced them to rise, and they wouldn't go away. After one of my counseling sessions, I started thinking about something that happened while we lived in Cheyenne.

One day, while the kids were at school and Adam had gone off to work, I received a phone call.

"Hello?"

The voice on the other end sounded vaguely familiar, like someone I once knew. "B.J., its Colin. I have something I want you to hear, and then you can choose to do with it whatever you think best."

"Colin, what are you talking about?"

"Just listen." Colin played for me that day a tape of a conversation between Adam and his wife, Vicki. It appeared that their affair had been going on for a while and, for some reason that he didn't go into, Adam wanted to break it off.

When the tape ended, I said, "You can destroy the tape," and hung up. I never told Adam, but I believe he found out from Vicki that Colin played the tape for me. I left things unsaid. Later, I remembered a note I found on top of Adam's desk with the name of the Donnelly Hotel, a scribbled date and time, and signed *MT*.

Again, I stuck my head in the sand and chose not to deal with life. Then it hit me that the initials M.T. were the initials of Melissa Tate, Adam's old girlfriend from college. Every boy in school had the hots for Melissa. Except for that enormous head, perhaps there was something attractive about this fair skinned girl or "high yellow" as we called it. Anyway, Melissa had all the boys chasing their tails. I turned a blind eye to Adam's other life. For the sake of my children, I forgave his indiscretions. Perhaps underneath all my bitterness, his womanizing was the real reason I blamed him for Nate's death. Those counseling sessions forced me to act upon my feelings of betrayal. Very slowly, the anger moved out and the even slower healing process moved in. It felt good. I got up and climbed into bed.

After Sunday dinner, Dannie, Amy, and I waited together for Kellee's call. I wondered what I'd say to make them understand. Adam called. He thought he should be the one to tell Dannie. I agreed but asked him to wait because I wasn't ready. I cried myself to sleep that night, and when I woke, I swore I'd never shed another tear over Adam Mirabeau. He never understood how deeply his lifestyle choices hurt me. After years of cleaning up and organizing our lives, this split felt like the right move. After all, he never organized our lives. I did that.

A few days later, Dannie and Amy stopped over to check on me. They looked so happy. Amy's face glowed. Before I could ask, Dannie said, "Mom, I've asked Amy to marry me." I screamed and ran toward them with arms extended. We hugged and kissed.

"Dad's not picking up his office or cell phone. I've tried several times. Have you heard from him?"

I lied. "Your dad went out of town, he'll call you soon." Dannie looked happy, but underneath I felt that something was troubling him. Amy and I talked about wedding plans while Dannie watched a football game. Kellee called. Dannie and Amy shared their news.

They left around seven, and as I settled in for the evening, Adam called. "B.J., the kids need to know what we've decided." I agreed, even though living apart had a nicer ring than divorce.

"I'll call you later," he said. I waited for Adam's call. A couple of days went by, so I called him.

"Adam, I'm going to New York on Thursday to talk with Kellee, I suggest you talk with Dannie. You know how close they are. It's best we tell them the same day."

That worked for Adam. Later that evening I called Kellee and told her I'd made plans to come out for the weekend to see a play.

"I'm thrilled," she said. I flew out on Thursday evening and took a shuttle into the city to my hotel.

I left her a message on her cell phone, checked in, and unpacked. An hour later, she called to say that classes ended at four. "I'll see you at six for dinner," she said. We agreed to meet at my favorite Thai restaurant around five thirty. The cab pulled up in front of the restaurant, where she waited outside. We hugged and went inside. I chose a secluded booth in the corner of the restaurant so that we could talk privately. We ordered ice tea. Her eyes lit up as she talked about her school, friends, and everything happening in her life. I forced a smile. She noticed right away and asked that powerful question,

"Mom, what's wrong?"

"Kellee, for a long time your dad and I lived unhappy lives. It took Nate's death for us to realize the truth. Adam stayed away so much it was easy for me to blame him. After all, everybody has shortcomings." *Why did I say that?* I thought. She fixed her gaze on me. After that, I chose my words with care to avoid saying something she might detect as spiteful. Tears filled her eyes. I continued. "Honey, we'll always love you and your brother, but your father and I have grown worlds apart. Of course, I'm hurt, angry, and disappointed, but it doesn't affect my love for you and Dannie."

She sat there and took it all in before she spoke. "Mom, I want nothing but happiness for both of you whether together or apart. I know I can't change the course of your lives, but I'm grateful that your parting is amicable." Then she looked at me with dread in her voice and asked, "Is Daddy having an affair?"

"Of course not."

It wasn't a lie. Her question spoke of the present. It didn't address the past. She relaxed. The difference between Adam and me—I kept my vows, he failed to see a need to keep his. I think he cheated because he kept searching for the "fireworks." I suppose someone told him that love should feel like a big explosion, and he believed them. He never asked me, and, if he had, I would've told him that it felt warm and gooey like melted chocolate.

Adam's affair with Vicki ended shortly after it started, a lifetime ago, and Melissa was just another short-lived adventure. Adam loved adventures. Affairs weren't things you could hide like birthday or Christmas presents. They tended to tumble out into the open when you least expected them to. I had had my suspicions about Melissa, and even Vicki before Colin called—wives knew. Adam, a true Mirabeau, cheated, but he'd never leave his family. It had to do with that Mirabeau code of loyalty to family, which didn't equate to faithfulness. However, because his leaving was about much more than being unfaithful, he knew he couldn't stay. Looking back over the years, I wonder who besides Vicki and Melissa shared my husband's affection. Not meant for sharing with my daughter, my private thoughts swirled in my head. However, her next pointed question caused me to focus. "Does Dannie know about you and Daddy?"

"Probably, since your dad and I decided to talk with both of you today."

"Oh!" she said.

"Amy will help Dannie deal with our news. Adam and I will watch over you from afar. Whenever you need us, just call."

I changed the subject and moved on to lighter conservation. We spent the rest of the visit doing the things I enjoyed. On Sunday evening, I kissed my daughter goodbye and flew home. As soon as I reached the door, I heard the phone ringing, but couldn't get to it in time. I looked down at the caller ID, saw Dannie's name, and dialed him right back.

"Hello."

"Hi, Dannie, how are you?"

"Good, I suppose."

"How are you doing, Mom?"

"Good, Dannie."

"Mom," he said" Dad and I talked a few days ago,

and he tells me that the two of you will live apart for a while. Are you okay with that?"

"Yes. Dannie, your father and I need to take some time and figure out if we can, or want, to stay together. Sometimes people grow apart. It's not that we don't still care for each other, but the hurdles seem too high. Can you understand what I'm saying?"

"I guess."

"This will in no way affect the love we feel for you and your sister."

"Mom," he said in a sad voice, "I'm sorry."

"So am I."

We said goodnight. After he and his sister talked, everything would work out. I picked up my luggage from the kitchen floor and walked toward the bedroom. Then I dropped everything and headed for the shower, no unpacking tonight. Short trips drained your energy. Tonight, I planned to curl up with a good book and fall asleep.

At daybreak, I woke with the lights on and the book resting on my pillow. On the plane ride home, thoughts of my future raced through my head. What future? I had no plans, no job, and no husband. Frankly, I wasn't worried. We'd done okay in the later years. I needed something to fill my days and thought about going back to the nonprofit organization. Instead, I looked for hobbies to occupy my days and joined the garden club, and a senior's tennis league. It felt great getting out and meeting people again. The kids called every other day to check on me until they figured out that I'd picked up the pieces and was skillfully putting them back together. Dannie told me that he and Kellee worried about me merging into the mainstream. They felt relieved when I did. Adam rather quickly moved on with his life and started dating. We talked often about the kids and other financial issues. *How did you stop loving someone you'd spent your entire life caring for?* I wondered. He was a great father and provider, despite that one despicable flaw.

Chapter 17

My Friend and My Sister

The strangest thing happened today. Out of the blue, I received a call from Edmond Stein. I'd just returned from a tennis match. When I stepped inside, I heard the phone ring.

"Hello?"

"B.J.!" the voice called out.

"Yes?"

"It's Edmond."

His call came as a total surprise and more surprising that Lee was not the caller. "Hello, Edmond, it's good to hear your voice."

"B.J., do you have a minute to talk?"

"Of course, I've always got time for an old friend." I sensed something was wrong, but I waited. It had been a long time since we last spoke. Lee and I talked last year when Adam and I visited DC on business. It appeared that our friendship happened somewhere in another galaxy then broke apart and drifted like atoms. It seemed like not so long ago, we shared everything.

"B.J., Lee has an aggressive cancer." I heard the pain

in his voice as I listened in horror. Cancer tried to claim another friend who fought this monster and won. "B.J., can you come? She needs you," he pleaded, as if afraid of what I might say. Edmond didn't understand that Lee and I became each other's conscience that evening in her basement. Maybe Lee had forgotten, but I hadn't, and, before he finished the last sentence, mentally I'd already packed my bags.

"I'll make my reservations and call you back."

"No, my secretary will handle everything. How soon can you travel?"

"Right away."

"Okay, good. It's good to hear your voice again, B.J.," he said as he hung up. The next day, tired and weary, I boarded a plane for a small town outside of Cheyenne. At one thirty in the afternoon, the plane touched down. Alan picked me up at the airport. He hugged me tightly, grabbed my bags, and didn't say much as he drove away from the airport heading toward the countryside. I sensed his weariness as he stared ahead.

"Alan, God holds the power of life and death in his hands. Your mom knows this. Remember, she's a fighter."

He looked over at me with misty eyes, "That's what my dad said, too."

"Listen to your dad." When we reached the house, Mia ran out to greet me. Fear had temporarily stolen her beauty and, in its place, deposited tiny worry lines all over her face. She was pale and much too thin, and I could see she wasn't eating. I held her close and whispered a prayer right there for my friend and her family. We walked together hand in hand, Alan on one side and Mia on the other as they guided me up the stairs and into Lee's bedroom. Edmond sat on the edge of the bed, but, when he saw me, he smiled, and came toward me, holding out his arms. He held me close for a moment then guided me over to the bed. Lee looked up, opened her arms wide, and received me with this big smile on her face and a look of surprise in her eyes. Perhaps, she feared that I wouldn't come. Surely, Lee knew me better than that. I didn't walk away from her, she walked away from me. Then I thought that maybe guilt and not surprise stared back at me. We hugged, cried, kissed, and hugged some more.

"B.J. when you're ready, I'll walk you over to the guest cottage," Edmond said.

"Edmond, if it's okay with you, I'd like to stay in here with Lee."

He smiled. "I hoped you'd say that. I'm in the guest room across the hall if you need me." Edmond and the kids walked out of the room, leaving us alone. Lee was no longer the strikingly beautiful redhead I once knew. Her outer appearance had undergone a drastic change. A scarf covered complete baldness, and her dull, washed-out skin showed signs of all the pain she now endured. For the first time in a long while, I thought of our Girls Night Out and all the fun we had watching movies while eating buttered popcorn, crying, laughing, or both. I remembered the conversation that she and I shared in the basement of her home and the unspoken pact we made that night never to speak of it again.

Lee and I talked into the night. "B.J., did I ever tell you why Edmond's mother resented me?"

"No, don't talk, just rest."

Of course, we had no secrets between us. Between shallow breaths, she told me that once Edmond made partner, she quit her job because they could afford it. Edmond's mother disapproved of her decision. "His mother thought I looked at Edmond as my opportunity. Far from the truth, I loved him," she whispered.

"I know, Lee." No one knew better than I how much Lee loved Edmond. She drifted in and out of a restless sleep and didn't want me to leave her side. Lee found out about six months ago that she had a rare type of cancer. The doctors tried some new treatments, along with the proven treatments of chemo and radiation, but so far nothing worked. She looked like a frightened little girl.

"B.J., forgive me for my foolishness. I owe you an apology for my bad behavior that day in Washington. I forgot what we once meant to each other and broke our special bond."

"I forgave you that day." Right then, I crawled up in bed next to her, and we spent the rest of the night locked in each other's arms. All during the night, the pain threatened her sleep. The more she struggled in agony, the tighter I held her. I wanted her to know that I'd never leave her.

The next morning, I got up moving quietly so as not to wake her. I showered and went downstairs for breakfast. Edmond sat at the kitchen table, drinking coffee. Maria, the housekeeper, poured me a cup while Edmond and I talked about everything: our lives, the kids, but mostly about Lee.

"B.J., do you mind if I stop by the office, A few things need my immediate attention?"

"Not at all. I won't leave her."

Then I wandered outside and found myself standing in Lee's rose garden. I began reciting out loud the third chapter of Ecclesiastes. The words usually settled me down and eased my fear.

> "'To everything, there is a season,
> a time for every purpose under the sun.
> a time to be born and a time to die;
> a time to plant and a time to uproot;

a time to kill and a time to heal;
a time to tear down and a time to build;
a time to weep and a time to laugh...'"

I sat for a long time, among the fragrance and the quiet, and then went back inside. The house felt gloomy and sad, draped in a veil of darkness. Everyone knew the end was near. Lee's eyes had lost the spark that once ignited laughter. We watched her vitality fade away, and we could do nothing. It seemed as if the people I loved always left me. Perhaps God had something for me to do, but I hadn't yet figured out what. I whispered, "Lord, show me the purpose for my life."

Edmond called the doctor. Lee's pain had escalated. He increased her morphine. She no longer recognized any of us. I saw the pleading in her eyes for God to release her. After he visited with Lee for a few moments, the doctor motioned to us. We gathered around. Edmond and I climbed into bed beside her. She smiled up at us as we held her hands. Alan and Mia kneeled next to her bedside, held hands and wept loudly. I kissed her forehead and said goodbye as she took her last breath. Lee died that day. At last, I walked out of the room to mourn the loss of one of my dearest friends.

All our friends came. Larry and Lynette, Winston and Ellie, Rita, and Adam came, too. He looked like the old Adam once more. People offered their condolences and well wishes. Adam walked up to me and hugged me tightly. "B.J., I know you loved Lee, and sometimes I just didn't get it. I guess I thought you loved her more that she deserved or perhaps you loved her more than me, and for that I'm sorry."

"Thanks." The last guest left late. I couldn't remember the last time I'd had a decent night's sleep. On those many days and nights when Lee wrenched in pain, I sat

and read out loud, hoping the words would soothe her
mind and her body. When she cried, I cried inside and
refused to let her see my tears. But now my tired body
ached. Alan and Mia headed upstairs to bed. I reached out
my hand and drew them near. "Cry for her a while, but
don't spend too much time mourning. She wouldn't want
that. She'll forever live in your hearts."

They kissed me on the cheek and said, "Goodnight,
Aunt B.J.," then continued upstairs. I found Edmond
standing at the kitchen window that overlooked the rose
garden. It came as no surprise to anyone who knew us
that Lee and I also shared a passion for roses. She played
tennis, volunteered, and spent the rest of her time in her
perfectly groomed garden.

Edmond turned around with tears welling up in his
eyes. "I'll miss her, B.J."

"I know and so will I." We hugged, and I walked out
the door over to the guest cottage. I undressed and collapsed into bed, tired and drained of all energy. The night
she died, I slept in the cottage for the first time. Lee
wanted me near, and, quite frankly I wanted to be near
her.

Early the next morning, after I said goodbye to the
kids, Edmond waited outside to take me to the airport. "If
you ever need me, call. I love you both."

He pulled up to the curb in front of my airline. "I'll
miss you, B.J., thanks for coming. You made a difficult
task less difficult. We couldn't have done this without
you."

We hugged and said goodbye.

"I had to come." And then I walked away.

I thought it unlikely that Edmond and I would ever
see each other again. With my boarding pass in my hand,
I sat down to wait. Instead of feeling sad, I thought of the
fun we had and the times when we shared the most inti-

mate and personal thoughts. I arrived back home at mid-day. An early-morning rain had left the streets wet under dreary and overcast skies. It had only been a few short weeks since I left, but it seemed like months. For years, Lee and I drifted further and further apart, but at least if I needed to hear her voice, I could still do that. Now, I would never hear her voice again.

I spent the rest of the evening relaxing with a book I started right before I left. I knew it wouldn't take me long to fall asleep. It was impossible to sleep while Lee lay next to me in so much pain. Lee Georgiana Mattson Stein became my friend, not a childhood friend like Maggie, but that didn't matter. Lynette and Ellie came to relieve me, but Lee never wanted me to leave her side. So, I stayed until the very end.

I dozed off and woke sometime after midnight then turned off the lights and slid under the covers. The next morning, I called Dannie. I missed him. Dannie wasn't home, but I spoke with Amy. She'd set their wedding date for next June and had already begun making plans. I offered my help. She said she'd let me know.

"Tell Dannie I'm back."

"I will," she said.

Then I picked up the phone and dialed Kellee's number. I'd called both of them several times while I was away.

"Hello, Kellee."

"Mom, are you all right?"

"Yes."

And then before I could change the subject, she asked, "How's Mia and Alan?"

"They're doing okay. Everyone's doing their best, under the circumstances."

"I'm glad. Are you sure Alan's okay, Mom?"

"I'm sure, honey." I didn't want to talk anymore

about Lee's family, not today. We spent a few more
minutes talking about school and her approaching graduation, and then we hung up.

Chapter 18

The Letter

While cleaning out some neatly stashed piles of junk, I realized precious memories lay hidden among the spoils. Adam left me, Dannie had his own place, Kellee was away at school, and Nate was dead. So, what about me? I pulled out boxes and started throwing away things. It reminded me of the years we spent moving from one place to another. By the time I finished organizing and preparing for each move, there were piles everywhere: a pile for Goodwill, a pile to keep, and a pile to throw away. The only difference, this time—my address wouldn't change. I found baby and school-age pictures of all the kids, clothes, and even toys that belonged to Nate. I couldn't bring myself to get rid of them. Carefully, I put them back in the box and placed it high upon the shelf. His things had to wait for another day. I fought back the tears, fearing, if they started, I couldn't stop them. That's how much I loved him.

Toward the back of the shelf sat a box containing letters that Mama Joe had written to me over the years. I sat there for a few minutes reading a few of them. Her role of mother-in-law changed over time. I knew she loved me. She always encouraged me to do something exciting with my life. "B.J., honey," she said, "try something new every once and ag'in."

Maybe she had some regrets. I read a few more of her letters and put the box away. I pulled out another box labeled "Anna's stuff." I didn't bother opening the box clearly marked with my cousin's return address. I figured such a small box could only contain some old costume jewelry or other trinkets. I put it aside and continued pulling things out of the closet. Adam left things behind, too. I put his things in the pile labeled "Trash." If he considered them valuable, surely, by now, he would've picked them up.

When I finished pulling out things, I stepped over the piles and walked out of the room. Rummaging through some of those boxes brought back deeply buried memories, some best left forgotten. The tape Colin sent me laid hidden deep under layers of stuff. I never wanted it, but Colin insisted. He said I'd do the right thing with it.

"I'm too hurt to make a wise decision. I believe you'll do the best thing for all of us," he said.

On the day the tape arrived in the mail, I tossed it into an old shoe box and hid it in the darkest corner of my closet. Never once had I considered listening to that recording again. I didn't need to hear it again to know that it held the truth. Perhaps, I thought that if it never saw the light of day again, it wouldn't matter. The funny thing about that sort of thinking is that what we don't deal with consciously will rise anyway. Whenever something is left unsaid, life ends up complicated.

Why had I kept that tape? It was time to let go of the past, so I smashed the tape and tossed it into the garbage.

Then I got up, went into the kitchen, and fixed a snack. I decided to call both my kids before I sat down to eat. I dialed Dannie's number, no answer. I left a message. "Hello, Dannie, it's Mom. Please call when you're free." Then I dialed Kellee.

She answered right away.

"Hi, sweetheart."

"Hi, Mom, how's your day?"

"Good." We talked for about a half hour about her plans after graduation. After we hung up, I grabbed the newspaper on my way to the kitchen. The news never changed, always the same—depressing and more depressing. I finished my snack and headed back to the bedroom to finish tackling the closet when I remembered the box labeled, "Anna's stuff."

I couldn't imagine what was inside the box. It didn't appear unusual looking from the outside, not too large and not too small, just an average size box. "Everything she owned could probably fit in it," I said out loud.

We never owned anything of real value, and when she died, we had no estate to settle. For the first time in a very long time, I thought of my mother.

I don't think I ever really knew her. She had no real friends and kept to herself mostly, with only Aunt Eva dropping in for a visit. What did I remember of her life? She worked hard and had a boyfriend once, but that didn't last long. My mother couldn't handle relationships. One day I asked, "Anna, why doesn't Mr. Michaels come around anymore?"

Rather sharply she said, "He ain't got my same values." That probably meant, knowing my mother, that he didn't spend every waking hour on a job. She was a workaholic, born of necessity, not of choice. Carefully, I picked up the little box, removed the lid and, as I suspected, it held costume jewelry and a few colorful buttons. At the bottom of the box, lay a piece of faded and wrinkled paper. Slowly, I unfolded the paper and discovered a letter in my mother's handwriting addressed to me. I glanced at the letter and wondered why my mother wrote to me. We never shared the kind of closeness I saw between the mothers and daughters of some my class-mates. Regardless, we claimed our mother and daughter status. Cautiously, I unfolded the letter and began reading her written words.

Dears Beatrice Johanna,

If you reading this letter, then that means I ain't here with you, but I here with you in spirit. I never call you B.J., even thoughs you wants me to. Sometimes I thought you hate your name to spite me 'cause I takes great pride in calling you by the name I gives you. My whole life I take care of you best I can. I sorry if I ain't what you want or deserve in a mother.

I was born in a little town five miles south of here. Too late in life, my mother gives birth to twins, my brotha and me. My brotha Bennie died of complikations to neu-monia when he was six years old, and my father never said another word to me from that very day. I was seven years old when I heard my father say to my mother, "God help me, Lena, but I wish that gal died stead of my boy." He blame me for living. I cryed myself to sleep that night. I ain't sure if he ever know my name 'cause he never called me by it. He say to my mother tell that gal to do this or that. I wait to hear my mother defend my life or say she loved me, but she never did.

My mother never hug me or tell me she love me, and my father turn his back on me.

When I turn fifteen, I meet a young soldier. His name was Cole Parker. He listen, and I did not feel invisible no more. I had never met anyone so grown up. We fell in love and, no surprise, I become pregnant. It was easy to love someone that showed affection you ain't never had.

When I tell my mother I was pregnant, she tells my father. He push me out the door with only the clothes on my back and my savings of ten dollars tuck in my pocket. My mother stand by and say nothing as my father shut the door in my face and said, "Don't come back, this ain't your home no more." His words did not hurt 'cause this house never feel like home to me.

Afraid and alone, I walk down the dusty road to town. I stop in the local store and call Cole. I ain't got no more tears. Cole says his sister on her way. I sit on a old stool outside to wait. Eva come take me home with her. My mother silence teached me them words I love you spoke casual is not how you show love. Cole come home the weekend 'fore he gets his orders. The young man I meet and fell in love with gone in a few weeks. We never married, and I live with the shame of a being with child and no husband. I ain't take nothing from Cole, not even his name 'cause it ain't belongs to me. I stayed with your Aunt Eva tills you was born. Then I move out on my own. His sister was good to me and loved you, but I cannot stay. I ain't except no charity. I found a place not too far from her and find work right away. Eva take care of you while I work. I ain't had no real education, barely sixteen. It so hard to find anything decent, I took in other folks clothes to wash and iron.

I miss out on many things in my life, and I sees many regrets. But I never regret you. B.J., there I say it. The only thing that I learned from my parents kept us apart. I did not know how to say I love you or hold you. But in my heart, I loved you more than my own life. Please forgive.

Anna

My mother's final words brought tears to my eyes. I once said that I understood my mother's life more in her death, but I never realized the entire truth in that statement until I read that letter. Anna Louise Marten's complicated existence was a result of a fruitless search for the happiness she never found. But this woman loved me without spoken words. I kissed the letter, placed it back in the box, and sat it on the top shelf of my closet right next to Nate's.

Chapter 19

The Graduation

Time marched to the drummer's beat like a band in a holiday parade. It didn't seem possible that a little over a year ago, I buried a son. And now Kellee's upcoming graduation drew near. Adam called. He'd ask his secretary to handle reservations for us. He said she'd call back later in the week with the final details.

"Thanks," I said.

From the moment we dropped Kellee at her dorm four years earlier, we looked forward to this day. I thought back to the crowds, the lines, and the noise of the city. None of us and especially Kellee wanted to look back at Nine/Eleven. Perhaps someday, but certainly not on such a joyous occasion. I remembered my graduation day and the pride on my mother's face. The light from her countenance shone as brightly as the sun at high noon. Kellee planned to attend medical school after graduation. Everyone looked forward to her celebration. Adam and I remained friends after our divorce, with him making more of an effort to attend every special event in the lives of our children.

Adam's secretary called midweek with flight and hotel information, and I passed it on to Dannie. On Friday, Dannie and Amy picked me up, and we headed to the airport. We found Adam waiting for us in the boarding area. "Hello, everyone," he said and gently kissed my cheek. Then he hugged Dannie and Amy. Everyone bubbled with the anticipation of witnessing Kellee's big day.

The flight to New York boarded quickly. We arrived early and took the shuttle to the hotel. Adam made dinner reservations at Nate's favorite Italian restaurant around the corner from the hotel. "Dinner's at six," he said.

"I'm going to the room," I said.

"I need to stretch my legs. See you later," he said. I'd known Adam my entire life and could read him better than anyone. He'd walk through Central Park and back over to the restaurant where he'd sit at the bar, order a gin and tonic, and think of Nate. Adam and the boys came here one weekend many years ago. Dannie later told me that, in that one weekend, he and Nate really got to know the man they called Dad. I settled in and stretched out across the bed, but I couldn't stop the onslaught of memories. Adam and I spent most of our lives together. We raised three children and traveled across the country in search of a better life, living as modern day nomads. Still, we remained a family, but not in the same sense of the word. Adam moved on with a new wife and a new life. He remarried the year after our divorce became final. I'll never forget the day he asked my permission to start over. He certainly didn't need my permission, but I think he felt he owed me something. I gave my friend my blessing only because he didn't bestow the honor of becoming the new Mrs. Mirabeau on either Vicki or Melissa.

I dozed off. The phone rang just as I got into a comfortable position. It was Edmond. We remained close and found time to keep in touch over the years. He dropped me a few lines sometimes or called just to say hello. We still missed Lee and reminisced on occasion about the good old days. He hadn't forgotten about Kellee's graduation.

"B.J., how are you?"

"Great."

"Please give Kellee my best wishes."

"Of course." Then we chatted about his life and mine. He didn't brag or boast about the job that kept him working around the clock on one important issue after another. I admired his modesty. He only cared about getting the work done and never took full credit for anything, always willing to share the spotlight. Lee and Edmond came from two different worlds. I invited him to the graduation, but he declined, saying that he didn't want to intrude on a family celebration. We continued to chat, and, finally, he got up the courage to ask if he could see me before I left town.

"How about brunch on Sunday?" he asked. "I have some business today, but after that my schedule's clear."

"Okay." I agreed to meet him Sunday morning.

"My driver will pick you up around ten-thirty." He hung up, then I dozed off again and woke to the blaring sound of the alarm clock. I got up, showered, and went downstairs to meet my family. We walked around the corner to the restaurant. The weather agreed with us. It was nice with a slight chill in the air. I draped my wrap around my shoulders. Adam said Kellee called en route to the restaurant and would meet us there. We arrived about the same time. Just as we walked up, she stepped out of a cab. We hugged and kissed. She literally glowed. The waitress escorted us to a table. Everyone started talking all at once, and then we laughed.

Kellee pulled from her memory a few of the funny and colorful stories. "Mom, do you remember when Nate ate so much he got sick?"

"How could I forget?" She laughed. "I stayed up all night with him. He slept on the floor in our bedroom. Adam was out of town." The waiter recognized Adam from earlier in the day and smiled as he took our drink orders. Without asking Adam, he returned and set a gin and tonic in front of him. Everyone pretended not to notice. We looked over the menu and placed our orders.

"Tonight, I'm ordering spaghetti and meatballs, Nate's favorite," Dannie said. We held our glasses up high in a toast to his memory.

And after that moment of reflection, Kellee took center stage. Adam raised his glass to toast her accomplishment, and we followed suit. "Here's to your acceptance into medical school," he said.

"In the meantime, a short vacation in Europe, compliments of Daddy, for a little rest and relaxation," Kellee said. We paused to take in the power and the magic of the evening. "Mom, Aunt Lynette and Aunt Ellie called to wish me well and said to check the mailbox."

As promised, Lynette, Ellie and I kept in touch. We shared all the special times in the lives of our families, like graduations and weddings. No one had any grandchildren yet. Kyle got married last year, and both Sam and Ted married the year before. Leah Ann got accepted into law school. We tried not to miss any milestones in the lives of the people we loved. After dinner, Kellee hailed a cab, and we walked the short distance back to the hotel. I wished Nate could see his baby sister graduate with honors. Dannie and Amy said goodnight and headed to the elevators.

Adam asked, "B.J., will you sit and talk for a while?"

"Sure, why not?"

We walked into the bar and sat looking out the window at the beautiful city lights. I could see that Adam wanted to ask me something. We ordered drinks, club soda for me, with a twist of lime. Adam ordered a gin and tonic. I could never forget that I'm an alcoholic. We indulged in some small talk for a few minutes. Then he asked, "B.J., when you found out about Vicki and me, why didn't you throw that tape in my face?"

I started not to answer. The past should remain in the past, but then I changed my mind. He needed an answer, and I deserved the chance to tell him how I felt. "Adam, at first I wanted to hurt you as badly as you'd hurt me. But then I realized that destroying you meant destroying our children, and I couldn't let that happen. They meant more to me than anything on this earth. Besides, Vicki and Melissa only made ripples in the pond."

He looked shocked but didn't say anything else, and neither did I.

Adam looked at me. "I didn't realize what I had."

"Perhaps, you didn't, and now you have a new life, remember?"

I changed the subject, and we spent the rest of the evening talking about our kids, his new family, and my life. Adam now had a stepson, Kellee's age, away at college. We talked for a long time, until I realized the lateness of the hour. We had a hectic day ahead. I got up, said goodnight, and took the elevator to my room. Adam said he wanted to hang out a few more minutes. I smiled. *He probably sat there trying to figure out how I found out about Melissa.* I thought. Vicki and Melissa belonged in the past with all the other stuff that no longer mattered. Too exhausted, it didn't take me long to fall asleep.

I woke to the sound of the phone. "Hey, Mom! Do you want to meet us for breakfast?" Dannie asked.

"No thanks, I think I'll order room service, and just relax for a few minutes before we go."

Several hours later, we grabbed a cab and headed for the school. Crowds of people, especially parents who sacrificed greatly filed into the auditorium and took their seats. We maneuvered through the crowds, found seats near the stage, and waited. The ceremony began promptly. Between the slightly subdued shouts and cheers, we heard "Kellee Josephine Marten Mirabeau."

We clapped and cheered, too. I smiled, and my heart skipped a beat. Kellee waved as she walked back to her seat, and I blew her a kiss, remembering Anna. Today I understood how my mother had felt. After the ceremony, we grabbed a snack at the hotel and in that true Mirabeau tradition, we went to an excellent off-Broadway production. Adapting to her role as a Mirabeau woman, Amy took charge of the arrangements. After the play, Kellee went off to meet up with some of her classmates. Dannie and Amy wanted to see the city at night. I decided to retire for the evening, but Adam asked me to go for a walk with him on that lovely night. I agreed. We walked up and down Times Square, over to Fifth Avenue and back. The crowded streets, crisp night air, and the lights dancing brightly overhead shouted, "Welcome to New York!" Full of electrifying energy, the city possessed the power to hypnotize. We left many times, but we always came back. Adam and I headed back to our hotel. I turned to say goodnight as Adam leaned forward and kissed my cheek. "Thanks for the evening."

"You're welcome."

Before I fell asleep, I called Dannie. "I'm having brunch with an old friend."

"Okay, Mom."

He didn't ask questions, and I didn't volunteer any information. Adam's secretary had scheduled us a late return, so we had no time restraints. I slept in and woke up refreshed with an hour to dress for my luncheon. I went downstairs and found the driver waiting. It was only a short distance from the hotel. I walked up to the maître d' and asked for Edmond Stein, and he immediately escorted me to a secluded spot on the terrace. Edmond stood as I approached the table. He hadn't changed, still breathtakingly handsome.

"Hello, B.J."

"Hello," I said and extended my hand.

"I was afraid that you might change your mind."

"I almost did, but thought, it too rude on such short notice."

"I'm so glad you came."

A few gaps needed filling in, but we'd done a pretty good job of keeping up with each other. Handsome, and still the serious guy, now with his hair slightly graying around the edges, he looked even more distinguished. We ordered and talked until I looked at my watch and realized the time. The day was more enjoyable than I'd imagined. Even though I'd known Edmond a long time, I had forgotten that he could be quite charming. As I stood to leave, he reached out his hand and pulled me to him. He kissed my cheek and held me for a minute.

"Goodbye, Edmond," I said and pulled away. While Edmond sat and waited for Alan, the driver took me back to the hotel.

On the ride back, steeped in thought of Edmond, a question arose. "What's happening?" But I shook my head and moved on. "Friends and no more," I said, over and over, as if trying to convince myself.

At the hotel, Dannie and Amy sat waiting for me in the lobby after going for a long walk in a city that never sleeps. "Mom," he said, "Dad will be down shortly. He's on the phone."

"Okay. I have time to call Kellee before heading out." I'd missed a call from her earlier. I went to my room and made the call. The phone rang twice, and then she picked up.

"Hello, Mom, where've you been?"

"Meeting an old friend." She didn't ask who, and again I didn't volunteer anything.

"Kellee, yesterday you made me so proud, and I want you to know that I love you with all my heart."

"I know you do, Mom, and I love you, too." Next week, because of her dad's generosity, she would begin an exciting vacation. He always had a soft spot for his little girl.

"Have fun and be careful."

"I will, Mom."

"Let's talk before you leave next week." She agreed and then hung up.

I finished packing and hurried down to the lobby. We took the shuttle to the airport and then flew home. I picked up my luggage and turned to walk out the door, but, instead, I walked over to Adam. I gave him a hug and whispered in his ear, "You didn't deserve me."

"Much too late, but I know that now," he said.

Dannie and Amy looked at each other and then back at me but said nothing as we walked out together.

Minutes later, we pulled up in front of my house. "I'll see you later," I shouted as they drove off. Despite a few bumps in the road, my family turned out pretty good. Nate's tragic death ended a life of promise. Some of the facts remained cloudy, and with some pieces still missing it was hard to see the complete picture. I'm still hopeful that one day I'll discover what will end this season.

Chapter 20

The Wedding

In a few weeks, Kellee would return from Europe to attend her big brother's wedding. Dannie, my oldest, became the pillar of our family after his dad left. This strong and supportive young man found the girl of his dreams and the last-minute countdown to their wedding had begun. He met Amy shortly before graduating from college.

"Awestruck by her inward beauty, I wanted to marry her the moment we met, but I also wanted her to finish medical school. She has a compassionate soul. No one deserves a career in medicine more than Amy. She's worked hard," he said.

Amy just smiled when he spoke so flatteringly about her. Of course, completing medical school mattered to Amy's parents, too. They had time and money invested in her.

Anyone watching could see why Dannie loved Amy. She was thoughtful and caring with the most alluring smile. Dannie adored his four-feet-eleven inch, brown-skinned beauty. She always wore her dark brown hair pulled back into a ponytail.

"I'm too busy to do anything with it," she said. As a little girl, she planned and mapped out her big day down to the tiniest detail. Apparently, her parents had been planning equally as long and would spare no expense on her wedding. Amy and her coordinator began to fine tune the festive and dramatic gala. Nothing would surpass the affair, except Amy's own beauty. I gave her my guest list, and she merged it with her own. Amy already knew the people on my list. They met at Nate's funeral. Edmond and I hadn't spoken since Kellee's graduation, but I understood the importance of his work. If he needed to, he knew where to find me.

Amy planned an elaborate, storybook wedding that would surely make every society page of every local newspaper, and perhaps a major one as well. Her horse drawn carriage with the six white horses and designer dress sounded like something out of a fairy tale. Amy mentioned the name of the Parisian designer, but it was unimportant to me. Besides, the day belonged to Amy, not me. However, I paused and remembered my own wedding day. Our small ceremony consisted of a gathering of a handful of friends and family. Her guest list already exceeded mine by two hundred guests. Amy's red bottom shoes probably cost more than my entire wedding. I laughed out loud at the thought, but it was true. Amy didn't care that Dannie couldn't afford the life she grew up knowing. Admittedly, Amy's wealth gave me some concern. I worried Dannie would try to keep up with her life of privilege. He had a good job, but it would never pay that kind of money. As I got to know Amy, I saw that she loved Dannie because he understood the true meaning of love, family, and commitment. Dannie gave Amy an elegant white gold band encased in diamonds.

When Amy first saw her engagement ring, she screamed and kissed Dannie. I guess that meant she approved.

What advice would I give to Dannie and Amy as they start their lives together? I thought for a moment. Perhaps, I should say, "Dannie and Amy, remember to love each other and never leave anything unsaid, no matter how ugly." Adam and I loved each other but failed to trust each other with the ugly. What advice would Amy's parents give her? I wasn't sure. Of course, age and wisdom, we all had plenty of that. Amy's wonderful parents loved her deeply. As an only child, she commanded her father's undivided affection. He owned a bank, and according to Dannie, her mother came from old money. It pleased me that both her parents loved Dannie, too. With the wedding now only days away, Amy's wedding coordinator had a checklist a mile long with not nearly enough time to check and recheck every detail. But, she'd get it done.

Kellee came home the day before the wedding along with the entire Cheyenne gang. We invited them to stay at the farm. Edmond called. "B.J.," he said, "As soon as the wedding ends, I must get back. I hope I get to say hello."

"I hope so." With my Cheyenne family here, it gave us a chance to catch up. We needed the time together. Winston and Larry asked about Adam.

"He's well." The news of our breakup reached across the miles. We regretted that we had to share such ugly news. Later that evening, Adam came by to see everyone. It almost felt like old times. Almost. The guys sat around talking politics and sports, as usual, while Lynette, Ellie and I visited separately.

Rita couldn't make the wedding but sent her best wishes. "She and her new husband left two days ago for a vacation in Australia," Lynette said. Ellie, Lynette, and I talked about our kids and the things going on in our lives. With some hesitation, I told them about meeting Edmond in New York, and that sometimes he called or dropped me a note.

They didn't look surprised or shocked, and then Lynette asked, "How is Edmond?"

"Very well," I said, not wanting to take this conversation any further. We stayed up much too late enjoying great company. Adam left sometime before midnight, and everyone turned in for the evening. A noon wedding meant we didn't need to rush, so the kids slept late. I rose early and prepared breakfast for the gang. Lynette and Ellie helped with the dishes.

Around eleven-thirty, we gathered in the living room, ready for a brief ten-minute drive to the same church where Amy got baptized. Interestingly, I also got married in the same church where my baptism was held. Of course, that's where the similarities stopped. Her beautiful church stood comfortably in the middle of downtown. That huge old building witnessed more of life and death than any of us could ever imagine. We waited outside to see the dramatic arrival of the bride. At a distance, we saw the carriage and the six white horses as they pranced up the street and then watched Amy step from the carriage. She looked stunning. Hand sewn pearls covered every inch of vacant space on her dress. It emulated the purity and freshness of snowflakes falling from the sky, and her train flowed from the top of her head for some distance behind her. A tiara rested atop her head, adorned with three rows of rhinestones. What could I say, other than, "Spectacular!"

Fresh cut flowers decorated the church, and a heavenly fragrance floated in the air. The processional began on time. Everything went as planned.

Dannie waited nervously, just as Adam had on our

wedding day. The older he got, the more he looked like his dad: handsome and tall, with smooth chocolate skin and that distinctly coal-black Mirabeau hair. The music changed, and the bride, on the arm of her father, walked in, poised and graceful. She looked like the princess in my mother's imaginary world. The bride and groom exchanged vows, and within minutes the minister pronounced them husband and wife. Daniel Marten Mirabeau took as his wife Amy Lucinda Jefferson. Amy and Dannie ran out of the church, as rice showered down like rain upon them. The carriage waited then it took them to an extraordinarily beautiful reception hall. It bowed gracefully and allowed its amazing transformation. Fresh flower arrangements sat on top of tables with some suspended from the ceiling. I'd never seen so many fresh flowers in one place in my life; not even at Longwood Gardens.

The bride's cake stood three tiers high, covered with white, glossy icing, with a tiny bride and groom on top. The groom's all-chocolate, two-tiered cake was a true chocolate lover's dream. In the center of the stage, a live orchestra played lovely soft music. The violins, cello, and harps made celestial sounds.

Amy and Dannie walked in, and everyone applauded. Unlike his father, Dannie was an excellent dancer. Then Dannie placed Amy's hand in her dad's and watched as she and her father danced together. The drinks flowed like running water, and the most delicious lobster and steak dinner completed the evening. Dannie and Amy said their goodbyes around eleven then escaped in their horse drawn carriage for the evening. Briefly, I got a chance to say hello to Edmond before he left. Around midnight, the reception ended. We settled in exhausted after an extremely long day. No late-night talks tonight. Everyone had early flights. Dannie and Amy, the recipients of Adam's generosity, boarded a flight early the next morning for the island of Hawaii. Just as Amy planned, her wedding turned out to be the event of the season, and, no doubt, her honeymoon would surpass all her expectations, too.

As I lay in bed, I thought about the breathtaking ceremony and wondered if Edmond made it back safely. The morning came quickly. I rose and went to the kitchen to prepare breakfast—too late. Lynette and Ellie had everything ready.

"Good morning."

"Good morning," they said. We cleared the breakfast dishes while the guys put the luggage in the rental cars. Then we exchanged hugs and kisses and said our goodbyes. I went back inside and sat down to another cup of coffee. Dannie called just as I was getting up from the table.

"Mom," he said, "we're at the airport, but I just wanted to say goodbye, and I love you. See you in two weeks. Amy sends her love, too."

"I love you both, enjoy your honeymoon."

"Mom, when I get back, I need to talk to you."

"Okay, should I be worried?"

"No, of course not."

"Okay, then have a good trip."

Chapter 21

Just Between Friends

As I walked out of the kitchen, the phone rang. I ran back in and picked it up.

"Hello," I said, surprised to hear from him so soon.

"B.J., how are you?" Edmond asked.

"Great! Thanks for coming to the wedding. Dannie and Amy thank you, too."

"Have they left yet?"

"Yes." We talked about the wedding and the weather and our friends from Cheyenne, and then, in the same breath, Edmond asked me to come to Washington for a visit. It was flattering that he wanted to spend time with me, but, of course, I made up an excuse.

"Edmond, I'm sorry, but I have plans for next week, perhaps another time." I had no plans for next week, but I didn't know what else to say. Our friendship started moving a little too fast, and it frightened me, although I had to admit that I knew him better than he knew me. I once shared a very close and intimate relationship with Lee. No secrets existed between us.

His honesty, purpose, and conviction shaped the man I came to know over the years and not just from what I learned from Lee, but what I saw as I got to know him more. I sensed the disappointment in his voice.

"I plan to stay in DC for a while. The kids have their own lives. The homestead's a lonely place these days. I'm thinking about selling the family house and maybe buying a smaller one."

"That's a good idea."

"B.J.," he said, sounding hopeful, "Would you consider coming out and helping me?"

"I'm—"

But before I finished my sentence, he jumped in.

"Hold on, let me grab my calendar." While he checked his calendar, I thought about Lee. A little over a year ago, her spirit went home. Interrupting my thoughts, he asked, "How about the third weekend in this month?" I couldn't think of another excuse, so I accepted. Besides, the spectacular weather there would make it worth the trip. So, I agreed to come help him locate a smaller house.

After I hung up, I thought, *Edmond doesn't need me to come all the way from Suellen to help him house-hunt. Our friend Ellie handles his real estate deals, and her office is only minutes away, not hundreds of miles.*

I knew an excuse when I heard one, but I went along. House-hunting again with someone other than Adam would seem strange. I'd moved from one place to another, and many times from one city to another, but always with the same person. It's funny how things worked out. Just when you thought you'd gotten it all figured out, you discovered you didn't.

I hung up and walked out to my rose garden. A long time ago, I thought I'd lost God's favor until I saw his hand moving again in my life. As Lee lay dying, I realized God was right there keeping His promise to never leave nor forsake us, so I thanked him for that same favor in Lee's life. He heard me and then, as He promised, he took my sister and my friend home to rest.

I walked back into the house. Tired, but not sleepy, I grabbed a book off the bookshelf, pulled a throw up over my legs and sank down into Adam's old cozy chair. I loved to read. Nothing relaxed me more than reading a really good book. I didn't prefer one genre over the other. I just enjoyed the adventure found in the pages of a good book. It was late when I looked up. I took a long hot bath soaking in the sweet, fragrant lavender bubbles with music playing softly in the background. Then I dried off and crawled into bed. Sleep came quickly.

I'd decided to get back into volunteering, so I called up an old associate and asked, "Where do you need me?"

"Everywhere, welcome back," she said. I jumped right into the middle of organizing food drives and fundraising. Still hectic and as political as I remembered, with too many people wanting to lead and not enough real workers bees to get the job done, nothing had changed. The long, grueling hours caused me to question why I loved it.

The weeks flew by. Edmond's secretary handled all my arrangements. He pushed my departure back as late as I felt comfortable with because I didn't like getting home at night and walking into that empty house alone.

After I finished packing my last bag, I called Dannie and Amy.

The phone rang while I stood thinking of Dannie and Amy's honeymoon pictures. I started to place the receiver down when I heard Amy's voice.

"Hi, Mom!"

"How are you, Amy?"

"Good."

"I'm on my way out of town for a few days visiting an old friend. Give Dannie my love. You can reach me on my cell phone if you need me."

"Okay, have a great time."

She didn't ask which old friend, and I didn't volunteer an answer.

The plane arrived on time, and I headed downstairs to wait for Edmond. I hadn't checked anything, so I skipped baggage claim and headed straight out the door to the sidewalk. A limo pulled up just as I stepped to the curb.

"Hello, B.J.," he said as he stepped out.

"Hi, there."

He gave me a hug and kissed me gently on my cheek. The limo driver picked up my luggage and placed it in the trunk. Edmond stepped aside, and I got in. He then slid in next to me.

"B.J., I'm so glad you came."

"So am I."

The ride to the hotel took about a half hour. We always had plenty to talk about and today was no exception. When we reached the hotel, the driver got out and opened the door. Edmond grabbed my hand, "I'll call you later. Dinner at seven, will that work?"

"Yes, that's fine, I'll see you then."

I checked in and sat down on the bed. *What am I doing here?* I thought. *Edmond surely doesn't need me to help him find a house.* I panicked, realizing something I'd tried to hide. I was falling in love with Edmond Stein. *But how does he feel about me?* He cared about me, but did he love me? I reminded myself that I came this weekend simply to help an old friend. Sunday, I'd head back home, and that would be the end of the story. I decided to go for a walk on this nice, but chilly day. The city bustled with tourists and the air felt damp and cool. After a few minutes, I returned to my room. Looking forward to the evening, I took a long hot shower. Then I sat down on the bed and called Kellee.

She answered on the first ring. "Hello, Mom."

"Hi, sweetheart, how are things with you?"

"Good, classes will be starting in a few weeks. Where are you?"

"I'm in DC."

"Oh!" Her voice sounded inquisitive, but she didn't pry.

Finally, I said, "I'm here visiting an old friend."

"Have a good time."

We hung up, and I finished dressing. I brought two of my favorite dresses with me, but couldn't decide which one to wear: the black or the red.

Oh, well, you can never go wrong with black, so I dressed in a basic and timeless black dress with a triple string of pearls. I wore a pair of black, high-heeled peep-toed pumps, and carried a small red jeweled clutch the kids gave me one year for my birthday. I picked up my wrap and stood in the mirror admiring my reflection when the phone rang. It was Edmond. He was in the lobby.

He walked toward me, smiling, as I got off the elevator and then extended his hand. People rushed up to him as we made our way through the lobby. He greeted them, and then we got into the waiting limo.

Edmond had reservations at this upscale restaurant that reeked of old money. Heads turned as an unknown woman walked in on the arm of this prominent senator. Edmond proudly introduced me to everyone who stopped at our table. We had a marvelous dinner, with the most entertaining conversation. My keen interest in politics didn't surprise him. Perhaps Lee shared the extent of our political discussions with him in confidence. We talked about any and everything from gardening to gay rights. I'd followed his work on Capitol Hill with a great deal of respect and admiration for both the senator and the man. After dinner, we left the restaurant and headed out of the city. Edmond turned to me and asked, "Will you stay with me tonight, B.J.?"

When the word "yes" tumbled from my lips, it surprised even me. In the back seat of a limo, we held hands like young lovers. It was a short ride to Edmond's home. When the driver pulled into the driveway, Edmond got out then came around to the passenger side and opened the door. I stepped out. Then he stuck his head in and said to the driver," I won't need you anymore tonight. Thank you and have a good evening."

"Yes sir," the man replied.

I looked around. It was not the home he once shared with Lee, but a place he rented to escape the prying eyes of the world. He escorted me in and kissed me passionately. Many nights, as I lay in bed alone, I imagined this night.

He unzipped the back of my dress and pushed it off my shoulders. It fell in a crumpled heap onto the floor. Then he lifted me high in his arms and carried me to his bed. It was the most sensational lovemaking, gentle and passionate.

We lay holding each other when Edmond turned to me, "I love you, B.J., marry me."

I sat up and looked deep into his eyes. "Now?" I asked in shock.

"Yes, now."

"What about the marriage license?" I asked.

"I've already spoken with Judge Crane, a long-time friend. I've known Jerry since law school. We can swing by his office on the way and pick up the license. He'll also waive the twenty-four-hour waiting period for the State of New York."

"It appears you've thought of everything?"

"I certainly hope so."

"Again, my reply surprised me. "Yes, I'll marry you, Edmond Stein."

We both laughed out loud.

He grabbed and kissed me hard on the lips. We spent the rest of the night making plans wrapped in each other's arms. Morning came very quickly, and I rolled over as Edmond entered the room with a tray in his hands. He'd fixed breakfast: bacon, toast, orange juice, and coffee. I wasn't hungry, but I ate because of his sweet and loving gesture. We dressed and headed to my hotel so that I could change.

Then the driver drove west, heading out of the city to a small chapel. Unaware of his plans until last night and totally unprepared, I wore the only other dress that I brought with me, the red one, and my pearls. No crowds invaded our private ceremony. Edmond had full confidence that the minister and his driver would keep our secret. He told me later that he and Reverend J.T. Kettle grew up together back in New York and attended the same university.

When the minister asked for the ring, Edmond pulled a gold wedding band from the inside of his jacket pocket and placed it upon my finger. On such short notice, I improvised. I took my gum wrapper from my purse, twisted into a circle and placed it upon his finger. Everyone laughed. The ring didn't matter, only the union, and when the minister pronounced us husband and wife, I kissed my new husband. Edmond told me that he purchased the ring the day after he returned from Dannie and Amy's wedding.

The outside world didn't need to know our secret. I

feared that the media would thrust me into the spotlight and swallow up the freedom I loved. Edmond, and I agreed not to disclose our marriage for a while. Besides, our kids needed to know first, and I didn't know how to tell them or Adam. I didn't need Adam's permission or his blessing, but I wanted to be the one to tell him. Why did we think we owed each other anything after all these years?

That remained somewhat of a mystery, even to me. Our lives had certainly evolved into a whole new dimension, filled with an accumulation of new family and friends.

As we headed back, Edmond turned to me, "I have one more surprise."

"I don't know if I can handle anything else," I said laughing.

He laughed, too. When the driver dropped us off, we got into Edmond's personal car. He drove back to the city but this time to a very special place he'd found. I learned on the way that he'd discovered this quaint, cottage with its dark gray shutters and window boxes that reminded him of the old neighborhood. He couldn't wait to show it to me. The well-landscaped front yard had ample trees and flower beds lining the long walkway. Both the living room and the master bedroom had large wood burning fireplaces and an oversized open kitchen, designed for entertaining, tied everything together.

The cottage had an amazing backyard. A deck extended off the back of the house and sloped deep, into the woods. From the kitchen window, we enjoyed nature in its splendor.

"B.J., what do you think?"

"It's perfect."

In many ways it reminded me of Ellie's backyard. Edmond and I spent the rest of our time touring the countryside. We stopped at a restaurant off the beaten path and enjoyed a quiet dinner. I tried to retell, with little success, some of Rita's funny jokes. Something always got lost in the translation, and they didn't seem funny, but to humor me he laughed anyway. Edmond was a very serious guy with one or two silly moments, but no more. We got back to the hotel later than I expected. He walked me to the elevator, and we said goodnight.

"I'll call you," he said, and then he walked away.

Edmond was a master at handling matters discreetly and, rightly so, because everywhere we went, people recognized him. I was in bed when he called. We discussed how and when to tell our families the news. I still insisted that we wait. He agreed to honor my request.

"B.J., my driver will pick you up early for Sunday worship, and then we'll grab a late lunch. I love you and sweet dreams," he said.

"Me too. Goodnight, Edmond."

Over the years, he'd allowed stuff to infringe on his relationship with God, but today, we planned to worship together in the nondenominational church of his friend, the very same Reverend J.T. Kettle.

I lay awake for hours, remembering the romance of the previous night, the surprise wedding, our lovely home, and our plans for the future. Sometime later, I fell asleep.

The sun woke me, pouring threads of sunshine through the sheer curtains that fashioned the hotel windows. I took a leisurely bath, dressed meticulously, and stood, studying my thin, shapely image in the mirror. Auburn highlights accented my naturally curly dark brown hair. Momentarily, I thought of Lee's beauty and how, despite our differences, we really loved each other. I wondered what she would think of Edmond and me, but I knew the answer. Lee would rejoice that her two best friends in the whole world had found each other.

Kellee recently ended a dead-end relationship. I prayed that she would find someone to share her life with, and, thank goodness, she started dating a young medical student. It looked promising. He was in his last year of residency with big plans for his future. He didn't come from a wealthy family and neither did she.

"He's extremely focused, committed, and he makes me laugh," Kellee said. A few days ago, when we talked she said, "Mom, I think he's the one."

I was happy for her and prayed each day that her life would continue to line up with God's will for her. I once thought that Alan would someday be the one. It looked like I was wrong. *Parents, what do we know?* I thought.

I spent too long lost in my thoughts. When I walked out, Edmond was waiting. The driver opened the door, and I slid in next to Edmond. We arrived promptly and found seats mid-way in the aisle just in time for the opening prayer. When the short, spirit-filled service ended, the driver headed uptown to the restaurant.

Different from Edmond's previous choice, this restaurant had an urban vibe. Delicious food, superb ambience, and the sweet sound of smooth jazz floated on the wings of hope.

"From our friendship long ago, I remembered that you loved jazz," he said.

We had a lovely time. On the way to the airport, we held each other and kissed goodbye in the privacy of the limo. I picked up my bags, waved goodbye, and walked inside. Although not a bad flight, it seemed that in the last year, I spent too much time in airports.

Dannie, Amy, and Kellee had their lives and were doing fine. I missed home, but I missed Edmond, too. I got home before dark, took a hot shower, and collected the pile of mail.

After a quick dinner, I called Amy. The phone rang a long time before she answered. "Hello, Amy."

"Hello, Mom, how was your trip?"

"Just great and, how are you?"

"Wonderful!"

"May I speak with Dannie?"

"I'm sorry, Mom, he's not home. He went out for a few minutes."

"I hear the wedding pictures are back. I'd love to stop by tomorrow evening after you guys get home from work to see them."

"That's a great idea! I'll tell Dannie."

"Good night, Amy. Give Dannie my love, and I'll see the two of you tomorrow."

Chapter 22

Hello, Old Friend!

Too tired to read tonight, I turned on the television and let it watch me. Around midnight, I woke up, turned off the lights, and went straight to bed. The next morning, I noticed a missed call from Edmond. From the very beginning, our separate and secret life started to get complicated. Why had I kept putting off sharing the news with our families? I was a divorcee with adult children who adored Edmond as much as he adored them. So, what did it matter? I loved my privacy and dreaded the thought of a media invasion.

I left Edmond a message asking that he call me when he got in. I hadn't heard from him by early evening, so I called the kids then drove over to see their wedding pictures. The wedding hit the front page of the local newspaper. Edmond told me that one of the major newspapers carried it, too.

Amy answered the door. She looked radiant with that newlywed glow. I smiled remembering that once upon a time my face held that same radiance, then I gave her a hug and stepped inside.

Dannie came from around the corner. "Hi, Mom."

"Hi, Dannie."

"Can I get you something?"

"No, I'm fine." Still beaming, Amy pulled out her wedding album. We sat for about an hour looking over and over again at those amazing pictures.

"The photographer did a great job," I said.

"Yeah, he did indeed!" Amy said.

"Mom, I need to talk to you," Dannie said.

Amy picked up the photo album and left the room.

"What's going on?" My body grew tense, knowing I'd waited for this moment. He sat down on the sofa next to me.

"Do you remember the girl Nate started seeing right before he died?"

"Yes, but I never got to meet her."

"I know."

"Lora, I believe that was her name."

"Yes, Mom." I saw pain in his eyes and, finally, the words came out. "She died last week."

"What happened?"

"She died of a drug overdose."

"Prescribed?"

"No."

I held my breath, as if I was afraid to breathe. Then he began to let go of what he kept inside for so long, too painful to discuss. Because of this tragedy, he had found the courage to tell me what I needed to hear—the truth.

"Lora had an addiction, Mom. When Nate met her, she worked as a nurse in a hospital across town. She'd had a bad car wreck that left her with severe back pain. Most days, she couldn't function without the aid of prescription drugs. Too often heavily medicated, her life started spiraling rapidly out of control. Her job was in jeopardy, so she begged Nate to help her. She forged prescriptions and got him to fill them. Lora knew eventually her sin would catch up with her, but she couldn't tolerate the pain. Nate loved her and would've done anything for her, and he did. Lora started buying drugs off the street and went into dangerous parts of town to get them. It was Lora's voice Dad heard the night Nate died. She sent Nate to pick up some drugs from someone she trusted. When Nate got there, they decided to rob him instead.

"I kept in touch with Lora after Nate's death. Honestly, I don't know why, but I helped her get into a rehab clinic. She had to deal with the physical pain, as well as the burden of guilt she carried for Nate's death. She blamed herself for what happened, and I blamed her, too, at first. Then suddenly, something happened to me, and I realized that Nate loved her and died trying to help her. He always took care of the wounded. I decided that if he loved her enough to risk his life, I could at least try to save her life for him. Amy found out from some nurses she works with that Lora committed suicide, Mom."

By the time he finished, tears were streaming down his face. We sat there and cried for Nate and for Lora. I never met her, but if Nate loved her, surely, she deserved my tears.

"Her funeral's tomorrow. Will you come with me?" he asked.

"Of course, I will." I hugged him. We cried until we had no tears left. I picked up my purse, hugged him again, and walked out the door.

I crawled into bed and cried myself to sleep. The next morning, I dressed, fighting back the tears as they welled up inside me. We arrived at the church ahead of the family and sat in the last pew. I watched as her parents, family, and friends piled soberly into the church. Her mother cried, and her father consoled his wife during the brief service.

When the services ended, we were walking toward the car when I heard my name.

"Mrs. Mirabeau!" a female voice called out.

I stopped and turned to face an attractive, but obviously heartbroken woman. She reached out and hugged me.

"My name is Lauren Jones. My daughter, Lora loved Nate. We're here today because she allowed guilt to steal her soul. I'm so sorry for our children. I wish we could've met under more pleasant circumstances."

"I know."

"Mrs. Mirabeau, please pray for me, and I'll continue to pray for you."

We hugged again and then Dannie and I walked away. My heart ached for Lora's parents. I had firsthand knowledge of their pain. Also, I knew that if they didn't grab hold of God's hand, they wouldn't survive the trial. *Perhaps I should keep in touch*, I thought. Not so much for me, but for her because Nate was that kind of friend.

Edmond called an hour after I got home. "B.J., sorry I didn't get back to you sooner. I've had a hell of a day, with too many problems on the floor that couldn't wait."

"I understand." Before I could say anything about my day, he told me that a reporter discovered a marriage license on file for Senator Edmond Stein and Beatrice Johanna Mirabeau.

"He wants to go public but would prefer an exclusive. What do you want to do?"

"Tell him we'll give him a private interview- if he'll give us time to tell our families."

"I can probably stall him for a day or two."

"Good, that'll give me the time I need."

A short conversation could only mean one thing— our fast pace lives finally caught up with us. We couldn't hide the tiredness, so we said goodnight. I sat down for a minute to think of how best to handle the conversation. Then I called Dannie and asked if he and Amy could stop by after work. Dannie said that Amy had a late shift, but he'd come over. I decided I'd call Kellee after Dannie and I talked, and perhaps call Adam later. I spent the rest of the day preparing dinner, along with what I would say to both Dannie and Kellee. My children trusted my judgment and were genuinely fond of Edmond. They thought of him as a great guy—and yet, for some unknown reason, I had an uneasy feeling in my stomach. Dannie arrived shortly after six.

"Hi, Mom! What's up?" He kissed my cheek and walked pass me with his sights on the kitchen.

At our house, everybody gathered in the kitchen. I sat down and asked him to sit down, too. Fearing bad news, he looked a little uneasy as he sat down.

"Dannie, Edmond and I see each other sometimes. He's a good man, and we care deeply for each other."

Before I could continue Dannie reached over and caught my hand. "Mom, Amy and I've known for a long time about you and Edmond. Didn't you ever wonder why we never asked, 'what old friend?' Come on, Mom, you know me. I want to know everything. Amy's parents saw the two of you together at brunch after Kellee's graduation in New York and again at a Sunday worship service. We've known for some time now."

I looked at him and smiled, somewhat relieved. Then I asked, "How do you feel about Edmond?"

"I think he's a great guy. I've known Mr. Stein most of my life, remember?"

"I guess I'd forgotten."

"Does Kellee know?"

"Of course. You know we can't keep secrets from each other and never could."

I then looked at him again and said, "Edmond and I got married last week."

He didn't look shocked or surprised. He jumped up and came around to the other side of the table and hugged me. "Way to go, Mom!" Then he got up and headed straight to the stove. "Boy! What smells so good?"

I laughed. "Help yourself, it's only spaghetti."

I kissed Dannie and held him for a long time. Around our house, everybody loved spaghetti.

"Mom, we hope the two of you will have a happy life together."

"Thanks, I guess I'd better call Kellee now." Then I told Dannie about the reporter and that he might get some questions. "Please decline to answer."

"Okay. Goodnight, Mom, I love you."

"Me, too."

Kellee answered on the first ring, as usual, as if waiting for my call. "Mom, how are you?"

"Terrific! I've got something to tell you, but I understand from Dannie that you already know more than I realized."

"If it's about you and Mr. Stein, yes, I already know that you guys are dating."

"How do you feel about the news?"

"Happy. I never wanted you to be alone, Mom. He's a nice man. You know we all love him."

"Kellee, Edmond and I got married last week."

Again, she didn't seem shocked or surprised. "Congratulations! Way to go, Mom!"

I laughed and whispered, "I love you," then hung up.

My thoughts swirled about in my head. I'd wasted too much energy trying to protect a secret that didn't really qualify as a secret. I picked up the phone again. Betty Jean answered.

"Hello, Betty Jean, how are you?"

"I'm fine, B.J., and you?""

"I'm well, too."

"May I speak with Adam?"

"Of course. Let me get him."

Adam picked up, "Hey there, what's wrong?"

"Nothing. Can you come over? I need to talk to you."

"Just me?"

"No, Betty Jean's welcome, too."

"We'll be there in a few minutes."

The one perk to living in a small town was the ability to get anywhere within minutes. Betty Jean and I saw each other in the grocery store, the dry cleaners, at church, and we went to the same beauty salon. I sat down to wait, and, within a few minutes, the doorbell rang. We exchanged greetings, and I escorted them into the kitchen where they sat down across from me. A deep trench formed in Adam's forehead, so I got right to the point.

"Adam, Edmond and I got married last week."

He stood up, walked around to the other side of the table, and hugged me. "Congratulations!"

Betty Jean hugged me and offered her well wishes, also.

"Did you know?"

"Sure did, the kids told me."

"B.J., I know you didn't need my permission or my blessing, but I'm glad you thought enough of me to tell me."

"Thanks."

"You're welcome."

They stayed for a few minutes longer and then left.

I remember saying once that my life had almost come full circle. Now, it truly had. More good days crossed my path than bad ones—what a blessing! I showered and fell face down on the bed, giggling like a school girl. My family accepted my life's choice without the third degree, and that called for a celebration. I went into the kitchen and poured a soda and sat there quietly sipping, and then turned in for the evening.

When morning came, and I hadn't heard from Edmond, I panicked. Surely Alan and Mia accepted our marriage. I'd known the two of them most of their lives and thought they loved me as much as I loved them. Would they now feel that my relationship with their father had gone too far? Suddenly, it occurred to me that because Edmond and I came from two different worlds, we'd made a mistake. With the die cast, would we turn back? What was I thinking? What had I gotten myself into? I walked outside, picked up the newspaper, and walked back inside. Instead of a late breakfast, I poured a cup of coffee.

I hadn't heard from Edmond. Mid-morning, I grabbed a sweater and walked out to my rose garden. No other place on earth cleared my head and gave me the solace needed to reason out my problems. In the deafening silence, I sat quietly and listened for God's voice. Then I prayed. "Lord, my family's hearts overflowed with joy over the knowledge of our union. Let Edmond's family feel the same contentment. If the relationship causes division and strife among his children, then give me the courage to do the right thing. Amen."

I sat there another moment, enjoying the beauty and the fragrance of the roses. Then I got up and left the problem in the capable hands of God.

The urge to do a little shopping hit me, so I grabbed my purse then headed out the door. My friend Lynette and I made great shopping companions. We shopped a while, broke the spell with a bite to eat, then shopped some more. I parked in the department store's garage, and then took the elevator up to the shoe department. I browsed through the large selection of shoes that sat invitingly on their pedestals before I noticed Betty Jean standing across the aisle from me.

"Hi, Betty Jean."

"Hello, B.J."

We exchanged a few words, and I asked about Adam.

"He's well."

I'm glad he found her. I thought. *She made him smile again.*

"B.J., I want you to know that we're very happy for you."

"Thanks." I walked away, feeling pretty good with my new pair of red pumps in hand. When I got home, I had a message waiting from Edmond.

"B.J., please call me."

The phone rang a couple of times, and then he picked up. "Hi, how're things?" I asked.

"Pretty great. How about with you?" he asked.

"Great, too, actually."

"B.J., I talked with both Alan and Mia, and they're thrilled we got married. I'm sorry I didn't get back with you yesterday, but we had a family emergency."

"What happened?" I asked nervously.

"Alan took a pretty nasty fall from his motorcycle and ended up in the hospital with a punctured lung and some broken ribs."

"Why didn't you call me?" I shouted excitedly.

"I know I should've called you. We've always been family. I'm sorry, B.J., I didn't mean it the way it probably sounded. I didn't mean to exclude you. He'll be in the hospital a few weeks. It won't happen again, I promise," he said jokingly.

"I'll come if you need me."

"No, I have everything under control. Alan's going to be okay."

"I'm glad. Give Alan my love."

"Alan said he'll call you in a day or two and Mia wants to know if she can come down at your earliest convenience. By the way, the reporter called. I'm meeting with him in the morning for the interview. Do you want me to cancel so you can come?" he asked.

"No, I'd rather you handle it."

"If he wants pictures, I'll call you."

"Try to discourage pictures."

"I'll do my best." We talked a while longer, and then Edmond asked, "How soon can you come home?"

"Soon, I need to finalize a few more things." Arranging this move would require more work than I anticipated, but fewer problems, I hoped. When Edmond hung up, I screamed out loud, "Oh no! Ellie and Lynette." I immediately picked the phone back up and dialed Lynette.

Larry answered. "Hello, Larry, how're you doing and how's the weather?"

"Great and great, and how about you?"

"Wonderful, may I speak with Lynette?"

"Sure, hold on a minute. She's on the computer." Before he could call out to her, Lynette picked up the other phone.

"B.J., how are you?"

"Very well, and how about you?"

"Fantastic!"

I didn't know how to start the conversation, so I just came right out with it. "Lynette, Edmond and I got married last week."

She let out this big roaring scream and then yelled for Larry. "B.J., I'm so happy for you."

I heard Larry in the background saying, "What's going on?"

She whispered, "B.J. and Edmond got married."

"Wow! Wonderful! Tell B.J. congratulations for me," Larry said.

Lynette and I talked for about twenty minutes. She wanted to know every detail. When we started dating? Where we went on our first date and where we got married? I was sure she had more questions.

Finally, I said, "Lynette, chill. If you want me to answer, you'll need to slow down." She laughed. Then I filled her in on all the exciting details. "I haven't told Ellie yet. Let me tell her, please."

"Okay," she said.

I thought I'd make Ellie my last call because once the tears started, I wasn't sure if we could stop them. Lynette's genuine happiness for me echoed loudly in her voice. We promised to talk later. Then I hung up and called Ellie.

"B.J., my love, how are you?"

"Terrific! How's Winston?" I asked.

"Good. He's en route and will be here shortly."

Again, not knowing how to begin, I got right to the point. "Ellie, Edmond and I got married last week."

"B.J.," she said in her high-pitched excited voice, "I'm so happy for you I'll try not to cry. I promise. And how's Edmond?"

"Very well. He's pretty busy right now, but that's the nature of his job."

Ellie then said, "If I tell you now that I'm shocked, it would be a lie. I think I knew even before you and Edmond knew. Whenever you entered a room, his face lit up. And right after Lee died, I ran into him in Washington on one of my girlfriend weekend trips. Our entire conversation centered on you. I knew then that Edmond was in love with you, and that time would handle the rest.

I know he'll bring you happiness. He's a great guy! I look forward to your homecoming, my friend."

"Stop! You sound like Lynette. I don't know all the answers yet, but I can say that I'm definitely coming home." Home! That sounded odd to me.

She screamed, "I can't wait!"

We talked a few more minutes and then hung up, promising to chat again later in the week.

I prayed for Alan's speedy recovery and looked forward to hearing from him, but a serious case of curiosity plagued me when I remembered Edmond saying Mia preferred to come for a visit. Alan and Mia had spent as much time at my house as they had their own. Lee and I didn't share the same bloodline, but we thought of ourselves as sisters. I needed to know they approved. Their approval meant as much to me as the approval of my own kids. That evening, I read for just a few minutes and then decided to turn in early. I had some decisions to tackle. This house once belonged to Adam and me. In the divorce, Adam signed it over to me because he knew how much I loved it. I thought about giving it to the kids or selling it if they didn't want it. I earmarked some of the furniture for good will, some for the kids, and the rest for shipment to my new home. Again, I started organizing yet another move. Mentally exhausted, I turned off the lights and slipped beneath the covers.

Early the next morning, I walked outside and picked up the paper. With a cup of coffee in hand, I sat down to read. The headlines talked about our messy economy, and then I flipped the page. On the second page an article caught my attention. The caption read: *Senator Edmond Stein Weds*. The story stated: *The senator married in a small chapel just outside of Washington, DC, and his new bride, a long-time family friend, returned to her home after the ceremony. Reverend J.T. Kettle, a close friend of the senator for many years performed the ceremony. Other than the couple, the minister, and senator Stein's chauffeur, no one else attended. The children of both parties only learned of the union a few days ago. Earlier sources told this reporter, now confirmed by the senator, that the children look forward to spending time with their new family. The couple hasn't officially lived together as husband and wife. However, after arranging their affairs, they'll live in one residence. Currently, the new Mrs. Edmond Stein resides in Florida, and reportedly was a close friend of the senator's late wife, Lee, and the person that the late Mrs. Stein requested as she lay dying. Senator Stein said of his new bride that she's a beautiful and intelligent woman, and he looks forward to a bright future with her.*

Some write-up, I thought, especially the part that talked about Lee requesting my presence as she lay dying. Did the world need to know that? Some reporters just had to go for the shock value. *Will my private and public worlds always collide with one another?* Oh well! Overall not a bad article, at least it hadn't portrayed me as desperate or lonely. I thought it was funny that the article failed to mention that, just like Lee, his new bride was several years younger, too. Now that was an aha moment that this reporter missed. *Oh well, the world knows all they need to know for now, and that's enough. Tomorrow we'll slip to the back pages, like old news, and no one will care about the marriage of Senator Edmond Patrick Stein and Beatrice Johanna Marten Mirabeau.* Just then the phone rang.

"Hello."

"Aunt B.J."

"Alan, sweetheart, it's good to hear your voice. I'm so sorry about the accident. I'm just glad you're going to be okay."

"I'll be fine. Thanks for caring. I guess I'll need to stop calling you 'Aunt B.J.,'" he said, laughing.

"Perhaps. How's everything with you and Darlene?"

"Not good. I don't think that's going anywhere. How's Kellee?" he asked.

"Well."

"I think of her often. Please send her my love."

"I will."

"Anyway, I told my dad I'd call and congratulate you personally. I'm happy for you and my dad. Aunt B.J., do you remember when I fell off my bicycle and scraped my knee, and you ran over to comfort a scared little boy?"

"I remember."

"Then when Dannie and I fell out of the tree in the backyard and sprained our ankles, you and Mom came to our rescue?"

"I remember."

"You and my dad belong together. Take care of yourself and my dad for me, I love you. I'll need to work on calling you something other than 'Aunt B.J.,' but that may take a while."

"I don't mind. Regardless, I'm still Aunt B.J."

We both laughed. His phone call brought a ray of sunshine at a most fretful time. At one point, I thought maybe Alan and Mia disapproved, and Edmond wanted to spare my feelings.

I hoped to hear from Mia soon. I had no idea what she wanted to say to me that she couldn't say over the phone. She had her mother's personality, and that meant she'd state her feelings, whether I liked it or not. She didn't have her mother's temper, thank goodness, but pretty much every other trait, including her good looks. I asked Edmond if he knew why Mia wanted to visit.

He just said, "Relax, honey, everything will work out."

I wasn't so sure. Men saw the world differently than we did, and, with that in mind, 1 felt just a wee bit ill at ease.

I spent the rest of the day cleaning out the stuff stored away in the remaining closets. I didn't want to ship a lot of unwanted junk. The move was a chance to do some general housekeeping. I hoped perhaps Adam and Betty Jean would want some of the furniture if the kids didn't want it.

I'd forgotten about the box labeled "Nate's stuff." Then I thought, *If not now, then when?*

I pulled the box down from the top shelf of the closet and sat down on the floor, crossed my legs under my body, and opened it carefully, as if the contents would break. Inside, I found baby pictures, baseball cards, a baseball, and copies of an interview he'd done after receiving the MVP at his first World Series game. That evening, everyone gathered around the television in our hotel room. He handled the interview with grace, giving much of the credit to his teammates. A deluge of memories covered me like dam waters rushing through a flood gate. I could smell him and thought I even heard his voice. Loving Nate was easy because he loved you back without condition.

The tears stung my eyes as they rolled slowly down my cheeks. I cried for the child I'd lost that awful night, for the generations that I'd never know, and for the chance to hold him one more time. For what seemed like hours, the tears kept right on coming and, this time, I didn't try to arrest them. My chest hurt and my eyes swelled shut.

When I caught a glimpse in the bathroom mirror of the pain and suffering that waited patiently for the inner me to grow strong enough to finish grieving, I sat down and prayed.

I hadn't cried so uncontrollably in a long while. Somewhere, I read that "crying cleanses the soul." Well, today my soul got a good cleansing. I put his things back in the box and placed the box among my personal belongings. They'd remain among my most cherished possessions.

I heard the phone ringing as I walked out of the bathroom.

"Hello."

"Aunt B.J, hello, it's Mia."

"Hello, Mia, how are you?"

"Good, I'm so happy for you and Daddy. Please accept my sincere congratulations."

"Thank you, honey."

"Aunt B.J., I'd like to come down and spend just a few hours with you tomorrow. I can catch an early flight leaving here in the morning, if that works with your schedule?"

"Of course."

"Great! Then I'll see you tomorrow morning around ten o'clock. I'll grab a cab at the airport."

"Are you sure?"

"Of course, I'm all grown up now."

We laughed.

"I guess you are. See you tomorrow."

I couldn't wait to call Edmond. His secretary said he'd just stepped away from his desk. She put me on hold and in a few minutes, he picked up. "Hello, sweetheart."

"Hi there." And before he said another word, I announced that Mia was coming down tomorrow.

He laughed. "B.J., honey it's okay. Remember, I love you, and nothing will change that."

We talked briefly about the plans for my move. After

giving Edmond the latest update, I set the date and noti-
fied the movers. With packing already underway, boxes
covered most of the floor and, in some places, with no
floor visible, I couldn't even tell what type of flooring hid
underneath. I had piles to take, piles for the kids, piles
possibly for Adam, piles for Goodwill, and piles for trash.
With my experience, I should've gone into the moving
business. Not surprisingly, Edmond offered his help, but I
declined, knowing his schedule would get in the way. I
didn't need any complications. Besides, I'd done this so
many times, I could probably make the arrangements in a
trance. By late evening, I'd filled and labeled every empty box for transport. The kids decided they didn't want
any of the furniture, so Adam and Betty Jean took it.
Then I placed the house on the market and packed the
rest of my personal belongings in boxes.

Amy prepared a chicken casserole, and she and Dannie brought it over. Cabinet doors stood open, exposing
bare shelves. Most of the kitchen sat in boxes. No more
cooking would take place in here—not by me, anyway.
Everything was done, so they didn't stay long. Too tired
to eat, I took a few bites and headed for the shower. Re-
living memories left me drained. I looked forward to a
good night's rest before Mia's visit. Without question,
Edmond and I loved each other. I kneeled and prayed.
Then I climbed into bed and turned off the lights.

I woke feeling anxious. In every move, something
popped up at the last minute that required my attention.
In another half hour Mia would arrive. I poured another
cup of coffee and sat down with the paper in my hand.
The morning seemed quiet. When I looked at the clock, it
was now a couple of minutes past ten. Right about then,
the cab pulled up in front of the house, and this beautiful,
tall redhead got out. If I hadn't known any better, I
would've sworn that it was Lee. Mia looked exactly like

her mom and walked with the same confident air. She paid the cab driver and walked up the sidewalk. I opened the door just before she rang the doorbell.

"Hello, Mia."

"Hello, Aunt B.J."

We both laughed because even to us, "Aunt B.J." sounded odd. We hugged, and she stepped inside.

"How have you been?"

"Swamped with class work, but that's the world I live in. Daddy said to tell you that he'll call later this evening."

"Thanks." We walked into the kitchen and sat down. "Can I get you something?" I asked.

"No thanks, I'm fine."

I couldn't stop staring at her. When she caught my stare, I turned away.

"What's wrong?" she asked.

"I just can't get over how much you remind me of Lee. It's not only that you look exactly like her, but your mannerisms are the same: the way you smile, and the way you hold your head slightly back when you laugh. It's uncanny."

She smiled. "Sometimes, I catch Daddy staring at me with this odd expression, like he's seen a ghost."

"I bet. Alan called yesterday. We had a long talk. He's recovering nicely, and he sounded good."

"Alan's just Alan," she said ever so sweetly.

He had a rebel streak like his mom. I knew that all too well. After all, Lee and I had no secrets. Abruptly, the conversation changed.

"Aunt B.J., do you remember when you, Mom, Kellee, and I got together for our sleepovers? We stayed up all night watching movies and eating popcorn. Well, let me rephrase that, you and Mom stayed up all night.

Somewhere around midnight, Kellee and I crashed. We really had some great times, didn't we?"

"Yes, the best times."

"Mom really loved you, Aunt B.J."

"I know she did, honey, and I loved her."

Then she said, "I'm sure you're wondering why I came to see you. A phone call seemed too impersonal for me. Mom would never have done that. She had her own style when it came to the handling of important things. You know, Aunt B.J., I don't remember a time when the two of you didn't hang out together. You and my mom made quite a twosome, like twins—one couldn't survive without the other."

"So true, I miss her."

"So do I," Mia said. "Aunt B.J., after Mommy died I couldn't go through her things without breaking down. She left specific instructions that she wanted me to follow, but I stood frozen in a puddle of my own sadness. I wanted to honor her wishes many times, but it hurt too much. Shortly before she died, she asked Daddy to place her safety deposit key on my nightstand. Too weak to leave her bed, she scribbled her wishes. 'Mia, this key opens my personal safety deposit box. The contents of this box belong to you now. I hope you wear each piece and enjoy them as much as I have. Over many years, your father gave me these gifts with his love. I hope they'll bring you the same joy they brought me. Open it when the time feels right.'" Mia sighed. "The day Daddy married you, I opened the box. It contained all her valuable jewelry, including her two-carat diamond and sapphire engagement ring and her gold wedding band. She removed them shortly after discovering she had cancer and placed them in her safety deposit box. The box also held other beautiful pieces I'd never seen, along with her favorite tiny gold cross that she wore every day. She loved jewelry, and Daddy showered her with the most exquisite pieces.

"A soft brown pouch lying in the bottom of the box caught my eye. I opened the pouch and pulled out a most exquisite brooch with a cluster of diamonds in the center and two rows of rubies encircling them. I recalled seeing my mother wear it on very special occasions. The note attached read, 'This brooch belonged to Edmond's great grandmother, passed down through three generations. Give this brooch to B.J. with my love. Until B.J. came into my life, I never knew the love of a sister. Over the years we formed a bond that not even death can steal. This brooch belongs to her now. I entrust this task to you because I know you'll understand and honor my request. Whenever I wore this broach, B.J. jokingly said, 'it's gorgeous, but you still outshine it, sweetheart.'"

"I know, girlfriend," I said and winked at her.

We laughed and laughed. Lee and I really did think of ourselves as divas.

I didn't know what to say, so touched by the generosity of my sister and my friend. I started to cry, then Mia started to cry, and then we just sat there bawling. Finally, we regained our composure and, when the downpour stopped, we reminisced about the fun times all over again. I couldn't resist. I had to know, so I asked, "Mia, did Edmond know why you were coming here today?"

"Yes."

Now I understood why he had gave very little credence to my concerns about Mia's visit.

He already knew, and that was why he kept saying, "It's okay, B.J."

Mia and I talked about her life and her plans before the cab arrived to take her back to the airport. We hugged, and she kissed my cheek. We promised to see each other soon.

As she turned to leave, I said, "I love you, Mia."

"I love you, too, Aunt B.J." As she dashed toward the cab, she turned and shouted back at me, "I agree with Alan. We've got to figure out something other than 'Aunt B.J.' to call you. It just doesn't have the right ring anymore."

She blew me a kiss and got into the cab. After Alan's call, Mia's visit was the second highlight of my week. I couldn't wait to call Edmond.

He'd probably just arrived home. I dialed his number.

"Hello, B.J., I'm so glad you called. Did Mia get there safely and how did her visit go?"

"Yes, and we had a wonderful time. Of course, you knew we would."

He laughed. "Feel better now?"

"Yes, as a matter of fact, I do."

We both laughed.

"I can't wait to see you. Everything going as planned?" he asked.

"Everything's on schedule. I should see you on Friday."

I scheduled the movers for early Friday morning. Adam picked up some pieces, along with a bed that belonged to his parents. Since my flight didn't leave until later in the afternoon, I had time to visit with Dannie and Amy.

They took the day off so we could spend some time together. *I'll miss them,* I thought. Every Sunday after church, they came over for dinner. There was one more thing to do, so I got in the car and drove to the cemetery. Usually, I visited once every month, and then on holidays and his birthday. Today, I walked along the brick walkway toward the back, and then across to the other side of the cemetery. When I reached Nate's grave, I sat down on the little bench that Dannie placed under an old oak tree to shield us from the heat of the day. "Nate, I'm going away, but wherever I go, I'll take your spirit with me. I know this place only symbolizes your resting place. I'm sure I'll feel your presence wherever I go. The most important part of you rests with God. Dannie will stop by while I'm away, and I'll never forget your birthdays." Tears filled my eyes. "I love you, my sweet boy." Just as I got up, a cool breeze blew gently across my cheek. "Thank you." Then I walked back to my car.

When I got back to the house, Amy and Dannie stood waiting outside. And, within a few minutes, Adam and Betty Jean came, too. Amy ran over and hugged me. Dannie followed. Adam and Betty Jean hugged me as well. The movers pulled up just as we turned to walk into the house. They wasted no time packing up the last few reminders of my life in Suellen. Within a few short minutes, they finished, and off they went. I'd loved this place from the first moment I saw it. Now, it held a reminder of another passing season.

"Mom, Amy and I think we might want to buy this house."

"Oh, Dannie, how wonderful! It's truly a lovely place. I think you and Amy would love it here. But if you decide you want it, consider it your wedding present."

They exchanged surprised glances then Dannie nodded his head. Amy ran over and hugged me again, "Mom, thank you for the best wedding present ever, we accept."

"You're welcome."

"Are you sure about this, Mom?" Dannie asked.

"Of course."

Adam hugged me again. "You've given the kids a truly unselfish gift. No one would ever expect anything less from you, B.J."

"Thanks, Adam."

Then he and Betty Jean left.

"Thanks, Mom." Then Dannie gave me this big bear hug and those wet kisses like when he was a young boy.

"Again, you're both welcome. Dannie, you don't have to worry about buying your sister out of the house. She and I have already talked it over and worked it out."

Kellee knew how much I loved that house and that I hoped it would stay in our family.

Finally, with all the farewells behind us, Dannie picked up my luggage, placed it in the truck, and the three of us headed to the airport.

Chapter 23

Full Circle

Tears formed in Dannie's eyes as he kissed me goodbye. Amy turned away so that I couldn't see her tears. I kissed them both and walked inside. Minutes later, I boarded and took a seat next to the window so that I could look out at the clouds. I thought about our first airplane ride together as a family and the many different trips after that. And I thought about all the people that touched our lives so positively and about the new life that awaited me. It would be exciting for sure. Perhaps, I dozed off while watching the movie, because shortly, thereafter, I heard the landing gear positioning for our descent. It was the beginning of September.

Many years ago, I arrived in September ahead of the most uncommon weather pattern that eventually turned into a snowstorm. *I hoped history wasn't about to repeat itself.* I thought. I left this city for a warmer climate, only to come back again. "Love makes strange companions," I'd heard.

As soon as I arrived, I called my old friends. "Hello, Ellie."

"B.J., I can't believe you made it!" she shouted.

"I'm here. I tried to call Lynette but didn't get an answer."

"She's here," Ellie said.

Lynette picked up the phone. "B.J. we're so glad you're back. We've missed seeing you."

"I've missed you guys, too."

"So, when do we get together for lunch?" Lynette asked.

"Tomorrow sounds good to me," Ellie blurted out.

We laughed. Everyone agreed.

"Ladies, can we do lunch at the house?" I asked.

"Sounds great!" they said.

"I'll see you both around eleven-thirty, does that work?"

"Sounds good to me, "Ellie said.

"Works for me, too," Lynette said.

"Then I'll see you ladies tomorrow at eleven-thirty. We've got a lot of catching up to do."

I hung up and went into the kitchen, where Maria busily prepared dinner. "Maria, a couple of my dearest friends are joining me for lunch tomorrow. I'd like something special, but I'll leave it up to you."

"Yes, Mrs. Stein."

"Thank you."

Edmond called.

"Dinner's almost ready," I said.

"Good, I'll see you soon. B.J.," he said. "Have I told you today that I love you?"

"No, but it's not too late."

"I love you, B.J. See you at six."

I sat on the deck and enjoyed the beauty surrounding me then went inside to dress for dinner. Edmond arrived promptly at six o'clock. We sat out on the deck and enjoyed iced tea and a beer. I had tea and Edmond had a beer. Edmond knew I'd gone through a really bad time, and that alcohol took control of my life for a while. I learned never to leave things unsaid. We spent the entire evening laughing, talking, and remembering a time long ago. Even with some unpleasant memories to contend with, I didn't mind looking back.

We sat, looking up into a star-filled sky, and then Edmond took this tiny box from inside of his pocket and handed it to me. "For saying I do."

I smiled as I opened the box, but my smile quickly changed as I stared at the most beautiful diamond ring. The two-carat center stone had a carat of baguettes clinging to each side. Edmond always had a love affair with beautiful jewelry. I sat frozen unable to move with my mouth still agape. Finally, Edmond said, "Silly, do you like it?"

I jumped up and onto his lap. "Yes, yes, I not only like it, I love it." I smothered him with kisses.

Later, we spent a romantic night locked in each other's arms.

I slept late. When morning came, I found a note on my pillow. *Stay with me forever, B.J. Love, Edmond.* I rolled over and jumped straight up in bed. I forgot to mention my lunch with the girls. I worried he'd drive all the way back out, thinking we could have lunch together. His secretary said he'd gone out, but she knew how to reach him, so I asked her to let him know that I had a luncheon engagement with friends. I hurriedly dressed. Surprisingly, it was a nice day to sit outside, but a little on the cool side. I pulled on a lightweight sleeveless sweater with a matching cardigan in a soft peach with navy slacks.

My friends arrived right on time, as expected. We had the same pet peeve. Tardiness drove all of us crazy. Lynette and Ellie looked lovely. Lynette had kept her

weight in check and looked beautiful, with those unforgettable blue eyes. Ellie's curly afro grew back after her
bout with cancer. She looked gorgeous. "Ladies, it's so
good to see you again."

We hugged and screamed as the tears fell. Maria
peered around the corner when she heard all the commo-
tion. We spent the rest of the afternoon traveling up and
down memory lane.

Maria set up lunch in my favorite spot on the far
edge of the deck, overlooking the forest. With so much to
say, we didn't know where to start. Of course, the conversation turned quickly to how Edmond and I got together. Answering that question caused me to think that
perhaps our spirits connected long before any physical
union formed. This man, my best friend's husband, and I
were friends long before we became lovers.

Suddenly, the sunlight bounced off my ring, and Ellie gasped. I thought she was going to hyperventilate. She
grabbed my finger, and then we laughed. We talked for
hours about everything. Lynette said Rita and her new
husband moved away. They hadn't heard from her. All
the boys had good jobs, and, except for Alan, all of them
had wives. We spent the day talking about our lives, our
hopes, our dreams, and the sad fact that no one had
grandchildren yet.

"What are they waiting for?" Lynette asked.

We laughed.

After lunch, they headed back to the city, and I settled in with a good book. Reading, one of my favorite
pastimes, started back in my childhood.

I fell asleep and, when I woke, Edmond was standing
over me. He leaned down and kissed my forehead, "Hello, sleepyhead."

"Hello, yourself."

"Dinner's ready," he said.

"Okay."

I rushed upstairs and washed my face. Again, with the weather so nice, we dined out on the deck while gazing up at the stars. My serious guy sat quietly. Edmond once told me that his parents never allowed him to play outside with the other kids. He spent all his time reading. I thought how sad. We stayed outside for a few minutes longer and then retired for the evening. Edmond slept soundly. In the middle of the night, I made my way to the bathroom. My eyes felt like I'd stuck my head in an oven. Because I'd left my contacts in too long, my red, irritated eyes burned.

Edmond left for work bright and early the next morning. I had an idea. Feeling much better, I got dressed, went into town, and found him the perfect gift. It wasn't his birthday or any special day. I arrived home only minutes before him.

"Hello, B.J.," he shouted from the kitchen.

Edmond loved to tease Maria by tasting everything in sight. She tried banning him from the kitchen until she had dinner ready, but it didn't always work.

"Go! Go! Mr. Stein," she shouted as she shoved him out of the door.

Edmond treated her like a member of our family. I knew I'd grow to love her, too.

"Hello, I'm going upstairs to change. I'll be back in a minute." I threw on a pair of jeans and an old football jersey.

When I walked into the room, Edmond whistled and said, "Wow! You look great!"

"You would think I looked great even if I had on an old terrycloth bathrobe."

"And you would. What's that?" he asked, pointing to the package I held out to him.

"Happy just because day."

He opened the box and inside was a football.
"Wow!"
"Let's go outside," I said.
"Let me change." He rushed upstairs and came back down in no time flat. The kid in him wanted to come out to play. We ran into the backyard and tossed the ball around. He had an amazing look on his face as we rolled around in the grass while playing our own version of touch football. I had fun just watching him. This day was a long time coming, but it was finally here. "B.J., thanks for the best gift anyone has ever given me."

"You're welcome." I couldn't give Edmond back his youth, but I could give him some of the joys that should've come with his childhood.

Definitely, we needed a shower before dinner, so we got cleaned up and sat down to dinner in our favorite spot in the whole wide world. We enjoyed each other's company and, not surprisingly, Edmond respected my political views. I'd had quite a few magical moments in my life, and tonight topped the list.

"B.J., starting tomorrow night, I'll need to work late on a new bill I want to get passed. When it's over, let's take a trip. We haven't had a honeymoon yet, and, in a couple of weeks, the weather will get cold. Perhaps we should plan on getting away to some warm weather."

"Where do you want to go?"

"As long as it's with you, I don't care."

"I'll keep that in mind," I said, winking at him playfully.

My antiques arrived, in time, to find a place among lots of other beautiful pieces in our new home. The interior decorator provided lots of good advice. I knew what and how I wanted things but needed her help to pull it altogether. Every day I kept my friends current with updates about the things happening in my world, and they kept me in the loop from their end. I told Ellie that Edmond asked me to choose a place to spend our honeymoon, and I didn't have a clue yet.

"Paris, of course," she said.

I hadn't thought of that, but Ellie loved Paris. I remember telling her while she fought her bout with cancer that I'd heard it was lovely in the springtime. Winston promised to take her, but he hadn't gotten around to it yet. Ellie and I talked for a few more minutes. Suddenly, I got an idea. *What if Ellie, Winston, Edmond, and I went to Paris together?* I thought. Hopefully, we could surprise Ellie with her lifelong dream. I couldn't wait for Edmond to get home. He got in late. I could see the tiredness in his eyes as he pulled me close. Maria had his dinner warming, so I fixed him a plate. He ate very little. We talked. "I love talking to you. It helps clear my head and keep me grounded."

"I'm glad, sweetheart." Then I leaned over and kissed him. After a brief pause I said, "Edmond, I'd like to go to Paris for our honeymoon."

"Sounds great, B.J. Have you started making the arrangements?"

"No, not yet, I have another idea."

"What's that?"

"What if Winston and Ellie joined us?"

"What a terrific idea. It would be fun to have them along." He grabbed his jacket and went upstairs. I stayed downstairs and worked on the details. I couldn't sleep. Edmond slept so soundly he didn't know when I came to bed. I didn't fall asleep until early morning, but when I awoke he'd gone. Disappointed not to find a note, I showered and came down to breakfast.

Maria tried her best to coerce me into a full breakfast. "Not today, just coffee," I said.

Maria brought me a cup of coffee and a note that she found near the coffee pot.

Bet you thought I forgot. Not a chance. I love you. Edmond.

Loving Edmond reminded me of loving Nate. They loved you with everything they had. I wished my mother had found someone to love her the way Edmond loved me. I loved my mother perhaps more than she knew, but she wouldn't let me get close enough to show her. She guarded her feelings to keep from getting hurt again.

I got Winston's buy in right away when I said Edmond and I planned to honeymoon in Paris and that perhaps he and Ellie should come along. "Ellie would love Paris. You did promise her Paris, remember?"

He gave me their itinerary and agreed we'd surprise her. Later that day, I spoke with Edmond's secretary and locked in his most available dates. Then I marked everything down on my working calendar and got busy.

No matter how late Edmond got home, we always made time to spend together, if only for a few minutes before he dragged himself upstairs. Sometimes when I came upstairs, I found him collapsed in his big old comfortable chair sound asleep. Three weeks into this madness, I couldn't wait for it to stop. I worried about him.

With the plans in motion, I counted down the days. We had reservations at a hotel right near the Champs Elysees in the heart of the city of romance. I planned guided sightseeing trips, with a few unescorted adventures. For Ellie, we planned to climb the Eiffel Tower just as she dreamed. We made Lynette swear she wouldn't utter a word. But we held our breath. With Lynette, if we wanted something to remain a secret, we had to make her swear.

Now with hotel accommodations and air transportation arranged, I invited them over for dinner. It was time for the big reveal. From the moment Edmond left the house, I looked forward to him coming home. Around six o' clock, Edmond returned in time to shower and change before the St. Claire's arrived. At exactly seven o'clock, they showed up. Winston looked both nervous and excited. He couldn't wait to spring the news. The guys got together at the bar, while Ellie and I made our way to the table. With all this excitement, I unintentionally skipped breakfast and lunch. Maria had outdone herself.

Winston blessed the food and then said, "I would like to propose a toast to my lovely wife and our upcoming trip to Paris."

Ellie's mouth flew open. She almost fell out of her chair. And to top it all off, she started to hyperventilate which was not an uncommon occurrence for her. After recovering, she asked, "Are you serious?"

"Yes. B.J. and Edmond will honeymoon, and you and I will live out your dream."

Tears rolled down her cheeks, and then she leaned over and kissed him.

"Thank you." Then she looked over at us. "Thank you too, my friends."

We laughed about worrying over Lynette's inability to keep a secret. We enjoyed dinner and spent the rest of the evening talking about the planned events. "We depart one week from today. Ellie, did I leave you enough time to prepare?"

"I can handle this," she said, and we all laughed.

They left after dinner, and Edmond and I spent the remainder of the evening listening to some jazz. We turned in before midnight, and by early morning he'd gone. This morning's note read: "Every moment that I'm away, I think of you. I love you. Edmond."

Friday arrived with us packed and heading to the airport. We checked in, got our boarding passes, and headed to the gate to find Ellie and Winston already waiting. Too excited to sleep, Winston said Ellie stayed up half the night checking and rechecking things.

We boarded on time. I settled in for a long flight with my book and a couple of magazines. Winston and I exchanged seats for a while. Ellie and I watched a tear-jerker that I'd seen, but I cried again. We sat together for a big part of the flight as excited as schoolgirls away from home without parental supervision. I returned to my seat and fell asleep on Edmond's shoulder.

Many weary hours later, we arrived in a beautiful and sophisticated city. Our elegant hotel overlooked the Champs Elysees, filled with shops, restaurants, and side-walk cafes. We unpacked and hit the streets. Then we walked until we lucked upon a little café that sat over-looking a man-made waterfall. The water gurgled as it cascaded off the side of the building. I felt lightheaded from all those intoxicating sights and sounds.

When Edmond and I returned to our room, I kicked off my shoes and fell across the bed.

"B.J., I hope you have the most memorable time of your life."

"More memorable than right now?" I asked.

He smiled and held me close. We fell asleep in each other's arms. When we woke, we hurriedly dressed for dinner.

I'd bought a new black dress and planned to wear the brooch that once belonged to Lee. Anxious to see Ed-mond's reaction, I carefully pinned the brooch to my dress.

When I walked into the room, the sparkle in his eyes said it all. "B.J., you look stunning. That brooch magni-fies your beauty. I've always believed that any woman courageous enough to wear that brooch has confidence in her beauty. You look amazing."

"Thanks." I'd spent too much time getting my

makeup perfect. I didn't want to ruin it. So, with a tiny bit of vanity on display, I stood in the doorway and blew him a kiss.

We met Winston and Ellie downstairs. People turned and stared.

"B.J., you look beautiful," Ellie said.

Winston gawked, speechless for the first time since I'd known him. Finally, the words found their way out, and he said, "Girl, you're hot."

Everyone laughed.

"It's the brooch," I said jokingly.

"It's not the brooch, sweetheart, it's you," Ellie said with confidence.

We took a cab to the restaurant. The brochure had done a great job of describing the famous La Maison Blanche with its spectacular panoramic view of the city.

We enjoyed a marvelous dinner, but I had one more surprise to unveil. Earlier, I'd let Ellie in on my surprise. After we finished dinner, everyone sat and enjoyed cocktails.

I lifted my club soda and faced my husband. "To my wonderful husband, may we love each other forever!" Holding the ring gingerly, I reached over, took Edmond's hand, and placed the ring on his finger. The gum wrapper had long ago disappeared, but not the memory. Misty eyed, he leaned over and kissed me gently on the lips, sealing this magical moment in time. Everyone applauded, including the other guests and restaurant staff. It was the end to a perfect evening.

We spent the rest of the trip touring museums and churches, not to mention the most famous Notre Dame Cathedral. We ate delicious food, from street vendors to fancy restaurants. It wasn't springtime, yet, but it was the most unforgettable season of my life. We didn't climb the Eiffel Tower, instead took the elevator up as high as we could go. From the top, we looked out at an awesome sea of city lights. It felt good knowing that my friend lived to see her dream come true. After midnight, we returned to the hotel, slept late, and the next morning ordered room service. Edmond and I decided to take one more walk around the city, just the two of us.

We walked hand in hand while planning our future.

Edmond stopped and turned to me. "B.J., when we get home, I'm going to throw a big party so that I can introduce you to the world."

"The world, Edmond?" I said, laughing.

"Maybe not the world, just my world."

"You already have. Finally, my life had come full circle, if only for a season."

About the Author

Bertha Connally Abraham is a retired ATT manager. She attended Southern University and, although the South is in her blood, she lived on the East Coast for a while. The love of traveling fuels her desire to write. She and her husband often hit the road for business and pleasure. Her hobbies include reading and gardening. She is a Master Gardener and public speaker. Wildly diverse and unforgettable characters fill the pages of her books. As founder of The Writer's Workshop for Children, she helps children realize their love of reading and writing. Currently, she is a member of (OTC) Off the Chart book club and The Red Hat Society. She lives in the countryside of Wharton, Texas. Her works include, *Woven*, *If Only for a Season* and *In the Pew*.